17 Days to Texas

A post-apocalyptic journey of survival

17 Days to Texas

A post-apocalyptic journey of survival

Deidre Whipple Lopez

Deidre Whipple Lopez

Copyrighted Material

Copyright ©   3 dogs Publishing House, 2022

All rights Reserved.

3 dogs Publishing House
Hitchcock, Texas

ISBN 979-8-9871516-9-3 ebook
ISBN 979-8-9871516-9-3 paperback
ISBN 979-8-9871516-1-7 hardback

Cover Picture by Dale, Alicia, and Ashlyn Thompson
Editing by Nancy Quarrell

Dedication

First and foremost, I would like to thank my mom Collene and my husband Josh for their love and encouragement to keep writing and finish my first book.

I would also like to thank my friends and family for the inspiration of my characters, I'm sure you recognized yourselves!!

TABLE OF CONTENT

CHAPTER ONE
Las Vegas

Day 1: D'Ann

The pain was unbearable. I couldn't move. Tears streamed down my face, as I've had this pain many times before. The muscle on the inside of my leg was making my toes contract and curl up and the pain would not allow me to straighten my leg.

My sobs and moans that escaped my mouth sounded like a wounded animal. "Breathe. Try to get up and walk it out." I heard his voice as plain as day, like he had told me so many times before, even though he wasn't here.

The screams under my breath were getting louder. My knuckles were turning white from gripping the headboard and squeezing it hard. Thinking this would ease the pain.

I tried to kick the sheets off and get out of bed, but something was holding the sheets down around my feet. Between the pain and the constriction on my feet, all I could do was cry. Realizing the constriction around my feet was dogs on either side of my legs, I kicked and yelled for them to get down off the bed. I heard the thuds and felt the release of the sheets from my legs.

Immediately, I threw the sheets off and grabbed the wall to pull myself up to a standing position. Trying to concentrate and regulate my breathing "breathe, relax, breathe, relax," I kept telling myself.

I had heard of a trick that if you twisted your upper lip, the pain would go away. "What the hell," I thought, as I twisted my top lip. "Crap, that hurts," but it also did the trick. The pain had subsided. I walked back and forth down the hallway, making sure the charlie horse was gone. The muscle in my leg released and my toes relaxed. "Dammit, I hate those things," as I wiped the tears away from my cheek.

I walked the two feet, which was our hallway, then down two steps and I was in our living room. Looking straight ahead out the windows, I noticed it was no longer dark outside. I could see that the big, bright yellow sun was just peeking into the camper windows.

It was going to be another miserable, hot day. The meteorologist had reported on the 10 o'clock news last night that we were in for another record day in the Las Vegas Valley. It was mid-August, and we had already had five 110° days in a row. The temperature in the RV was already getting warm. I walked back up the two steps and checked the thermostat "79 already". I pushed the button and turned it down to seventy-two, hoping it would cool the RV down before it got too hot. But I knew once it got over ninety outside, the RV's A/c would not keep up.

The RV was an older model. It was our second one. The first one we had traded a pontoon boat for it. It being older than this one; we did a lot of work to it to make it livable. But it had worked for us, we lived in the first one for almost 2 years. It actually made it to Colorado, where we spent our first summer managing an RV park. We turned around and sold it once we got back to Texas the following fall. And purchased this one, which was a little nicer.

Walking to the kitchen area of the RV, I reached for a glass out of the cupboard. "Water, I need to drink more water," I said to myself. "Maybe the charlie horse that I just experienced wouldn't have happened." Taking a long drink of the nice cool water, the words of my mom came to mind, "who camps in the desert in the summertime?" she said when we told her we were heading to Las Vegas to be hosts on a gun range.

Glancing at the clock on the microwave, 5:16 AM. Jay would get off work soon from his graveyard shift. But because it was my day off, I still had plenty of time to go back to sleep. I never got to really sleep in on my days off, because of the dogs and Jay getting home early, kicking me out of bed so he could sleep. Sleeping in was a luxury. I set my glass in the sink and headed back to the bedroom, climbed into bed. It didn't take long before I was fast asleep.

Without opening my eyes, I reached on the nightstand and grabbed my phone. Pushed the dismiss button to shut the alarm off. "Damnit, I forgot to turn it off last night," knowing I wanted to sleep in this morning. First, opening my email as my eyes became accustomed to the light, "nothing but junk mail, delete, delete." Next, as I did every morning, I open Facebook. Nothing seemed out of the ordinary as I scrolled through the same old funny dog videos and cute kid saying the darndest things videos. A friend posted how awful her date was last night and my cousin changed her profile picture, "cute a new hairdo." My sister-in-law had posted "miss you" on my page as my mind wandered to the last time I saw her.

The last 2 years had been quite eventful. We had quit our jobs and sold everything we had and moved into a 32-foot fifth wheel, hoping to travel the country, and working at RV Parks along the way. Doing my research and sending out several resumes to different RV parks, I finally got a response. Our dream job was going to happen in Colorado in the summer.

We spent 2 summers working in the Rocky Mountains. Colorado was beautiful. On our days off, we would pick a trail, pack some snacks and water, and take off on our ATVs. It was a great time. But at the end of the summer, we would close the RV park for winter, load our ATVs, and head back to Texas.

We hadn't been home very long when we got the call for an opportunity to be host at a gun range in Las Vegas, Nevada.

Jay had never really been out of the state of Texas before, so this had been quite an adventure for him. Jay was 26 years old and had worked as a Repo Man driving a tow truck when I first met him. Now at 43, he was about to live a dream life.

Being 17 years older than Jay, I have traveled to many states. Visiting Las Vegas on a couple of girl trips several years before, I loved the idea of living and working in Vegas.

Before we hit the road again, we spent a couple days at his brother's deer lease just getting ready for the long trip to Vegas. Spending as much time as we could with his wife and kids. The job in Vegas was going to be a long-term job, maybe up to several years if we wanted to stay.

The last night before we left his brother Doug and his wife, my best friend, Barb's house. We sat around a little campfire, trying our best not to cry. None of us wanted to mention that tomorrow we would leave this place. The place where our two families came together and bonded over campfires and hanging out one week every year. We sat in a circle surrounding a little fire. Quietly watching the dancing flames turn yellow and blue. The night was black, and the air was still. The only sounds were the crackling and popping of the little bonfire we had built for the last time until we all got together again next year. Barb and I were already planning their trip to come visit us in Las Vegas as soon as the girls were out of school for the summer. They were going to drive to Las Vegas along Route 66 and stop to see all the sites along the way.

"You guys know, if anything happens, we all need to make our way back here," Doug said, disturbing our conversation. "What do you mean, if anything happens?" I asked, startled at the unexpected, random comment he had just made.

"Haven't you been watching the news? There is so much unrest right now. Who knows what Russia or China are doing? Politicians going after each other. Local terrorist groups causing havoc. The rioting that had taken place in the cities. Cities wanting to defund the police departments. All the shootings that have been happening it just don't look good for a future."

"Do you really think something could happen?" Barb asked, looking across the flames at the serious frown on her husband's face. "I don't want to talk about it. It's our last night together, plus I think everyone will come to their senses and work it out," I said. "Well, it never hurts to be prepared and have a plan," my husband piped in. "Right, this would be the most secure place I know of, where we could set up a perimeter for security. Live off the plenitude of all the wild hogs and deer. Plenty of room to grow a garden, and we have well water and generators. It would be perfect." Doug said.

The deer lease was about thirty miles from any major city in the middle of east Texas. It was so secluded you would get lost if you didn't know where you were going. 750 acres of forest surrounding a compound that had solar panels for electric and well water for drinking, plus a few outbuildings that held our annual hunting and camping gear and supplies.

For the next hour, we jokingly made "what if" plans if something actually happened. None of us really thought anything would really happen, and we would be right back here next hunting season.
The fire had died to just embers. "We better get to bed. We got a big day tomorrow," Jay said, as he threw a bucket of water on the smoldering embers.

We folded up our chairs and carried them to the RV as Doug and Barb carried theirs to their house. "Good night, see ya in the morning," I yelled back to them. "Good night, love you guys," replied Barb.
The morning arrived quickly. There was dew on the grass and a chill in the air. Fall had come early to Texas. I finished packing the lawn

chairs into the under-storage area of our camper, while Jay made sure he strapped the ATVs down securely to the small trailer that we were pulling behind the fifth wheel. "I'm going to miss you, D'Ann. Vegas is so far away," Barb whispered, as we held each other. "I know. I'm going to miss you as well. You all need to come and visit. You can stay in the camper with us," I said, smiling, trying to lighten the mood. "Once the girls are out of school in the spring, we just might do that," Barb sniffled. "I just put the dogs in the truck. You ready to go?" Jay asked. "I guess so. I'm just going to miss them. No telling how long it will be till we see them again," I said, as I climbed into the truck. Jay started the truck and slowly started out of the driveway. I looked back to see Doug and Barb waving as they stood there, holding each other. We pulled our little "home on wheels" hooked to the back of our truck out of the driveway and onto the dirt road.

The trip was long; it took over 18 hours, and that was only stopping to potty and get something to eat along the way. We arrived in Las Vegas, Nevada in October. The RV park at the gun range was so beautiful. It had big canopies over all the sites to keep the sun from beating down on the RVs.

It had thirty-five covered sites and further up the mountain there were several more sites for the hosts and the public. There were eight rows of 6 RVs. We were at home in the second row from the entrance with neighbors on both sides.

The first night, after getting all set up and taking the dogs on a walk to get familiar with the area, we were mesmerized at the sight of the lights of the entire valley. You could see the Las Vegas strip, downtown and from one mountain to the other. "The fireworks on New Year's Eve are going to be spectacular from up here," Jay said, as we stared at the view.

Besides the beautiful views of the Las Vegas Valley at night, we were surrounded by desert, cactus, sagebrush, and lots of creepy crawlers everywhere, and at night you could hear the coyotes singing to each other.

It didn't take long before we settled into our RV, as much as we could in such a small space. The park seemed to be very quiet. Other hosts kept to themselves, only seeing them when they walk their dogs. Most of them were of retirement age. It seemed like we were one of the youngest couples there, well at least Jay was. There were so many varieties of RVs, motorhomes, fifth wheel, old ones, new ones, from tiny to huge.

Our neighbors to the north of us, in site seven, were Curt and Liz. They were the first to welcome us to the neighborhood. We thought we should get to know our neighbors and make them aware we had barking dogs and to let us know if they annoy them.
The gun range was a 5 Star facility and one of the best in the country. It spread out over several hundred acres. There was BLM land between us and the nearest residential neighborhood. We often saw hikers and people running their dogs on the BLM land. From where we were, we could see the entire area and anything that moved. To the east of us was military land, belonging to the Air Force base. On the west side was an Indian reservation. It was like being in our own little world.

Our contract required us to get up at 6 AM, two days a week, and do maintenance on the shotgun field for 15 hours each. There were twenty-four fields and close to fifteen miles of sidewalk that we had to blow off with the leaf blower. We would walk the fields and pick up bullets and shotgun shells. Getting to keep any live rounds we found. All of this in exchange for our RV site, and full hookups.

Our gun range boss, Benny and his wife Nadi, had become quick friends of ours, spending Thanksgiving at their house. Going over to their house to play pool or watch a football game. Benny and Nadia were avid Seahawk fans. Benny collected any and every bar or beer sign he could get his hands on. I don't think there was a square inch of their walls that didn't have one. Nadia was a collector also, but her collection would save her someday.

Benny and Nadia had invited us over to watch the Super Bowl that year. While the guys played pool and watched the game, Nadia and I sat and talked. Nadia loved to can vegetables, and according to Jay, made the best salsa he had ever tasted. As we sat and talked, I noticed on her kitchen counter were jars and jars of canned items. I pointed and said, "you've been really busy," as she turned and looked where I was pointing. "Ahhh, this isn't even half of it, come see." I followed Nadia back to her bedroom and as she opened the door to her walk-in closet, I stood there with my mouth open. She had rows and rows of canned food, dried food, and MREs. She pointed out the big tubs full of medication and first aid supplies. There were shelves full of books on prepping, survival, and what plants were edible. Any and everything you could imagine on how to survive off grid if needed. "Wow," I said in disbelief. "And this is not all," she said as we walked out of her bedroom.

Down the hall was a door that was closed. She reached into her pocket and pulled out a key. She unlocked the door and let me go in first. The room was a fairly large bedroom that was lined with shelves. The shelves again were full of canned goods, powdered foods, and dehydrated food. She pointed to a row of tubs and said, "those are full of medical supplies, medications, plant seeds, soaps, stuff to make soaps." I was speechless. "How long did it take you to collect all this stuff?" I asked. "Over a couple of years," she replied. She said her father had been a prepper/survivalist growing up, and she always showed an interest in it. "This is amazing," I said. "I'm coming here if something ever happens," I laughed.

Leaving all my friends in Texas, I had not made many in Las Vegas, but I really liked Nadia. I knew we would be longtime friends, and not only because she had a grocery store in her closet.

Living and being a host on a gun range, you had to own a gun. It was just a given that everyone living there carried a gun. Jay carried a 45, and I carried a little pink lady revolver. In the RV, we also had a hunting rifle in the closet next to the front door and an AR 15, which was a gift to Jay from his brother the first year we went to the deer lease. It was tucked safely under our bed. And a mean dog named Diamond. A cabinet full of ammunition completed our little arsenal. "I dare anyone to break into any of the RVs in this park." Besides, most of the other host shot every weekend, it was a gated community and a half a mile up the side of the mountain surrounded by desert. Most definitely the safest place you could live in Las Vegas.

We spent most of our free time exploring the city. After losing our money several times in the casinos on the strip, we decided it would be best to avoid the strip as much as we could. "It's the red zone" we named it because we never won down there. Only going down on the strip to get our favorite drink, a "Frozen Baileys" at O'Shea's. And dropping off family and friends when they came to visit. But luckily for us, there were several casinos on the outskirts of town just for the locals. Between spending money keeping them in business and frequenting the local marijuana dispensaries, the money was getting tight.

Marijuana had just become legal for recreational use that year. Jay was in heaven. Being able to walk into a store, buy marijuana, and walk out without the worry of being arrested was the craziest feeling ever.

After about a month, as we made our way back home from a losing night at the casino, Jay wondered out loud, "I think I would like to see if I could actually get qualified to work in a dispensary." he commented. "I bet you could, as long as your schedule works with the gun range," I replied. So, the next morning Jay set out to get all his licenses and started applying for bud tender jobs. In the meantime, while waiting for a dispensary to call him back, he picked up a job as a tow truck driver. In the short time he was there, Sean, his supervisor, and he had hit it off from the beginning, becoming great friends.

It didn't take long for him to find a job he was born to have. He was ecstatic when he got the call. "I mean, the man was an expert on marijuana." His brother introduced him to it at the very young age of twelve, smoking daily ever since.

The world's largest marijuana dispensary was right here in Las Vegas Valley. And he was now an employee. In a short few months, he would become top sales and, on his way, to being a manager.
Jay worked the graveyard shift and loved it. As he slept during the day, I took care of our four fur babies. But boredom overtook me. I knew I needed to find a job outside of the gun range, plus we could use the extra money.

It, too, didn't take me long to find a job, working as the assistant property manager of a mini storage facility in a part of Vegas that was called China Town. I only work part time, working Friday and Saturdays, which was great. I still had plenty of time to work at the gun range and be at home with the dogs.

When we had time off and when we weren't gambling, we often went out to eat or went bowling with Jay's friend Sean and his girlfriend, Andie. Sean was like a professional bowler, had his own bag with his own balls and shoes. We often teased Sean, "remember that one time?" Jay would say, referring to the time Jay had beaten Sean's score. We would all burst out laughing, and all Andie would say is "I can't wit you Jay!"

The marijuana business was very lucrative, and between his job and mine, we were able to buy an SUV for Jay to drive back and forth to work, and still have gambling money. We were finally in a great spot in our lives. Life was good!

Putting the phone down on the nightstand, I noticed the charger had come unplugged from the wall. "Great, it didn't charge fully last night," I said, as I rolled my eyes. "Damn dogs pulled it out of the wall again," after plugging it back up to fully charge, I was struck by the urgent need to go pee.

I opened the door and let the dogs go out to do their business. Four dogs were a lot in an RV, but there was no way we were going to get rid of them just because we moved into a smaller place. They were our kids.

Diamond was our big dog, part bull mastiff and pit-bull. She was the protector. No one dared come into our RV with her in there. She was a beautiful dog, but at about nine years old, had become very protective and had bitten five people because they moved too fast towards her. Sean being one of them. The RV didn't have a screen door, so we put up a baby gate to keep the dogs in when we opened the door to let some fresh air in. We knew Diamond could go right through the gate if she wanted to, but she never paid any mind. Until one afternoon when Sean came over to watch a football game with Jay. "Hello, anyone home?" As he stepped over the gate and came in. Diamond was on him before he could even think. She had his brand new "Raiders" jogging paint in her mouth and ripped a big hole in them, grazing Sean's skin. From that day forward, Sean knocked before he entered.

Our other three dogs were a little family of their own. Brooklyn, our little female, was the queen of the house. The others did nothing unless she okayed it. Bronx, "Lil Man," as we called him, my male, had recently become less of the man of the house when I had his pretty little balls cut off. He still gave me that look like, "I can't believe you did this to me!" Then there was Tator. He was the product of Brooklyn and Bronx, a Singleton, the only puppy born in the litter, and one of the cutest little Shih Tzu I had ever seen. We knew when he was born, we had to keep him.

I always knew when the dogs were ready to come back inside, Lil Man would run up and down the steps make a loud banging noise and Brooklyn would sit at bottom of steps and bark only once, unless I didn't come right away, then they would both do it again, "bang, bark." I opened the door. "Get in here, yawl get on my nerves," I yelled, as I let them back in. They all ran towards their water bowl; it was already hot. I could tell the meteorologist was going to be right. It's going to be a hot one today.

Turning the ceiling fan up to high, I reached in the fridge for my morning caffeine. "A can of Diet Coke," not a bottle nor a glass with ice, only a cold can would do. I admit it, "I'm completely addicted."
I glanced at the time on my phone that I had in my hand. Jay should be on his way home by now, unless the first shift was late. Then he would have to work till they were on the floor and ready to work.

Looking around on the floor for the remote to the TV, "damn dogs, what did you do with the remote again?" I asked. But knowing it was most likely Jay that miss placed it. It seemed to always be in the same place, though, under the only chair we had in the RV, a rocking chair I had gotten off Craigslist with a footstool. "I'm going to throw this footstool in the trash one of these days. I just don't have room for it," I thought. Finding the remote tucked oh so cleverly under the chair, I pushed the power button, turned and scooted Brooklyn out of the rocking chair. "Get on the couch with the others," I said as she jumped down, then climbed up onto the sofa.

Scanning the channels this early in the morning, not much was on, so I settled on the local news. A reporter was doing the traffic report, "Man, I'm glad I don't have to commute anywhere today," I said.
Suddenly, I heard a low rumble coming from outside the RV. The sound got louder and louder and the vibration stronger. The RV windows started to rattle. Knowing exactly what it was, I still peeked out the curtain just in time to see the Blackhawk helicopter flying right above us. "Dang, that's noisy. Why they got to fly so low this early in the morning?" I wondered.

Seeing and hearing the Blackhawk helicopter was nothing unusual. The Air Force Base was just a few miles away and our RV park seemed to be right in their flight path. They were a sight to watch, flying just a few hundred feet above us, and then there were the fighter jets. "Talk about loud!" They definitely rattled the RV. When we first arrived, the dogs used to bark something fierce when they flew over, but like us, we all got used to them.

It quickly drew my attention back to the TV, as the familiar music and voice came on, "this is a special report!" I waited, then the TV went blank. "Oh, come on really!" In this area, there was no cable TV available, so we all had satellite or internet and streamed our TV stations. It was not unusual for it to buffer for several minutes, and usually it was at the most inconvenient times. I waited a few minutes for it to come back on. "Nothing."

Then the unmistakable sound of a gigantic explosion rang in my ears, shaking the RV. The only picture I had room for on our small RV walls rattled, shook and fell to the floor. All four dogs started barking. As the RV was still shaking, I sprang to my feet and headed towards the door. "What the hell was that?" I yelled.

I hurried to the door and down the steps. Because we were in the middle of the park and surrounded by RVs, I could see nothing except the big bright yellow ball in the sky almost blinding me. But the sounds were almost deafening. Explosion after explosion, one right after another, was all I could hear. Ducking and covering my head with my arms, not knowing what was going on, and wondering if something was going to fall out of the sky, I ran to the end of our RV. "What in the world?" yelled our neighbors, Curt and Liz, as they came running from around their fifth wheel towards me. "Oh my God, look!" As they pointed towards the Vegas Valley.

Turning my head to look where they were pointing, the unbelievable sight of the Vegas valley came into view. The resorts were on fire! Explosions and fireballs everywhere. We stood there horrified and watched as several airplanes descended on to the unsuspecting neighborhoods and burst into flames. Just to the east of us, just past the main entrance gate, one of the Blackhawk helicopters was in flames on the ground.

Covering my mouth with both hands to cover the screams that wanted to come out, all I could do was watch. I close my eyes, "is this a dream?" I whispered. "No, more like a nightmare!" Curt replied.

A couple more people begin to appear from their RVs. Although the RV park had thirty-five spaces, it was hot, and most of the hosts fled north to cooler temperatures. Leaving at the end of May and returning in October. Most of them leaving their RVs in the storage area. They would return in the fall to pick up where they left off. We could've had our pick of spots with only 10 RVs left, taking up spaces.

Screaming and crying between the explosions, as they started realizing what was happening. "My kids!" One of the neighbor ladies cried, "John, we got to go save our kids!" as she ran back to her RV to grab the keys to her car. "If this is what I think it is, the car will not start," John replied. Knowing what he was talking about, several pulled their phones out of their pockets and stared. Not a single phone worked.

An elderly man at the end of the row slowly came out of his RV. The man could barely walk, and we knew he was hard of hearing because of many years of not wearing ear protection while shooting. "Did yawls' electricity go off?" he asked in his southern drawl.

Curt, our neighbor in site seven, trying to comfort his wife Liz, looked at me and asked, "what is going on?" We all stood there in horror at the sight of the Vegas Valley going up in flames. Curt turned and noticed the helicopter. "Maybe we should go see if anyone survived," as he helped Liz sit down at our picnic table. He ran to his RV and came back outside with a fire extinguisher, "I don't think that's going to work," I said. "Probably not, but we have to do something," as he started running towards the helicopter. I sat down next to Liz as she cried, but no words were spoken, none needed to be spoken. We were all in the same boat. We had no idea what was going on and what had happened to our family and friends.

Curt and Jim had finally reached the helicopter. Because of the intense flames, they could not get very close. Fully engulfed in flames, they knew no one could have survived that, and the little fire extinguishers Curt was holding would do nothing to put the flames out. Curt walked around to the other side of the helicopter to see if there was any way to get closer to it. As he rounded the tail, he saw what looked to be a body lying a few yards away. He dropped the extinguisher and ran over to the body. Through the blood and mangled bones and flesh, he could tell it was just a kid. "Couldn't be much over 21," he thought. Looking down at him, he knew there was nothing he could do. Jim caught up to him and looked down at the young man. "Oh, man," Jim said. Being the religious man that he was, Jim kneeled next to the body, bowed his head, and said a prayer. The two men then walked back to the RV. A small crowd had gathered around our table. Catching the looks from everyone, Liz looked up at me from where she was sitting and looked at me straight in my eyes. "Where's Jay at?" she asked. Tears formed in my eyes. I could not speak; all I could do was point. As she looked in the direction I was pointing, the Las Vegas Valley.

Curt went to his RV storage area and pulled out a shovel. "I think we need to bury him. How about in the Grove under one of the few trees?" The Grove was a small park on the west side of the complex. Although there was no grass, it had a couple of trees, picnic tables, a horseshoe pit, and a BBQ grill.

A couple of elderly men and Curt walked to the park as Liz, and I continued to comfort each other.

We had no idea if what had happened was only in Las Vegas or elsewhere. It was like we were on a deserted island up there. No communication about anything from anyone.

Even though we are pretty safe up here, we are cut off from the city. We will run out of food and water quickly. "We will die out here in this desert," Curt said, approaching the table after walking back from the Grove. My eyes went vacant. "Oh my God!" I thought. "Our family, our kids, JAY!"

Most of our family members lived in Texas, most of them not far from the Galveston coast. Jay's dad Nate, and his new wife Veronica, were retired and lived near the beach. Fishing was a big part of their lives now.

He had three siblings: his older brother Doug, his wife Barb, and their two twin girls, Abby and Ally. They owned a small gun and ammunition store in a small town near the deer lease.

His two younger sisters, Estelle and Megan, both lived with their family in the suburbs of Houston. Estelle had two kids, pregnant with their third and ran a large company from her home. Her husband, Ron, traveled a lot for business. Megan had three children and was a stay-at-home mom. She was married to Landon, a Houston Firefighter. Jay's only child, Gail, was a single mom to our only granddaughter, Lynn. She was 5 years old now and a ball of energy. Gail went to college in Houston, and we were so excited that she was in her last year of medical school. We were going to have a doctor in our family. I had two grown sons, Jordan, a local known dog whisperer, lived with his wife, Ashlyn, a local artist, in the same area as Jay's family, and owned one of the largest pet rescues in the area. My oldest son Thain and his wife Kris, and their two young kids, Heaven and Reece, lived a minimalist life in the mountains of Colorado, living off grid and unreachable most of the time. I knew they would be alright being a prepper and survivalist.

My mom, Kay, lived on the best bass fishing lake in Texas. My youngest brother, Jace, and his wife, Peggy, and their three daughters; Jenny, Lexi, Bea, and son Collin moved closer to my mom to help her out after dad died. They were only a couple of hours away from the deer lease. But my other brother Mike, his wife Sue, and their sons Taylor and Joel, lived eight hours away in El Dorado, Kansas, in the home I grew up in.

I couldn't believe what I was seeing. The panic set in. "Where was Jay? He should have been home by now." I cried.

CHAPTER TWO
Trying to get home

Day 1: 7am Jay

Jay was exhausted. It had been one of the busiest nights he had had in a long time. A huge order had just come in and they needed as many managers as possible to check the merchandise in before they went home. Besides having to deal with customers that were just downright rude.

He had clocked out about 10minutes late when the HR manager caught him before walking out the door. "Can I talk to you just for a second? I know it's your Friday and you're exhausted, but I wanted to let you know we had approved your promotion," she said with a smile on her face. When the club opened, he was going to be the general manager. He thanked her and ran out the door with renewed energy. "Wait till I tell my wife," he said to himself, smiling from ear to ear.

Since they had held him up, he knew he would be in the beginnings of rush hour traffic, and there always seemed to be an accident or hold up on the interstate. Even though it would take him a few more minutes, he decided to take the back roads home. Decatur Blvd was always the best route, three lanes and long stretches between lights. Plus, he could stop at Dutch bros and get his favorite cup of coffee,

"The Kicker." It was a very strong coffee, but not as bad as the "911", which he had gotten once and said never again.

Singing along with his favorite CD and drinking his coffee, he thought about the upcoming promotion. The things he would get to see and do, headliners he would get to book, and stars and celebrities he would get to meet.

The last couple of miles of Decatur went parallel to the North Las Vegas Airport. Usually for smaller aircraft and helicopters. The traffic light had turned yellow and the car in front of him had stopped abruptly, forcing Jay to slam on his breaks, and making his last couple drinks of coffee come flying out of his hand. "Damnit!" he yelled as he came to a stop. He looked down to find his cup before the last of the coffee came out of the little hole in the lid. "Crap, all over my pant leg," he grumbled as he glanced up to the light, "still red," and wiped the coffee from his leg with the only napkin he had.

Suddenly, the car died. He looked up just in time to see two cars collide in the intersection, and several more swerving to miss them but coming to a stop in the middle of the road.

At this point, he wasn't concerned about his car dying. He needed to see if the people in the other cars were okay. He jumped out of his car and ran to the car closes to him. The car had been hit on the passenger side. In the driver's seat, a man sat stunned. The airbag hadn't deployed. The man seemed to be okay. "Are you okay?" Jay asked the man frantically. "I think so. I'm not sure what happened," he replied. Jay looked up towards the other car and noticed several people had gathered around it. The man took off his seatbelt and Jay helped him out of his car. They walked slowly over to the other car where the others were standing.

They all seemed to stare towards the small airport. "Oh my God!" a lady standing there screamed. As Jay turned and looked, he saw a small airplane that had just started taking off crash back down on to the ground. Looking right past it, he could see plumes of smoke rising from the downtown area. Off in the distance, a big blue plane caught their attention. Everyone stood there in horror as they watched a huge jumbo jet fall from the sky in the eastern part of the valley.

Jay reached for his cell phone to call 911, but his phone was dead. "Hey someone call 911, my phone is dead," he yelled out. As several people reached for their phones, they too started yelling that their phones were dead as well. "What the hell is going on?" someone asked.

A crowd of people had gathered now in the intersection talking about how their cars just stopped, their engines just died. The radios wouldn't come on. They compared cell phones, and a couple had brought out their iPads, "nothing," everything was dead.
Explosion after explosion could be heard coming from all areas, and smoke rising from all around. Knowing that no one was seriously hurt, Jay walked back to his SUV. He turns the key to see if it will start. "Nothing," he said under his breath.

Just sitting there watching the others trying to start their cars, Jay just stared thinking to himself, "this started out to be such a great morning, now what?"

Day 1 9am D'Ann

The TV didn't work, our phones didn't work, the electricity was off, most importantly, no air conditioning. I opened the windows and sat down in the rocking chair. Surely it will come back soon. Thinking about what I had just witnessed, I just kept shaking my head in disbelief. "Where is Jay" I said looking up at the ceiling. He had to be on his way home. "Is he stuck somewhere on the interstate?" I wondered. Never even contemplating that he could have had a wreck or a plane fall on him. I pushed those thoughts out of my head. "He is fine," I said, as I scratched Diamond's head that she had in my lap. Dogs know when something is wrong, or someone is sad. I put my head back against the chair and closed my eyes. Tears seeped out around the edges.

Suddenly, the dogs started barking, and then I heard a knock at the door. "You okay in there?" came a man's deep voice. I jumped up and opened the door. Benny was standing there with a concerned look on his face. "Is Jay here? I need his help." He asked, "No, he never made it home this morning." "Oh my God, I hope he is okay," he commented. "Me too," I replied. "I don't know what to do," I cried, as Benny came in and sat down on the sofa. "I know," he said. "I needed his help to help me get to my house to make sure Nadia was okay." We both sit in silence for a couple minutes.

"If the cars stopped, he would have to walk home," I said, "depending on how far he got. That's a long walk." I added. "Do you think everything will come back on?" I asked. Benny looked up at me. "From all the things that Nadia has taught me, I think it's going to be a different world from here on out," He replied.

Wiping the tears away from my face, I stood up with a determined look. "We can't just sit here. We got to do something," I exclaimed. "So, none of the vehicles will start, correct?" I asked. "Nothing newer than the 1990s, the older the better," he replied. "Well, that leaves my truck out. It's a 2003. Going to the door, I looked around the park as much as I could see. No vehicles seemed to be old. "Hey, doesn't Mark have an old side-by-side that he keeps next to his RV?" I asked. "He's not there. He went to visit his daughter in Arizona," he replied. Glancing to the front of the RV, I remembered we had brought our own ATVs with us. But I realized the keys were on Jay's key ring. Benny and I walked out of the RV and down the row and then up two rows until we came to Mark's trailer. Benny was his boss, as well. They had both started at the gun range at the same time 8 years ago when the range first opened. Mark was one of the first hosts in the park.

Mark had gone to visit his grown kids several times a year, so Benny knew where Mark hid his extra key to his trailer. "Hopefully, the keys are hanging in the trailer," Benny said as he unlocked and opened the door.

I didn't feel right about going into someone's home when they weren't there and rummaging around for the keys to a side-by-side we were about to steal, or better word "borrowed."

After several minutes Benny came back out of the trailer, holding the keys in the air. "Found em," he exclaimed. "Let's see if this puppy has gas," he said, heading towards the front of his trailer. "And let's hope it starts," I added.

The tank was full, and better yet, Mark had three gas cans that seemed to be full, strapped to the back end. The side-by-side actually had four seats. Jumping in the driver's seat, Benny put the key in and turned it. "Nothing." He tried again, then again, still nothing. Just as he was about to give up, he remembered that during a lunch break they were all sitting around talking about their 4-wheelers and ATVs, and Mark had mentioned he had installed a "kill switch" on his so people couldn't steal it. Benny reached down under the steering wheel and found a small switch, flipped it in the opposite direction, and turned the key again. The side-by-side roared to life. "Yay!" I said, clapping my hands. I ran around to the passenger side and hopped in. "Wait, what are you doing?" Benny asked, startled. "I'm going with you; we can look for Jay on the way to your house," I replied. "It might take us a while. Let's stop back at my RV and grab some bottled waters and some snacks," I added.

I grabbed a backpack and stuffed several bottles of water into it. I looked around the pantry and noticed I hadn't been to the grocery store that week and we had little in the way of snacks, a few granola bars and some pop tarts was about it. "This will have to do," I said as I stuffed them in the bag as well.

Looking at my dogs, I knew they were going to be hot in the RV, so I ran out the door, held up a finger to Benny, indicating one second, and ran over to Curt and Liz's door. I knocked hard and fast; I could hear Liz come to the door. "Are you okay?" she said, breathing a little hard. I must have scared them. "I'm going to look for Jay and help Benny get home to Nadia," I said, all out of breath. Curt and Liz stepped out of their RV, "I know it's hot in my RV and I don't want to leave my dogs inside, will you watch them for me, I'm going to take Diamond with me for protection," I continued. "Yeah, yeah, sure, we can keep an eye on them. No worries, but do you think it's a good idea to go looking for him?" Liz asked. "I can't just sit here, he maybe so far away that it's just far to walk in this heat," I replied. "We will be careful, and you too," as she waved at Benny. "Thank you so much. I owe you," I said as I ran back to the RV, grabbed Diamond's leash, and snapped it to her collar.

The other dogs started getting excited. I'm sure they thought we were going on a walk. But as I led Diamond to the side-by-side and she jumped in, the other three just stood watching as we drove to the exit. The gun range sat on several thousand acres of desert. There was nothing north of us except the mountains. On the west and east side, there were only miles and miles of cactus. The entire city lay just south of us. There was about a one-half mile from the entrance of the park to the nearest neighborhood, and approximately three miles to the nearest Walmart, the closest gas station was about 6 blocks from the entrance of the gun range. Beyond that, within five miles was any kind of shopping you could imagine.

Benny and Nadia lived several miles away from the gun range. In the opposite direction of where I needed to go to find Jay.
The ride was loud and bumpy. Looking around, I could tell several neighborhoods were on fire. Cars were everywhere, just sitting there in the middle of the street. People were out trying to figure out why their cars didn't run.

There were still groups of people standing outside the stores, just looking around, like the electricity was going to come back on any minute, as we drove by. "Maybe we should stop and see if they know what is going on?" I asked. Benny shook his head. "They probably don't know any more than we do," he replied, driving right past them. We kept driving what seemed like forever, dodging cars and trucks, and even a couple newer motorcycles. Occasionally, we would spot an older model car or truck driving by. All the signal lights were dark, so we didn't bother to stop at the intersections, figuring no one else would be going through them either. People were everywhere, standing or sitting outside. It was way too hot to be inside now. They seemed to be just waiting. Waiting for something to happen.

We passed several buildings that were on fire, one even exploding right after we had passed it. "Dang, that was close," I said, ducking my head.

We were just a few blocks from his street when we noticed most of the houses were burning, or had exploded or were not even there, just a pile of rubble. The urgency grew in Benny as we got closer to his street. The side-by-side seemed to go faster and faster. I watched house after house on fire.

As we turned down his street, the houses seemed to be untouched. Then we saw it, his house was still standing, we pulled into the drive, and he slammed on the brakes, got out and ran to the door.

I slowly got out, took hold of Diamond's leash, and walked to the door. It was wide open. They were talking to each other. "I'm so glad you're okay," Nadia said. "I'm fine," Benny replied. Standing in the entryway of their house, watching them embrace. I thought about my own reunion with Jay.

Day 1 9am Jay

Jay sat in his car with the door open. "Of course, the windows won't roll down," as he pushed the buttons. He looked around his car to see what he needed to take with him. "Can't forget this," as he put his bag of marijuana samples into his backpack. He always carried his handgun on him, but while at work, he put it inside his middle console. Grabbing it and a couple of lighters he had thrown in there a few days ago. He also had a half a bottle of water he had grabbed from the fridge at work. "Better take this, it's going to be a long walk," he said as he stuffed it in the side of his backpack.

He shut his car door and hit the remote to lock it. "Well, that won't work!" as he opened the door and manually pushed the lock on the door. Without taking his hand off the door, he whispered to the car, "take care of yourself, you've been a great car," and then walked away.

The area he was in was a residential area. Houses and apartments lined the streets. As he walked, he could see lots of people, some still in their pajamas, coming out of their homes to see what was going on. Mothers and fathers, children and grandparents, everyone was so confused.

People standing by their cars that had just stopped in the middle of the road, confused and in a daze. Some people gathered in groups, trying to figure it out.

Jay kept his head down and just kept walking. He didn't want to converse with anyone, he just wanted to go home. And he knew it would take hours.

The sun was getting hot, and the only water he had was gone. Thirst was creeping in, and he knew he needed to get more water. As he walked, he started looking at the homes he was passing to see if there was a water hose or a source he could get water from. He knew the nearest store was still several blocks away.

Most houses along this street had desert landscaping, which meant very little water. But he kept looking. The people seemed to have disappeared, only a few still looking at their cars and refusing to leave them in hopes they would be rescued, or they would magically start back up.

The sweat was dripping off Jay's head. He knew he was losing more water. So, the next person he saw outside their home, he would ask if he could have some water, and if that didn't do the trick, he would force his way in to get water.

Searching ahead, he looked for movement. He was still walking at a pretty good pace. "There," as he nodded with his head toward a man that just came out his front door. It was the next house. "Excuse me, sir," he yelled across the yard, "could I bother you for some water?" he asked. The man looked around and seemed a little frightened. All he saw was a shaved headed man, with tattoos all over his arms, and a gun on his hip. The man turned and looked towards his front door, which was only about 50 ft away. "Umm, yeah sure," as he hurried to his door, "hold on," as the man opened his door, went in, and closed it in a hurry. Jay walked up to the porch and stood on the step and waited for the man to come back.

Several minutes passed, and no one came back out. Jay knocked on the door to see if he could still have some water. But no one came. He tried turning the door handle, but it was locked. "Well, shit," he said, as he contemplated whether he was going to enter the house and demand water, or just try the next place.

A few seconds more and with his throat really becoming dry, he walked down the steps and back onto the road. Passing a couple of abandoned vehicles, he thought, "maybe someone would have had a water bottle in their car. People always seem to have water in their cars, especially in this heat," he thought.

The next car he came to, he tried the door handle. "Locked." He looked through the windows, searching for any liquid he could find. "Nothing." So, he continued to walk.

The sun was really getting hot, and it was taking a toll on him. He had stopped sweating, which he knew was not a good sign.

Occasionally, a person or family would pass by him, but he could tell they were in worse shape them him. "Do you have any water?" they would ask him. "No, I'm looking for it myself," he would reply, as they all kept moving.

Jay knew he was getting overheated. "I need some shade," as he looked at the next house and saw a little shade as their home blocked the sun. There was no grass, and the pavement was boiling from the sun, but he knew he had to sit down. He felt like he had been walking for hours, even though the sun told him differently.

As Jay sat down in what little shade there was, he leaned up against the garage door. There were no vehicles in the drive and before he sat down, he took a peek in the garage window, no cars.

He wiped his head on his shirt and took some deep breaths. He brought his knees up to his chest and laid his head down on his knees. "I just need a little break," he thought.

Day 1 10am D'Ann

"I'm going to go look for Jay," I said, interrupting their conversation. They both looked up at me. "You want me to go with you?" Benny asked. "No, no, you need to take care of things here. I'll be fine," I replied. "I'm hoping he made it most of the way home and he won't be too far," I continued. "Here, I got some more gas in the garage. Let's fill up the side-by-side." As Diamond and I followed Benny to his garage.

After emptying the gas can, he strapped it to the roof, "in case you need to get more gas." Benny said, "hold on," Nadia yelled as she ran back in the house.

A few minutes later, she came out with a small backpack. "I put some more water bottles, a gas siphon kit and some high protein snacks in here," as she handed me the pack. "Take care of yourself," she said as she leaned in to give me a hug.

"I will," I replied. "Pack your stuff up and be ready. After I find Jay, we will come for you and get you up to gun range. It's probably the best place to be," I added. They both shook their heads, and Diamond and I walked off towards the side-by-side.

Diamond jumped up in the passenger site as I tied her lease to the roll bar. I petted her head and then held her face in my hands, putting my nose to hers. "Let's go find your daddy," I said. Kissed her forehead and went around the side-by-side and hopped in.

I knew Jay took the freeway to work and back, thinking he might be stranded somewhere along the way. I back tracked the way we came to the entrance to the freeway. Cars, trucks, and semis were scattered everywhere on the freeway. I could see groups of people walking around, trying to make their way to the exit ramps. I surveyed the crowds looking for Jay but stayed far enough away that if they tried to get to the side-by-side, I could speed off.

I knew with a full tank I could go about one hundred miles more or less on a tank. And it was twenty miles, give or take a couple miles to his work. I drove down the side of the freeway that he would have been driving on.

People tried flagging me down to stop, but I tried not to look at them and kept going. I saw a few cars on fire, looking like they had crashed. Even seeing what looked like a body or two lying beside their crash cars. I tried not to look at or think about it. I just kept scouring the highway for Jay's SUV, or him walking.

As I got to a long stretch of highway between exits. Most all the people were gone. Up ahead, I could see a black SUV. My heart started pounding hard. But the closer I got; I could tell there was no one in it. "Could I have missed him? Could he have gotten off at one of the exits?" So many thoughts were going through my mind.

Then suddenly, movement out of the corner of my eye caught my attention. Standing by a car was a woman with a toddler running around kicking a ball, and a baby's car seat sitting next to the woman. I could tell as I got closer the woman was crying uncontrollably.

"Damn it," I thought to myself. "I can't leave her out here with two kids all alone." Shaking my head, I drove towards her. Looking around to make sure there were no other people around, I drove towards her.

As I got closer, the toddler ran to his mother. She looked up. All I could see was despair on her face. Her eyes were puffy from crying and her face was red from the heat.

She grabbed her toddler and stood up, moving the baby between her and the car. She stared at me with a scared look face. I took one more look around, then turned off the motor. I pulled out one of the water bottles and handed it out to her. She was reluctant to take it, but her toddler started crying and said she was thirsty. "Here, take it, it's okay," I said to her as she took a step towards me and took the water bottle. "What's happening?" she asked in a shaky voice. "I'm not sure. I think it was an EMP," I replied. "A what?" she asked. "An EMP, will fry all electrical things," I said. "My cell phone doesn't work," she said. "I had just dropped my husband off at work and was heading home when my car just stopped," she added. "I just couldn't carry both kids, and it seemed like everyone else was so scared they just kind of left me here."

She reached down and took the baby bottle from out of the baby's car seat, opened the bottle, and poured her water into the bottle. She then put it down and little fingers grabbed it. "It's so hot. I really thought we were going to die."

I reached into my bag and handed her another bottle of water. "Here, I've got more," as I handed her the bottle.

"So, you were coming from the south. You dropped your husband off at work?" I asked. "Yeah, he works at Mountain View Hospital off Cheyenne and the 95," she replied. I looked down the highway, which was only a few more miles down the road, and not out of my way. "It would be best if you and the kids came with me. I can drop you off with your husband," I said. "That would be so wonderful. I wouldn't know how to thank you," she cried.

I made room for her and the kids in the back seats. The toddler strapped on her mama's lap. We rode towards the hospital. Still looking around to make sure I didn't pass Jay's SUV.
Smoke filled the sky all around. The neighborhood beside the hospital was on fire. We could see several homes completely engulfed in flames. I pulled my T-shirt up over my nose and mouth as the smoke got thicker the closer we got.

I exited the highway and pulled into the hospital parking lot. It seemed like hundreds of people were standing outside the doors. I suddenly stopped, and turned around to the lady, "I'm so sorry, but I don't think I can get any closer without someone trying to steal this," I said to her. "I understand. Here is fine, and again, I don't know how to thank you," she replied. "Take care and I hope you find your husband," I said as I jumped out and helped her out of the side-by-side. She reached out and gave me a hug. As we were standing there, I could see a couple of people from the crowd pointing towards me and then started walking my way. Diamond starting growling. "I gotta go," as I pulled away from her. She picked up the car seat with one hand and held her toddler's hand with the other and started walking towards the crowd and the doorway. I jumped in the driver's seat, put it in drive and took off. "Good girl," I said, putting my hand on Diamond's head.

The hospital was right at the exit to 95, so I was back on the highway in seconds, and back looking for the black Dodge Journey.

With my arm shading my eyes from the sun, I looked up at the sky. "Looks to be getting close to noon," I thought to myself. Still keeping on my path to Jay's work, I passed by car after car empty and some with people still standing around, wondering if their cars would start. Every once in a while, an older model truck or car would drive by, full of people going who knows where. Several times I had come up to an SUV that looked a lot like Jay's, but once I approached it, I knew it wasn't.

I could see lots of smoke plumes coming from all directions. Buildings and entire neighborhoods on fire. Then the last curve that turned back towards the strip I could see it. Several of the huge casinos were burning. "Oh my God!" I said under my breath. The Vegas Valley was burning.

Jay's job was only a block or two from the strip. Although people knew in Vegas a block or two was really a long way. Interstate 95 met with I15 at what they called the spaghetti bowl. From there, I15 ran north and south. North took you to Salt Lake City, and south would take you to Los Angeles. As I approached the spaghetti bowl, I knew I could no longer ride on the shoulder. I would have to cross several overpasses, and that could be difficult, I thought. There were more and more stalled and crashed cars. My heart was beating just a little faster the closer I got. I had to slow down to about 15 mph to navigate through all the cars. Then I saw it, a huge pile up. It looked impassable. I drove until I couldn't get through anymore. I stopped and hopped up on the seat to see if I could see a black SUV and take a thorough look around for any movement. The pile up looked to be several cars deep. I could tell on the other side of the pileup; a few cars had gotten stopped in time. "No black SUV!" But I could see several bodies slumped over in some of the crashed cars. "Damnit, I'm going to have to go back to the last exit and get off." I said. "This is a waste of time, ugh."

Taking one last look to see if there was any way to get through it. I put the side-by-side in reverse and backed up to the end of the overpass.

Coming to a stop, I looked at the drop off and thought to myself, "this is a freaking 4wheel drive, I could do that," I said, as I looked down the embankment to the street below. "I could catch that street go around the overpass and back up the other side." "I can make sure Jay is not on the back side of this pile up. Hang on, Daimy, we're going down." I said, petting Diamond on the head. I reached down and pushed the 2-wheel drive stick into the 4-wheel drive. And eased forward to the edge.

CHAPTER THREE
Two black fur balls

Day 1: 11am Jay

Jerking awake, Jay opened his eyes and lifted his head, confused for a moment. He looked around, wondering where he was for just a split second.

The sun was really beating down on him now. The sweat had beaded up on his forehead and his shirt was soaking wet. Even though he was half Mexican with a permanent tan and had already been working outside at the gun range, his head still felt burnt. He got to his feet, a little off balance and lightheaded. He leaned against the garage door and looked around. No one was in sight. He listened for noise but heard nothing except for a few dogs in the neighborhood barking. Still needing water and fast. He could tell his blood sugar was getting low as he shook.

He walked over to the front door. "Locked." He knocked several times with a loud knock so that anyone could hear him that was inside the house. But no one came. The house had a privacy fence that started at the corner of each side with a wooden gate on the garage side. Walking to the gate, "locked." He surveyed the height on the wall and decided he would most likely not be able to scale the wall. He felt the sturdiness of the gate by putting his shoulder against it and pushing a little, no give. It was very solid. "Well, crap," he said. Still looking around for any signs of movement. He walked back around to the front door. Again, he knocked loud, "nothing." The front door was solid wood, but beside the doors were side windows. "Guess I'm going to have to break it," he said out loud as he reached for the butt of his gun. The crash was loud as he used the butt of his gun on the window closest to the door handle. He reached in and felt for the knob and felt for a deadbolt. Twisting it, the door clicked. He turned the handle and walked in, closing the door quickly behind him. With his gun still in his hand, he walked through the entryway to the living room, kitchen area.

There was a huge TV hanging over a gas fireplace in the living room. Directly in front was a huge comfy looking sectional sofa. A couple of toy trucks in the corner and a big Barbie house with half naked barbies lying next to it. Across from them was a desk littered with papers and a small laptop. He surveyed the room and saw on the wall next to the sliding glass doors that went to the backyard, bookshelves with pictures of a bride and groom, several pictures of babies, and a couple pictures of a little boy looking to be about 5 or 6 years old. "I wonder where these people ended up?" he thought.

The house was an open concept, with the kitchen being completely open to the living room. He walked around the kitchen island/bar that separates the two rooms to the refrigerator.

He opened the door to see if it held any water. "Bingo" he had struck gold. He grabbed the first one, unscrewed the lid and drank it all fast as he could. "Oh, wow, that is good," he said as he grabbed another one and opened it. All of a sudden, he heard a noise coming from the bedroom area. "Oh, shit," he whispered to himself. He sat the water bottle down and, with his gun in his hand, walked cautiously towards the bedroom.

Peeking around the corner, the first room he came to was a child's room. Cars and Legos were everywhere, all over the floor. Slowly pushing the half-opened door all the way open, he could see the child's bedspread, with dinosaurs all over it, crumbled up and halfway on the ground. He stepped in, trying not to step on any toys, walked slowly to the closet door. One side of the bifold doors was closed. He took a deep breath and slowly, making no noise, opened the closed door. He waited a second to see if he could hear any sounds coming from the closet, and then peaked his head in. "Nothing." He moved the hanging clothes around and looked from top to bottom. No one was here. As he turned to tiptoe back to the door, another noise came from the hallway, but he couldn't quite figure out what kind of sound it was. It was a small quiet bang, and then a noise like a scratch.

He stepped back into the hallway and headed towards another closed door. He stopped to listen. "Maybe I should just get out of here," he thought. "I'll just go grab a couple more bottles of water and walk out the front door," he continued.

Listening a few seconds more, he turned back towards the kitchen. Walked as quietly but as quickly as he could open the fridge door, grabbed four bottles of water, and reached in the back and grabbed the only two Gatorade bottles, unzipped his backpack and threw them all in. He swung his backpack over his shoulder and headed towards the front door as quickly as he could, but it was too late. Out of the corner of his eye, he saw movement in the hallway. He stopped, frozen in his tracks, and slowly turned toward the hallway.

Two big black fuzz balls came running at him. The cats were chasing each other down the hallway. Jay grabbed his chest. "Oh my God, you almost gave me a heart attack," he said to them as they ran by.
He stood there a little longer to see what else was going to come down the hallway. But it was clear. He turned and watched the cats playing tag and running around the kitchen island. Walking back into the kitchen, he grabbed the largest bowls he could find and filled them with water. And set them on the floor, then went over to the cupboard

to find the cans of cat food and a big bag of dry cat food on the bottom self. He took the bag out and dumped the entire bag on the floor. "That should hold you for a while," he said, "but what if no one comes?" He walked towards the sliding glass doors, unlocked it and pushed it open about a foot. "Well, at least you might have a chance."

Day 1 11am D'Ann

Easing the side-by-side over the edge, I creeped down the concrete embankment. By the time I had gotten to the bottom, the sweat was dripping from my face, and not just because it was hot out. I sat at the bottom and literally had to peel my fingers and hands from the steering wheel after grabbing it so tight they almost became embedded in the vinyl. I looked over at Diamond and the "big, bad, ferocious man-eater" was shaking like a leaf. Reaching over, I petted her on the head, "I'm sorry, girl," I said to her as she licked my arm.

After a few minutes of composing myself, I drove under the overpass, looking up to see where the best place to go back up, where I was clear of the pileup, would be. I looked down the street a little further and saw an area that was not nearly as steep as this area was and decided I would go down there and up in that area. I knew I would have to backtrack a little to go back to the pileup and double check Jay was not there, but at least it wouldn't be as scary as it would be right here. Climbing slowly back up the other side, I reached the interstate. Turned back to the north and back to the pileup. From what I could tell by the mangled mess of vehicles, his SUV wasn't one of them. Looking over the vehicles, I could tell several people didn't make it out of there. I knew deep down there was nothing I could do for anyone, so I turned around and headed back towards Jay's job.
The exit to Jay's work was just about a half a mile more down the highway, which also meant a lot closer to the burning casinos and resorts on the strip.

I made my way to the exit, which was actually the on ramp since I was still going the wrong way in the northbound lanes. Several cars were blocking the lanes to get on to the interstate.

Since it had already been hours since this began, the people that inhabited these vehicles were nowhere in sight. I maneuver around vehicles, most of the time riding on the shoulder and reached the street. Sahara was the closest street to Jay's job. But once I got off the interstate, I still had several blocks of street to get there. The street his job was on ran behind the resorts. Thank goodness it was before the big resorts, for looking up at the newly opened Resorts World, which was one of the biggest resorts on the strip, the resort had almost imploded on itself; the hotel was on fire and one tower had come crashing down on to the parking garage. "Man, I wonder how many people were in that garage?" I said to myself. The street was empty, only a car here and there. But looking ahead, I could see smoking coming from the direction in which his building would be. I gave the side-by-side a little more gas and pushed it as fast as I could get it to go.

His building was a mess. I could still see flames coming from the building and a couple of walls had fallen into the store. I knew employee parking was on the opposite side of the building, but a privacy fence made of concrete blocks surrounded the parking area, with only one way in and one way out.

I eased around the parking lot and to the entrance of employee parking. The gate was made of solid metal, allowing no one to see in. A car looked like it had just gone out when it stopped.

I hopped out of the side-by-side and walked up to the gate. There was about a 1ft clearance at the bottom of the gate. I got down on my hands and knees to see if I could see under it, knowing I was too big to crawl under it. I couldn't see anything. There were several cars still in the parking lot.

Walking along the concrete wall away from the building, I search for a breach in the wall. Suddenly, I heard Diamond barking, which I had left tied to the roll bar on the side-by-side. I had walked too far. Not being able to see her from where I was. I ran as well as I could with my legs to get to her. As I rounded the corner, I saw the side-by-side but no Diamond. Hanging there from the roll bar was a lease and a collar. "Oh, crap," I thought to myself.

Running to the side-by-side, I heard growling coming from the other side of a low concrete wall. I ran over to the wall and saw Diamond standing over a man that was on the ground. She had pinned him and had a mouth full of black material.

I reached into the back of my pants and grabbed my gun. Walked around the wall. "Get your dog off me," the man said in a terrified voice. "Diamond, come here," I commanded. She looked at me, then looked back at the man. "DIAMOND!" I said louder, with a sternness to my voice. Diamond backed off the man and dropped part of the man's uniform that had once covered his arm. I reached down and put the collar back on her neck, making it a tad bit tighter.

The man sat up, and I noticed he had a security guard uniform on. Hoping this was a "good guy," I apologized, "I'm sorry, she is very protective." I said. "I see that," the man replied, as he stood up, brushing off his uniform. "Did you work here?" I asked. "Yes, I had just come on shift," "Do you know Jay Zepola? He's a graveyard shift manager," I asked with hopeful eyes. "Yeah, I know him. He's a great guy," he answered. "I'm looking for him. He never made it home," I said. "Yeah, I saw him leave. He was running late, though. I was already on the clock when I saw him walk out. He had a big smile on his face, seemed to be thrilled about something." He continued.
"I had to have missed him," I said under my breath. "I'm sorry," the guard said, "I'm sure he's just stuck somewhere on the road between here and your house." "Yeah, I'm sure that's where he is," I agreed. "I wonder if he took the back streets home, because of leaving late and rush hour traffic?" I asked. "I'm going back north. Can I give you

a ride? Oh, and sorry about your sleeve," I said. "No, I'm going to stay here and try to keep this place secure until I hear from someone about what to do," he replied. I walked to the back of the side-by-side and grabbed a couple bottles of water from the pack and some granola bars, walked back over and handed to him. "Thanks, I appreciate it," he said.

Diamond and I jumped back in the side-by-side and looked around. "I'm thinking he would have gone down Decatur Blvd. That would have been the best route home from here," I said out loud.

We back tracked the way we came, until we got to the interstate, and instead of getting back on I went straight under the overpass and continued to Decatur Blvd. This part of Vegas was well known for homeless encampments, and it did not disappoint. It seemed like there was more than ever on that stretch of road. People sitting around under any shade they could find. "These people will most likely make it. They already live with nothing and scrounge for food every day. It's the people like us that will hurt, living in all the comforts of life, until now."

Turning off Sahara on to Decatur, I tried to calculate how far Jay would have gotten this morning. "Shit, I have no idea. I'm just going to keep going and hopefully I'll find him walking towards home."

Day 1 12noon Jay

Jay walked out the front door. He had a renewed energy as he walked up the street. He had a few bottles of water now and figured he could make it at least to the store that was still several blocks away.
Jay was in great shape. He walked miles and miles every day while at work, back and forth across the showroom floor. A couple weeks after he started his job, we had bought him some expensive walking shoes cause his feet were killing him. Especially now he was very glad we had spent the extra money and got him the best ones we could find.

The sun was still hot. Beating down on his head, he slipped his T-shirt off and put it around his head like he used to do when he was little. He passed a few houses that had people sitting on their porches. "It was way too hot to be inside now," he thought. Every once in a while, he would hear the faint sound of an engine getting closer. He would look around to see what it was, but only a couple of times caught a glimpse of an old truck or old car driving down the street.

As he was walking, he occupied his mind by trying to devise a plan on what he was going to do once he got to the gun range. He knew D'Ann was most likely scared and did not know what was going on and where he was.

He thought about the conversation they had had before he left for work, about buying groceries. "Dang it," he thought. They had discussed, since today was payday and tomorrow was Saturday, they would go grocery shopping tomorrow. He knew the pantry was bare and there was not much in the fridge. "I wonder if they have electricity up there," he thought. "Probably not," he said out loud. "But we have a generator, which might keep the fridge cold for a bit," he continued. He took good care of the generator, turning it on every week and letting it run. It had been about a month ago he had drained the gasoline out and put new gas in it, till he knew it was full. The two propane tanks were full. The only thing we used the propane for was mainly the cooking stove (which we hardly used) and hot water. But the water temperature coming out of the hose was hot from the sun. We hardly used it either.

As he walked, devising a plan, he hardly noticed how far he had gotten. Up ahead, he could see the gas station sign. The LED lights that had pronounced how expensive gas a gallon is weren't lit up. He approached the station with caution to see if there was movement. Standing in front of the doors was an employee with a baseball bat in her hands. As He approached her, he could tell she had been crying, and she was shaking.

"Ma'am are you okay?" he asked, as he stopped just out of reach of the bat. The look on her face was total fear. She didn't look to be much over eighteen. "I don't know what's going on," she replied in a shaky voice. "I was working and all of a sudden, the lights went out and everything shut off. There were customers in here, and they just grabbed a handful of stuff and ran out the door. We keep this bat behind the counter in case we are robbed. But I just didn't know what to do. I was terrified," she continued.

"Listen, I don't think the electric and stuff are going to come back on soon. And it's going to get ruff out here. Do you live close?" He asked her. "I live with my parents up by Ann and Decatur," she replied. "They usually pick me up after work, but I don't get off for another couple hours."

"You need to go in the store, get a bag and put some bottled water in it, enough that you can carry it. I'm walking home and going in that direction. You can walk with me," Jay said. The girl looked apprehensive, then she noticed the embroidery on his shirt. "You work for P13?" she asked. "Yes, I'm a manager there," he replied. "My dad works there," she commented with a slight smile. "Javier Segornia, do you know him?" She asked. "He works during the day," she said. "Yes, I see him in the mornings when I leave," he replied. "Today was his day off, so he should be at home," she said. "So, go get some water, we will lock the place up, it may not help, but at least you know you did everything you could to secure it, and then we will start walking, it's going to be a long walk," Jay continued. "By the way, I'm Janie Segornia," as she turned and opened the door as they both walked in. "I'm Jay. Nice to meet you," Jay replied.

Janie grabbed a bag and put in several bottles of water and a few bags of chips. It was heavy, but she commented she could do it. Jay grabbed a couple of bottles also and some beef sticks and put them in his bag. They locked the door behind them and started walking. They were at the corner of Craig and Decatur, and Ann Road was almost two more miles. Once they got away from the intersection, it was all residential from there. They could see a large plume of smoke up ahead but didn't know what it was.

They walked in silence most of the way, only encountering a few people walking in the opposite direction. As they approached a group of five, what looked to be older teens sitting on bicycles, Janie walked closer to Jay with fear on her face. She had noticed he was wearing a gun. And figured she would be safe next to him.

As they approached the teens, one, which seemed to be the leader of the pack, got off his bike, dropping it where he stood and walked a few steps from the pack. Jay looked him and the other four up and down and noticed they too had bats and large sticks. "So, hey man, you got some smokes on you?" the leader said. "Nope, don't smoke," Jay replied as he and Janie kept walking. Jay grabbed Janie's arm and guided her to the other side of him, so he was between her and the teens. "What do you got in the bag?" he demanded. As one of the other teens approached them with a bat. As he was banging it against his other hand. "It's water," Janie replied in a shaky voice. "Shhh, say nothing to them," Jay said as he looked at Janie, who had tears in her eyes.

"Well, maybe we will take your water. We are all a little thirsty," the teen replied. Jay stopped in his tracks, turned towards the teen, and pulled his gun, keeping it at his side but making sure all the teens saw it. The last thing he wanted to do was shoot someone, especially a teenager.

The teens immediately saw the gun and backed away. The leader picked up his bike and walked away. "Come on guys, let's go," the leader yelled as they all rode away.

"That was so scary," Janie said, trying to calm herself. "It's only going to get worse. When you get home, you and your parents need to stay inside and lock your doors." Jay said with concern in his voice. "Does you dad own a gun?" He asked. "I don't know, I think so," she replied.

"Well, he needs to keep it close, at least till everything is back to normal, but that could be a very long time," he replied.

Jay looked up at the sun and could tell it was past noon. It was hot and only getting hotter. He took a bottled water out of his pack and poured it over his head and poured a little in Janie's hands as she splashed it on her face. "The water was not cold anymore, but it sure felt good," she thought.

Before long they could see the intersection of Ann Road and Decatur. Janey's pace quickened a little, as she knew she was almost home. From that point, it took them a good 15 minutes to get to the intersection. "I only live a couple more blocks east on Ann, right on the other side of Smith grocery store," she commented.

As they approached the parking lot of the Smiths, Jay looked around the lot. There were a few cars still in the parking lot, but the store had only been open a short time when it happened, so few people shop that early. The doors were closed to the store, and the glass was still intact. "Wonder how long that's going to last?" he thought to himself.

"Can you make it from here by yourself?" He asked. She whipped her head around quickly with that frightened little girl look on her face and look him in the eyes. "Do you think it's safe?" she asked. "If you go straight home, don't talk to anyone, and remember what I said, secure yourself. If the electricity doesn't come back on, you guys are going to have to get supplies. Just be careful," he said. She walked over to Jay and gave him a hug. "Thank you so much. I will tell my dad how you protected me," she said. "Now, go, hurry, get home safe, and God be with you," Jay replied as she turned and starting jogging away.

Day 1 1pm D'Ann

The Side-by-side could reach about 80mph, but with all the vehicles stalled and all the crashes, I didn't dare go that fast. On good stretches of road, I probably got up to 30mph, but I was also trying to conserve gasoline. So nice and steady was my motto.

As I made the corner where Decatur and Rancho merge over to my right, I could see the North Las Vegas Airport and where a couple of planes had crashed. The sight was horrifying. As I approached the intersection of Cheyenne and Decatur, the bottleneck of cars and trucks was too many to weave in and out of, and what looked to be a major crash in the intersection. It was a good thing the sidewalk was wide enough for me to go around. As I drove by the cars, I searched for the dodge.

Suddenly, I spotted a black Dodge Journey. It was right in the middle of the traffic, close to the intersection. I knew it was too congested to drive the side-by-side in there, so I parked it, hopped out and walked towards it. Diamond sat quietly, watching me walk away.

As I approached the SUV, I could see the familiar decal on the back window. "Wish I was on Galveston Island" it read. The last time we went home to visit family, we had gone to one of the souvenir shops on the island and stocked up on T-shirts, and a couple decals, one for his car and one for mine.

I went around to the driver's side door and noticed the window was broken, glass everywhere. I opened it and looked around inside. Everything was gone. "Either he left and started walking, or someone attacked him," I thought, as my stomach went to my throat. I looked around at the cars beside the SUV and noticed their windows were also busted out, and they left doors open. I calmed down a little, thinking this was an "after he left" job.

I went to the passenger side and opened the glove compartment to make sure he had taken anything that was left. As I was examining the glove box, I felt something hard push up against my shoulder blade. "Can I help you with something?" a man's deep voice said. "Put your hands where I can see them and slowly back up," he continued. "This is my husband's car. I was just making sure he got everything out," I replied. My mind was working overtime. "This must be a cop, by the way he was talking," I thought. "Turn around," he said. "Keep your hand where I can see them." I slowly turned around, thinking I would see an officer in a uniform. But that is not what I saw. Two men who looked to be in their late twenties, scruffy and dirty looking. One was holding a large metal bar which looked to be like a tire iron, which he had used to poke me in the back with.

The man held the tire iron just under my chin. And look at me straight in the eyes with a wild look. "These are our cars now, and everything that's in them," he threatened. I stared back at him, too shaken to say anything. "Go look at that other car, see what's in it, I'll take care of her," he said as his partner turned and trotted off towards the intersection.

The man looked me up and down, and fear rose in my chest. I didn't dare reach for my gun I had securely under my shirt in the front of my pants, "Thank God, he didn't see it," I thought.

"Come over here with me, missy," he said, as he poked my neck with the iron. I let out a little grown as the sharp end of the iron dug into my skin. "Look, I don't know what you want with me. I'm old and fat. I'm sure you would have a much better time finding someone else," I pleaded. "I like em old and fat," he replied. We had our backs to the side-by-side, but I could hear the faint rattling of Diamond chain on her lease. Praying to myself that I didn't tighten too tight that she couldn't get out, I made shuffling noises with my feet so he couldn't hear her struggling to get loose.

Just as he grabbed my arm, I heard it and saw her. Diamond lunged at his arm and with a mighty bit, she clapped on, whipping her head from side to side, ripping his skin. Blood everywhere. As he started screaming, he dropped the tire iron to the ground as I reached for my gun. I could hear his partner yelling what was going on. The guy was in so much pain he couldn't answer. He dropped to his knees, sobbing for her to let go, but she hung on. I reached down and grabbed the tire iron. Not wanting to kill the man, I swung and hit him in the head. Diamond let go as the man fell the rest of the way to the ground. I could hear his partner running towards us. As he came around the next car, I pointed my gun right at him. "What did you do? Is he dead?" He screamed. "Stay where you are unless you want to end up like him," I replied, trying not to show him I was shaking. "Diamond, come on," as we trotted back to the side-by-side. We jumped in and sped off down the sidewalk as I looked over at the men. The partner was helping the other one up off the ground.

I hit the gas and tried to get away from the intersection as quickly as I could, but tears where affecting my vision, so as soon as I knew I was far enough away, I stopped and put my hands to my face and sobbed uncontrollably. Diamond, with blood all over the front of her, put her head in my lap. "Thank you Daimy, you saved my life," as I held her and cried.

I sat for a few more moments and tried to calm myself down, but not wanting them to find me, I wiped my face with my shirt and started it back up. I drove slowly in and out of cars as I approached intersections.

The sun was scorching now, and my emotions were all over the place. I looked in the rear-view mirror to see why my neck was still burning and could see a small gouge where he had sliced it. It wasn't deep enough for stitches, but it was bleeding. With the mix of the man's blood from holding Diamond and my blood, my clothes and face were covered in it. "I looked like I had been in a horror movie, and it almost was," I thought.

I was now approaching Decatur and Ann Road. I knew there was a Smith grocery store there and thought I might get some antibiotics and bandages for the cut. As I approached the parking lot, I saw him. He was about a block away, almost out of the parking lot. Tears welled up in my eyes again. "JAY!" I screamed as loud as I could, as I sped towards him. "I would recognize that bald head and walk anywhere," I thought. The man stopped and turned around. He couldn't believe it. A Hugh smile came across his face. As I got closer, the smile disappeared as concern appeared on his face.

"Oh my God, what happened to you? I can't believe you're here," he said as I came to a screeching halt. I jumped off the side-by-side and ran up to him and threw my arms around his neck and sobbed again. He held me tight and didn't press me for answers. He helped me back to the side-by-side and noticed the blood all over the front of Diamond. But didn't say a word. He knew I would tell him as soon as I composed myself. "I think I need to go in to Smith before we leave and get some bandages and antibiotic cream, and some sanitizer to get this blood off. It is not all mine." As he looked at me again with concern in his eyes. "I will explain everything when we get on the road," I promised.

We drove up to the doors of the Smith Grocery Store. They were closed but not locked. We got off the side-by-side and told Diamond "to stay." Jay pulled the doors apart, and we walked in. "Hello, anyone here?" Jay yells loudly. At first, we walked to the pharmacy area, but we heard nothing. No one answered our yells if anyone was there. But as we got closer to the pharmacy, we heard voices. "Hello?" we both yelled. "Yes, hello? We are over here in the pharmacy." As we walked towards the counter, two women came to the counter. They looked straight at me with a horrified look on their faces. "Oh my God, are you Okay"? They both asked in unison. "Is there any way we can buy some bandages and antibiotics and maybe some hand sanitizer or hydrogen peroxide to clean her up?" Jay asked.

"Well, we don't have any way to ring you up. The computers are down," the pharmacist responded. "Well, I can just leave you some cash and write it down, so when and if they come back up, you can pay for it." Jay said. "Do you know what's going on out there?" the cashier asked. "I think it was an EMP. All cars and everything electronic have quit. Planes fell out of the sky. The strip and neighborhoods are on fire." Jay continued. "It's going to get bad. You two need to get home if you can. It will not be safe here. If it gets really bad, people are going to ransack this store for supplies," he said. "I was attacked already. I thought I was going to die," I quietly explained. But tears welled up in my eyes again, and I couldn't continue.

"Come on, let's get you washed up, and bandage that cut," the pharmacist said in a soft caring voice, as she came out from around the counter. "If you guys want to go get some supplies, get what you can," she continued.

She took hold of my arm and led me to the back of the pharmacy to their private bathroom. The water was still on. She grabbed some paper towel and soaked them in water and handed them to me. I put the towels on my face. The water was so cool it felt so good. A knock on the door and Jay's voice came through, "here's the bandages and stuff," he said. "Are you, Okay?" He asked. "Much better," I replied. After she applied the cream and bandages, we walked out of the restroom. Jay had taken a seat on the floor right outside the door. As the door opened, he got up and came over to me with a big hug. "You look a lot better," he said. "We better get out to Diamond," I said.
I turned around to the pharmacist, "Thank you so much, I really appreciate it," I said. "Where do you guys live? Is it close?" I asked.
The cashier spoke up. "I live within walking distance," she said. "I don't," the pharmacist replied. "I live over off of Ann and Simmons' area. I can't walk that far," she said. Jay met my look when I looked at him. Without even saying anything, we both knew we had to take her home. "Well, you can't stay here. You need to get as much food and supplies as you can and get home. I guarantee it's going to get bad," Jay said.

The two women looked at each other and shook their heads. "I don't know how I'm going to get home," the pharmacist said. "You can make it home?" He asked the cashier. "Yeah, it's just around the corner. My husband is at home," she replied. "Get a shopping basket, fill it up with nonperishables, and push it as fast as you can home, then stay in your house," Jay said. "We can take you home. We have an ATV out front," Jay continued. "You too. Let's get some supplies and fill up the side-by-side and get out of here."

Jay and the girls grabbed shopping carts and filled them with as much as they could, while I grabbed a gallon of water and went out to check on Diamond.

She was exactly where we left her, standing watch. I opened the water and poured it on her face and tried the best I could to wash the blood off. I moved my bags and stuff in the back to make room for some supplies. It wasn't long before all three came out with shopping carts full of supplies and food. We loaded it in the side-by-side and the three of us hopped in, me in the back seat with Diamond.

We followed the cashier all the way to her apartment door, where a man and a girl came out. Jay's eyes met the man's eyes and then looked at the girl. "Oh my God, that's him," she squealed. As Jay recognized Javier and Janie. "This is my mom," Janie exclaimed. "Thank you so much for helping my little girl and now my wife get home safely." Javier cried.

"No problem," Jay replied. "We gotta get going, you guys stay safe," Jay exclaimed as we drove away towards the pharmacist home.
We reached the pharmacist's house pretty quickly. Her husband came out and thanked us for bringing his wife home. We split the supplies, said our goodbyes, and got back on the road and headed towards the gun range.

We had a generator, but we would need that to just keep our refrigerator and deep freeze going so our food wouldn't spoil. The temperature was already in the high nineties, headed to 100plus outside. The temp in the RV was going to go even higher, even with all the windows open. This time of year, in Vegas, the temperatures could reach 115 and there was no breeze, making it deadly. After we unloaded the supplies into the RV. We made an inventory list of what we had and what we still might need. I sat down in the rocker and in seconds I was out, exhausted from all that had happened that day.

CHAPTER FOUR
Watching Las Vegas Burn

DAY 2

I had woken up still sitting in the rocking chair, and still wearing my blood covered shirt. I got out of the chair as I groaned. My body was stiff and sore. I walked to the bathroom to see if we still had water. "Yes!" I exclaimed. I pulled off my clothes and got in the shower. I let the water run over my head for several minutes as the water mixed with tears. Eventually I got out, got dressed and put clean bandages on my neck. It looked like it was still seeping a little blood, but not too bad. I could see a slight bruise forming around the cut.

Jay had let the dogs out to potty and run around in their little pen, then they settled down under the RV in the shade.

Curt, Liz and Jay had sat down at our patio table, trying to figure out what to do next.

We had only known Curt and Liz a short time. They too had worked on the shotgun fields. Only in passing did we know they came from Alabama. And most of their family still live there.

"Do you think this is happening all over the country, or even the world?" Liz asked. "We won't know, not having any television or radio, or any way to communicate. We just won't know. But we have to be prepared like it is happening everywhere," Jay said.

I opened the door and slowly stepped down the steps. Liz noticed me walking slowly and like I was in pain. "Are you Okay?" she asked, as I walked over to the table and sat down slowly, letting out a groan. "Yeah, I'm Okay, just a little sore." I replied. "Oh jeez, what happened to your neck?" she asked, as all three looked at me. I had realized I had not even told Jay the story yet.

"I had gone out looking for Jay, and when I finally found the SUV, the window had been broken, and someone had gone through the car. As I was looking in the glove box to see if anything was left. Two men attacked me. They put a tire iron to my neck, then Diamond attacked him, and we got away," I exclaimed, leaving out the part of almost getting raped. As I looked up at them, all three of them had their mouths open. "Wow, I'm so sorry that happened to you," Liz said. "Thanks, my body is just a little sore, but I'll be okay. Just need to take it easy for a couple of days," I replied.

"I'm going to go back inside and lay down for a bit," I said, as I got up and headed back to the RV. "If you need anything, please let me know," Liz hollered at me as I left. "Thanks!" I replied. As I opened the door, Diamond wanted to go back inside, so I let her go first. As she stepped inside, she looked back at me to make sure I was coming in. I walked back to the bedroom, even though it was getting quite warm. As I crawled into bed, Diamond jumped up on the bed and laid her head on my chest with her face right next to mine. I wrapped both arms around her and buried my face in her neck. Before I knew it, I was sound asleep.

Waking up completely soaked by sweat, I wasn't sure if what had happened yesterday was real or a horrible dream. I stared at the ceiling for several minutes, thinking about the events of the day before. Stretching and feeling for Diamond, the bed was empty. "Must have got too hot for her," I thought. I sat up, feeling every sore muscle in

my body. Looking at the battery-operated clock on the side table, it read 6:45pm. "Wow, I must have been exhausted," I said out loud.
I slowly walked to the living room. Jay wasn't in the RV. I walked past an open window and heard voices outside. I peeked out the blinds and saw Jay, Curt and Liz still sitting at the table.

"We need a plan; we need to get to our kids in Alabama," Liz said tearfully. Shaking his head in agreement, "Yes, we need to get back to Texas ASAP!" Jay added. "But how? John said the cars won't work," Liz exclaimed. "If we can find a car that is older than the 1990s without all of that electronic crap on it, it just might start," Jay said. "Where in the world are you going to find something that old?" Liz asked, looking defeated.

All at once, all three of them looked towards the end of the row. The old man that could barely walk and couldn't hear lived in an antique motor home, a Winnebago. "It has to be from the 1980s," Curt said. "I believe the old man is from Louisiana, as well. Maybe he will let us use it and get us all back home," Liz said. "Hopefully it still runs and will start," Jay commented. In the morning, we will go ask him and see if it is in running condition.

As the sun set behind the mountains, the four of us sat in silence watching the Vegas valley burn. It was going to be a long, hot night. We had pulled our cushions off the couch and used them for bedding outside on the patio. After the sun went down, it cooled off a bit. It seemed late when my eyelids could no longer stay open. Since Jay worked graveyard shift, he was wide awake. Sitting in one of the lawn chairs with the dogs sprawled out around him, one by one, he cleaned his guns and listened to the sounds of the night.

CHAPTER FIVE
Guns, Guns, and More Guns

DAY 3

The morning came quickly; I opened my eyes and saw Jay and Curt walking towards the old man's RV. "D'Ann, get up and get as much together from our RV as you can, water, canned food, anything we might need," Jay yelled back. Watching them walk away, I struggled to get up off the cushions. "Ugh, that hurt my back," rubbing my lower back. I grabbed a big bag on wheels and started throwing all the canned goods into the bag. Turning to open the next cabinet, I heard a gunshot and then yelling. I froze.

Jay and Curt had no sooner reached the old man's RV when Randy, the rifle and pistol maintenance guy, jumped out with a gun and fired a shot into the air. "Stop right there!" He yelled at Jay and Curt. "I guess we all had the same idea, huh?" He said. "But I got here first, so just back off before I put a bullet in you." Jay and Curt stopped in their tracks. Jay knew Randy was no match for him. He could have taken him down in one punch, but a gun was another matter. Not wanting to act stupid and get shot, they both backed away.

"Now what?" Curt asked in a low voice. "Let's just get back to our RVs and figure out what our next step should be." On their way back, an idea struck Jay. "I got an idea," he said, as he walked past the RV door to the front of the RV. He reached down and pulled the cover off his ATV. "Let's see if this baby will kick start," Jay said. "Wait," Curt yelled, grabbing Jay's arm. "We should probably wait till dark and push it out into the desert to start it, so no one else can hear. That's all we need is someone trying to take this away from us." Jay agreed and let go of the cover.

Still standing frozen in my spot, I heard the RV door open. Knowing my pistol was in my purse, but my purse was up in the bedroom, I waited to see who or what was coming in the door. I grabbed a can of peas ready to hurl toward whomever was coming in. A flood of emotions came over me as I saw Jay's face. I dropped the can and ran over to him, throwing my arms around his shoulders. "I was so scared, I didn't know what happened," as tears ran down my face. "We're alright, we just won't be using that motor home now. Randy beat us to it and won't let anyone near it. We need to find something else to get home in," Jay said.

"Come here and sit down. I want to talk to you," he said to me as we sat down at the dining room table. "As soon as it's dark, I'm going to take my ATV down into the city and try to get an idea of how bad it is and see if there are any supplies," he said. "No, that's too dangerous!" I cried. "I have to. We have no choice. We have to find transportation and supplies, or we will die up here," He replied. Again, tears rolled down my cheeks. "This is just unbelievable," I cried. "I know, baby, but you gotta stay strong. We will make it through this, together," he said, holding my hands. "I will be very careful, and we will get out of here as soon as we can. Just keep packing everything you can," he said. "Even though the truck wouldn't start, put all of our supplies inside and lock it up in case someone tried to break into our RV," he continued. I just stared at him. After a few seconds, I nodded my head in acknowledgment. I stood up, my legs shaking and continued throwing all I could find in bags.

Sitting on the patio trying to cool off after working inside the RV most of the day, I put my head back and shut my eyes. Trying to shut out the sounds coming from the Las Vegas valley. The dogs gather around my feet, not leaving my side, panting and shaking. I knew they were nervous, too. They knew something was going on.

Liz poked her head out her kitchen window. "Are you okay?" She asked. I opened my eyes and lifted my head, looking towards her.

"Yeah, it's just hard. I'm still in shock," I replied. "I got a cold beer if you want one?" she asked as she disappeared from her window.

I was not a beer drinker at all, but anything cold sounded great. I finished my last cold Diet Coke last night before going to bed.

She handed me the can and pulled up a lawn chair. I had just put the last of the bags in the truck and sat down. She sat at the picnic table beside Curt and handed him and Jay a cold beer. "Won't be cold much longer," she commented as they each open their cans.

Just as the sun was sitting behind the mountains, we heard an engine start up. We all looked at each other and knew that the old RV had started just like we thought it would. Screeching and clanking out of the driveway, we all kind of hoped it would break down and we would pass him sitting along the highway.

Jay and Curt took a walk around the park to see who all was left, and to get an idea of what they plan to do. After making the rounds through the entire park, they found two couples in Sites 11 and 12 left that were making plans to just hunker down in their RVs and wait for someone to rescue them. But the couples were old and set in their ways and felt more secure in their RVs. Jay and Curt knew this was where they would die. Jay and Curt both tried to tell all the couples it was not wise to stay here, that they should make their way into the city and at least get supplies.

The other RVers must have talked Randy into giving them a ride, or they walked into the city because they were gone.

As the sky got darker, the Las Vegas Valley was still bright as day due to all the fires that were still burning. From up where we were, you could still see pockets of the valley that were not touched. You knew people were still alive and as scared as we were. You couldn't hear any engines or sirens, just the sounds of minor explosions.

As Jay went to see how much gas was in the gas cans for the generator, I took a flashlight and searched the storage area for the battery-operated radio we had bought one summer when we went boon docking in the Rocky Mountains. "Maybe we can get some kind of reception with it," I thought.

The batteries were dead. "Put that on the list, get some D batteries," I said to myself. Jay went over to the side-by-side and got the last of the gas cans and put what was left in his 4-wheeler. Our list was getting long, but who knew how long we might be without supplies and if we'll even be able to find any.

Not believing the unimaginable scene, we watched as the Vegas Valley burned. Every once in a while, you could hear what sounded like gunfire or minor explosions. "What do you think you will find now when you go down into the city?" I asked. "I don't know. I'm sure it's way worse than it was, but I will be armed just in case." Grabbing a backpack, he tucked his pistol into its holster and an extra clip in his side pocket. I put two bottles of water in the main compartment. He grabbed my arm and pulled me close. He said nothing, nothing needed to be said. My tears flowed freely down my cheeks. "Please be careful and come back to me," I cried.

Day 3

Jay knew he would probably have to make a couple of trips to get all the supplies we might need. Pulling out his hunting binoculars, he scoped the road leading from the park into the city. Although he saw no movement, he could see the fires that were burning in that general area were really close to where the gas station would be.

As the sky drew black with a little orange because of the fires, Jay quietly pushed his ATV down the road away from the park till he knew he was out of earshot of the others. The ATV kicked started to life and Jay took off towards the city.

I stood outside watching his taillight getting further and further away. Curt and Liz walked over to where I was standing. "He's going to be okay. He'll be back soon," Liz said. "We should go up to the field house and see what will be useful up there," Curt said. "I'll grab a bag and my flashlight," I replied.

The walk to the field house was about a quarter of a mile up the mountain. As we walked, I kept turning towards the road where Jay would have been, again saying a little prayer. You could see more neighborhoods on fire. The higher up the mountain we went, the more of the valley we could see. Explosions and what sounded like gunshots could still be heard.

We reached the building in under 30 minutes. The building was locked. From what we could tell, it was still secure. Which meant the contents were still in there. Because Liz worked in the office there, she produced a key, and we went right in. The blackness of the building felt eerie. I had only ever been there during the day. I knew there were several mounted deer heads and a huge buffalo head hanging on the walls, but when my flashlight shined near them, it took my breath away. "Shit, that scared me," as I giggled under my breath. The gun range had been open to the public 5 days a week, selling ammo and renting guns if you need one. Liz knew in the gunroom there were rows of guns. Handguns, rifles and shotguns, and boxes and boxes of ammo. There was also an archery section, bows and arrows for rent. Liz grabbed her key and opened the door. I shined my flashlight around the room, gun after gun. "How are going to carry all these?" I asked. In one corner of the room, my flashlight caught the pile of gun bags, some hard cases and some soft. I walked over and picked up one of the soft side bags, looked it over and figured I could stuff at least five long guns in the bag. We each grabbed two bags, stuffed them with as many guns as we could, and sat them by the door. There were also bags that would be perfect for the ammo. Knowing if the bag was too full, I wouldn't be able to lift it. I searched until I found a stack of bags with wheels. Grabbing a couple, we stuffed it full of as much ammo as we could. "We might need to come back and get more. I think it might be good to grab some bows and arrows, just in case." I commented. We gathered all the bags and moved them to the front door. "No way can we get all this down to the RVs," Liz said. "Maybe we should put all this stuff in the maintenance garage. There are no windows, and we can secure it so no one can get in," Curt said. "Sounds good to me. This is heavy," I claimed, struggling to carry the bag.

It took several more trips to transfer everything we thought would be of use to the garage. Several bags of guns and ammo, bows and arrows, at least eight cases of water, and batteries of all sizes. We grabbed another bag and stuffed scissors and tape. There were several bungee cords and anything that looked useful. The kitchen area had boxes of granola bars and beef sticks they used to fill the vending machine. They had four vending machines, two with chips and snacks, and two with beverages. The glass broke easily with a chair as Curt slammed it against the machine. Being careful of the glass, we put all the snacks in a bag and took it with us.

"Well, that took my mind off Jay for a minute. I hope he's okay," I said. As we headed back down to our RVs.

The dogs started barking as I opened the door to the RV. "Shhh, it's just me," as I pointed my light at them. At least with the sun setting, it wasn't so hot inside the RV. I lit a candle and started packing clothes and shoes into another bag. Looking at the clock, I realized Jay had been gone for almost 3 hours. Letting the dogs out to go to the bathroom, I stood looking toward the road. "I should have gone with him," I thought to myself, looking over at my ATV.

We had gotten our 2 ATVs a couple of summers before. We loved riding them at the deer lease and in the mountains of Colorado. They weren't pretty by any means, but they did the job. We mainly rode them just for fun, but every once in a while, we would use them to haul deer and wild hogs that we had hunted back to the compound to clean, cut up, and put in the freezer. We had decided to take them to Las Vegas, when we heard we could ride them right there next to the gun range.

The dogs started barking, which brought me back to the here and now. I looked to see if it was Jay finally returning home, but it had only been a lone coyote running scared past the trash dumpster. I hurried the dogs into the RV and shut the door.

Day 3 Jay

As Jay got closer to the edge of the city, he decided it might be safer to not be heard or seen. So, he parked his ATV behind a brick wall and set out on foot. Ducking into the shadows until he knew it was safe, he made his way to the market. He could see it wasn't on fire, but the houses behind it were. The glass of the front door was lying all over the ground. Because of the noise of the fires behind the store, he couldn't really hear anything in the store. He pulled his gun and stepped through the door.

Before he turned on his flashlight, he listened for any movement. Not hearing anything, he turned on his light. The store had been ransacked. It had only been a few hours since this hell started and already looters had been here. Looking around, it looked like they were only after cigarettes and beer. He grabbed energy bars, canned meats, and anything he knew wouldn't spoil and stuffed his backpack full. Suddenly, he heard voices. Turning off his light, he froze.

Jay held his gun down by his side, almost holding his breath as he squatted down behind the shelf. There were three male voices. One man yelled to the other, "go check the back to see if they have any more cigarettes." Knowing that he was in the direct path of the man headed to the back, he crawled around the end of the shelves so he wouldn't be seen. As he moved, his elbow bumped some candy on to the floor. The crash caught their attention. "Who's there?" The one closest to Jay yelled. As another man's light caught his face. "Stand-up," he said. As Jay rose, he tucked his gun into the back of his jeans before any of them saw it. With his hands in the air, he walked out from behind the shelf. "I'm just trying to get food, that's all I want,"

Jay said. Since it was dark and a light was shown in his eyes, he didn't know if they had guns.

Jay was an intimidating man, had only just turned 43 years old. He was over 6ft tall and approximately 250. When we met, he was only 26 years old. Still a kid, living at his grandpa's house. Our relationship was fast and furious. Only 2 months he had moved in with me. Jay kept his head shaved, mainly because of losing his hair over the last few years. He had his favorite tank top on that showed his muscles and all his tattoos.

The three men stared at him as he came out. "Look, I'm not looking for any trouble. There's enough for all of us," Jay claimed, keeping them from seeing his gun in his jeans. "All I want is some food. You can have the rest." "What's in the bag?" one man asked. "Just food," Jay replied. "Dump it out, let me see," the man commanded. All three of the men had flashlights. One man kept shining his light at the other two men. Jay observed that there was no obvious gun in their hands. Knowing he had an extra gun clip in his bag, he knew if he dumped it out, they would discover it and know he most likely had a gun. Wondering whether to pull his gun or to fight them was a decision he didn't want to make.

The men stepped towards Jay, shining their lights on the bag. In a split second, he had decided. As he grabbed the bag by its straps to dump it out, he swung and hit all three men, one right after another. Hearing the cans of food connected to their faces and seeing flashes of light fly in the air, he ran out the door and into the shadows.

The three men were a little stunned when they picked themselves up off the floor, grabbed their flashlights that had been flung across the aisle, and stumbled to the door. One man walked cautiously to the north and around the corner of the building, shining his flashlight all around. Seeing nothing, he went back to the door; the other two men looked all around the parking lot but saw nothing. "Come on, let's get this shit and get out of here," the man standing by the door yelled to the other two guys. They all walked back inside the store and continued to gather items to put in their bags.

Before Jay had gone into the store, he had scouted around for places to hide in case he needed them. There were cars in the parking lot and a large box truck that had running boards, so the driver could climb up into the cab with little effort. As he stood on the running board so they could not see his feet, he watched through the driver's side window as the flashlights disappeared back inside the store.

"Damn, that was close," he whispered under his breath. "Next time he would not make the stupid mistake of putting his clip in the bag and put it on himself," he thought.

Shaking and walking slowly and quietly, he made his way back to the ATV he had hidden behind the wall about a block away. He knew he hadn't gotten a lot of items, mainly because of being so rudely interrupted, and knew he was going to have to go out again for more supplies. He also knew it was urgent that he go back out as soon as he could before others had gotten everything.

As I was dozing off in the lawn chair, I heard the engine of the ATV coming up the road. I watched as he drove right up to the RV. "Oh thank God you're alright, I was so worried," I cried, running up to him and throwing my arms around him.

CHAPTER SIX
Attack at the Gun Range

**Day 4**

The morning sun was shining through the windows. I jerked awake thinking the last 3 days were all a dream, but nope, it was a nightmare and it had only begun. I felt the bed next to me as I rolled over, empty. The dogs were not even in bed with me. I pushed myself out of bed, holding my head. The stress of the night before had given me a horrible headache. Jay and I had stayed up most of the night talking about what we had just experienced the last 3 days and hoping our families were okay.

I opened the door to the bedroom. He only closes it to allow me to sleep in, so I don't hear any of the noise he makes.

"Good morning babe, how did you sleep?" he asked. I know he knew exactly how I felt with the sour look I gave him on my face. "This stress has given me a horrid headache," I replied. "It was so hot last night. We might want to sleep outside again tonight," he commented. I opened the refrigerator door, expecting a relief of cold air to hit me, but the only thing that hit me was the smell of food going bad. I grabbed a "warm" Diet Coke. "Omg, I just don't know how I'm going to survive without a cold Diet Coke," I complained. Taking the Tylenol bottle down from the shelf, I opened it and shook four pills out. Popped them in my mouth and took a big drink of Diet Coke. Almost choking, I shook my head. "Yuck," I exclaimed. As I was putting the Tylenol bottle back, I realized, "shit, I better pack all these medications. We are going to need them," I said. "Wholly shit, what am I going to do when my prescription runs out? Not like we can call the doctor and get a refill," I moaned.

Three years ago, I was as healthy as a horse. I could keep up with the men at the deer lease doing all kinds of manual labor. Then one week in July, it had all changed. I couldn't get out of bed. My whole body was in pain. Within 2 weeks, I had gone from being physically active to not being able to walk or lift my arms. Jay had to help me to the bathroom, brush my hair and basically take care of me full time. After a month, I finally got into the Rheumatologist, the blood test had come back with the diagnosis of PMR "Polymyalgia Rheumatic" an autoimmune disease. The doctor explained to me that the only medication that help was a steroid, "Prednisone." After 48 hours of being on the medication, I was a new person. Now 3 years later I cannot go a single day without it, or I end up not being able to move with severe pain. I learned that by forgetting a dose every once in a while.

The dogs were sitting at the door whining to come in as soon as they saw me. I walked to the door and opened it as they all ran in, jumping and whining for their treats. We always gave them after they went out to potty. "Okay, Okay hold," I said, as I reach in the bag of treats sitting on the counter. "We are going to have to get a bunch of these also," I said, looking at Jay.

"What's going on?" as I saw him repacking his backpack. "There's something I gotta do," as he looked at me with a sad look on his face. "What, what is it?" I asked. "I must go to my job, when the electricity goes out the doors lock from the inside and no one can get out. I would never forgive myself if my friends and coworkers were trapped in the building," he said. "Plus, there are a few things I need to get from there," he said. "The building exploded and most of it burned. I saw it," I exclaimed. "It's been 4 days. Do you really think they could survive that?" I asked. "I have to try," he sadly commented.

I didn't argue. I knew he had to do this. "How are you going to do it?" I asked, "I think if I run along the city and down Decatur I can get there pretty quickly, barring any roadblock or fires." I could see the plan hatching in his head. "Well, maybe I should go with you. My ATV is full of gas, and you may need my help," I said. "I don't want to risk it. We don't know what it's like that far into the city, and I can go faster without worrying about your safety," he replied. "Well, will you at least take Curt, if he will go? I just don't want to worry," I asked. "I just think it would be better with two people. You could have each other's back."

"I would rather just go by myself. I know what I'm doing, and it will be a lot quicker, plus I can scout out for a vehicle we could use to get out of here," he added. He said it in a way I knew not to push him. He was exhausted and arguing with him wouldn't help.

The sun was just halfway over the mountains. At this point where the sun was, I knew it had to be around 10am. With cell phones out and never wearing a watch, what time it was is no longer an issue. The Las Vegas valley was on fire and seemed to smolder everywhere you looked. I could tell most all the resorts on the strip were burning still, downtown was in flames, and most neighborhoods I could see were still smoking.

After putting extra water bottles in his bag, we walked out to his ATV. I grabbed him and held on tight, not wanting to let go. "Please be careful, don't take any unnecessary risks, and return safe and sound to me," I whispered in his ear. "I will be careful. Take care of my dogs and try not to worry," as he kissed my forehead. I stepped back, letting him go as he kick started his bike and drove off towards the exit of the park.

The sound of Jay leaving had gotten Curt and Liz's attention. "How did last night go?" Liz asked as she stepped out of her RV. "He said it went okay, but I could tell by the way he acted something happened," I replied. "Where's he going now?" Curt asked. "To check on his people at his work and get a few things," I replied. Curt may not have known what I meant by "get a few things" but I knew exactly what he was getting.

I sat down at the picnic table and rubbed my temples. "Come on Tylenol, kick in. I got too much to do today," I murmured under my breath.

"We probably should go through and make a list of all the stuff we still need," Curt said. "I'll go get pen and paper," I replied. Jay had only been gone for a couple of hours. Rummaging through drawers for a pen, I heard the faint hum of an ATV motor. "Well, that didn't take very long. Wonder what happen?" I thought to myself.

Running back outside, I put my hand up to my eyes to shade the sun. I could hear the engine but couldn't see him. Then I saw the movement coming over the hill still several hundred yards away. But there was not just one ATV but two. Still standing there watching them approach, the hair on the back of my neck rose. Now they came into view. Neither one was Jay. There were two people on each ATV, and I could see the outline of guns strapped to the front of their ATVs.
I crouched down and slowly crawled back to my RV. Grabbing my purse, I reached in and grabbed my "pink lady" and tucked it in the back of my pants. The noise of the ATV caught my dogs' ears, and they barked. "Oh shit," whispering to the dogs. "Shhh, quite, come on, who wants a treat?" as I grabbed a hand full of treats and shoved them in the bathroom and shut the door.

As I peeked out the blinds, I watched the 2 ATVs ride right past the RV host area towards the clubhouse and the shop garage, where we had stockpiled the guns and supplies we had found. Once they were out of sight, I snuck out of my RV and ran to Curt and Liz's open window on their RV. "Curt, Liz?" I yelled softly into their window. "Yes, we saw them," Curt replied. "We locked the shop, right?" I asked. "Yes, I don't think they can get in unless they break the lock. Hopefully, they will see it and just move on," Curt answered. "What are we going to do if they come back here?" Liz said nervously. "I have my pistol," I said. "I have my rifle," Curt commented. "Just go back in your RV, make sure all your shades are closed and close your windows and lock your doors. Try to keep your dogs quiet," Curt said urgently.

I did what he said and ran back into the RV, let the dogs out of the bathroom, and hurried them into the bedroom. I quickly shut the door, went to the front door, locked it and, one by one, closed the window and curtains. The dogs were all whining again, so I grabbed another treat and went back to the bedroom. They were confused but excited, not knowing why they were getting another treat, but couldn't leave the bedroom. I sat on the bed, petting them all, asking them to please be quiet, and waited. Sitting there for what seemed like an hour, I heard the familiar sound again, only this time it was getting closer. My heart stopped as my dogs started barking. Sweat rolling down my face. Trying not to move too fast so that the RV rattled, I grabbed Tator, which was my biggest barker, and held him tight. "Please be quiet," I cried. As they settled down, I heard yelling and screaming coming from outside. Not close enough to think that they were next door, but close enough to figure they had found one of the other couples in the next row over.

I crawled along the floor to one window that faced toward the screams, slowing I pulled myself up and spread the blinds open just enough to look out. I couldn't see. Our truck was about a foot too far in the way. I couldn't tell what was going on, but I could hear the lady in site eleven screaming "please, please take anything you want just leave us be."

My heart raced, I was shaking, tears filled my eyes. "God, what do I do?" I said to myself, "I just can't sit here while they hurt them."
I knew my front door was hidden from view of their RV due to how we had parked the truck a couple of days before. As I sat next to the window listening to the screams, I tried to devise a plan.

Taking a deep breath, I crawled to the closet where we kept Jay's hunting rifle. It was always loaded and ready to go in case of intruders. I just never thought we would need it for that reason.

Knowing I had only seven bullets loaded in the gun, I knew I had to be an excellent shot if it came down to it.

My youngest brother, Jace, was a police officer in Texas and was the first person who taught me how to shoot. He used to tell me if you're going to shoot someone for your protection then aim to stop, in other words, kill. I never thought I could really kill someone, but if it was them or me, or someone I loved, I would sure try.

This was not someone I loved, and I hardly knew this family, just in passing, they had a big brown dog, which looked to be a cross between a German Shepard and a lab that they would walk every night right past our RV and if my dogs heard them, it drove them crazy, barking and carrying on all crazy.

I knew, though, that I could not let someone hurt another person without helping. I just hoped it wouldn't be me that ended up hurt.
As quietly as I could, I opened the RV door and moved down the steps, closing my door as quickly as I could before my dogs started in. I moved around the side of the truck to get a better look at what the situation was.

At first, I saw three men outside the RV in site eleven, but only noticed one had a rifle in his arms, just holding it like he was on patrol. The other two were tying the lady's hands and feet to a lawn chair. Suddenly, I noticed the fourth man coming around the side of their RV with the lady's husband. He had a hold of the back of his neck and shoving him towards his wife. The elderly man had his hands bound behind his back.

"I will not ask you again, old man. Where are your guns?" The fourth man was yelling as he shoved him to his knees. "I will shoot your old lady right here if you don't tell me, NOW!"

I could tell the elderly man was sobbing, "Please, we keep our guns locked in our locker in the clubhouse," he cried. "I told you, old man, we already checked the clubhouse and there are no guns there," man number 4 said as he come down hard on the elderly man's head with the butt of his gun he had been holding.

The elderly man crumbled to the ground as his wife let out a scream, "and I told you to shut the fuck up!" one of the other two men, which had tied the lady up, yelled as his fist connected with the lady's face. My heart beat uncontrollably. My hands were sweating around the butt of the rifle. "I couldn't just sit there and let them beat this poor, helpless, defenseless couple to death."

As I stood and aimed my rifle towards the men and started walking around the side of the truck, I saw out of the corner of my eye, the other elderly man that lived next door in site twelve, come from around his truck, he too had taken aim at the four men. A shot rang out. I watched as man number 4, the one with the gun, drop to the ground, moaning and grabbing his left shoulder.
"That was just a warning shot," he yelled towards the four men. "The next one will not be," he continued. "Drop your gun!" he directed to the other man that had reached for his gun. He cocked his rifle, and the man dropped the gun.

About that time, I saw Curt run across the road and grab both guns. I slowly walked towards them with my gun still pointed at the men.
"Now, if you want to live, pick up your friend there and get on your bikes and get out of here. Don't think of coming back here. Next time we won't be so nice," as the older man point his gun and motioned to the other men to pick up their friend and get going.

I continued to point my gun in their direction as they drove out the park and down the road. Once I could no longer see them, my nerves kicked in. My knees got weak, and my legs buckled underneath me.

Day 4 Jay

The building that Jay worked in was huge. Besides being the largest dispensary in the world, it had a coffee shop and a pizzeria, and the newest part of the building had not opened ye. A very large dance club, where people could come dance, smoke weed and party all night long. Jay was going to be the general manager of the club when it opened in just a couple of months. His coworkers had become like family to us. We would all get together outside of work for barbecues and pool parties. They were our family away from home.

Jay knew if he stayed on the side streets, he could probably avoid roadblocks and people that might want to cause him harm. Going slow not to cause too much noise and having to dodge cars and debris in the streets, he made his way to the dispensary. As he got closer, he could tell the building was smoldering, it had partially collapsed on the east side. "Oh, God," he whispered out loud.

Again, he thought it might not be the wisest decision to drive right up to the building, not knowing what to expect. So, he parked his ATV on the back side of the building so it would be hidden from view, grabbed his backpack and walked towards a big hole in the building's side. Walking so lightly not to make any sounds, he listened for movement or voices. Peering around a wall, he could see that people had already destroyed the place. The glass cases were all smashed. Everything on the shelves was on the floor. The cash registers were lying on the floor and pried open. At the back of the building where the pizzeria and coffee shop had been, smoke was still rising from the fire. There was nothing in there to salvage.

He walked around, checking all the rooms for anyone that might have been there or still might be there. When he got to the employee break room, the door was closed. With his hand on the handle, he turned the knob. The door was stuck. Something was on the other side up against it. He pushed and pushed, putting all his strength and force into it. Little by little it opened, just enough he could stick his head in to see what was holding the door.

Being that the break room was in the middle of the building and had no windows, it was pitch black. With all his strength, he rammed his shoulder into the door and pushed again. Opening it enough to stick his head in, he pulled out his flashlight. The room had caved in on itself and underneath the rubble against the door were two security guards.

Aiming his flashlight at their faces, he could tell they were dead. He knew if anyone else was in that room; they were gone as well.
He backed out and closed the door. Standing there, he looked around the big showroom floor, where he had just worked the day before, helping people pick out the type of marijuana products they wanted. He bent down and picked up a container of CBD lotion, looking at it like he had never looked at it before. That was all that was left. Everything THC was gone. "Go figure," he said.

But he knew something the public didn't know. There was a locked, fireproof, indestructible vault almost half the size of the showroom. Behind a hidden door that only managers and inventory personnel knew about, most employees didn't even know it existed. Once you find the hidden door, you have to know the combination to the lock on the vault.

Pieces of the building covered the path to the door. Jay made his way, knocking stuff out of the way, throwing sizeable pieces of metal and boards to the side. As he picked up the last piece of metal, he saw it. A human leg sticking out from under the rubble, he hurriedly began lifting the debris off. As the last board was lifted, he saw his face, Danny. Danny was one of the day shift managers. He had transferred to this location about 2 months after Jay had started. Jay didn't know him that well, but knew he was a great guy and was a hell of a manager.

Jay reached down to see if he had a pulse, not really knowing what he was feeling for. He quickly pulled his hand away. Jay knew he didn't have to feel for anything. Danny's body was cold.

Jay closed his eyes and asked the Lord to keep Danny and make a special place in Heaven for him. After a few more minutes of silent prayer, Jay rose and stepped over Danny's body, and walked towards the hidden door. The door was behind a false wall, but because of the damage, the wall was on the floor, which left the door intact but exposed.

Jay took his keys out of his pocket and unlocked the door. Immediately behind the door was the door to the vault. Jay turned the numbers to the combination lock and heard a click, which meant it had just unlocked. He pulled it open.

Jay shone his flashlight around the vault. The vault had drawer after drawer of marijuana products. Bags and bags of flower, vape cartridges, edibles, and concentrates. He knew the vault drawers were full because they had just had a huge delivery. He knew he had to stuff as much as he could into his bag.

Figuring this was not only local but country or worldwide, he knew paper money would be worth nothing now. But he banked that marijuana would be a significant form of currency. And it would be as good as gold. "Green Gold!" he whispered. This may come in handy along the way.

Grabbing a couple more bags, he stuffed them till they could barely shut. Struggling to carry all that weight, he walked out of the vault and locked it. "Just in case I need to come back," he told himself.

Slowing walking through the hole in the building's side, he looked around, not believing that he was just at work the day before. He stopped just outside the building, set his bags down on the ground and took one last look through the building to make sure there was no one left alive.

Not finding anyone, he went back to grab his bags and headed to the ATV. As he rounded the corner, he saw a man standing over his bags. Jay pulled his pistol out of the back of his pants. "Excuse me, can I help you?" Jay asked as he pointed his 45 at the man.

The man stood up and held his hands up. "Just looking for some smoke," the man said in a shaky voice. Jay could tell the man was scared. "He's just a pothead," Jay thought. "Back away from the bags and I'll help you out," Jay commented.

The man backed away, still with his hands up. Jay unzipped the bag and grabbed a bag of flower and handed it to the man.
"Thank you, thank you," the man said as he took the bag from Jay. "Everything else is gone. People already hit this place," Jay said as he grabbed the bags and swung them over his shoulder and put his gun back in his pants.

Jay walked back to his ATV, looking over his shoulder to make sure he wasn't being followed. He secured the bags to his bike and headed towards the used RV dealerships.

Day 4 D'Ann

Closing my eyes, I took some deep breath to calm my nerves. I could hear footsteps heading toward me. "Are you okay?" Liz asked, as she ran towards me. "Yeah, yeah, I'm fine, just went a little weak in the knees," I replied. She reached out her hand to help me up. I grabbed it and got to my feet. We both looked towards the couple that had been victimized. Curt was untiring the lady, as the man from site 12 was kneeling over the man from site 11.

Liz and I hurried to help them, but it was too late for the old man. "He's gone," the man from site 12 said, looking up at us. "The blow to the head was fatal," he said. Sucking in the air, I put my hands to my mouth. "Oh God, I should have tried to stop them sooner." As tears filled my eyes.

Liz put her arm around me. "We couldn't have predicted this would happen. Let's check on the misses," she said as walked away from the man and towards his wife.

Curt had gotten her untied, but the lady still sat in the chair. Curt looked up at us as he was bent over, looking at the side of the lady's head where the man had punched her. "Not good," he said. "She might have a broken jaw," he claimed. "Let's get her inside and clean her up. You men do something with him," I said as we tried to help her out of the chair.

The lady was too weak to walk on her own, so with Liz on one side and me on the other, we carried her into her RV, laid her down on her sofa and tended to her injuries.

Curt and the man from site twelve carried the body of the man from site eleven to the west end of the park. "I'll go grab a shovel," Curt said, as they decided they should bury the man in the park.

Liz rummaged through the lady's cabinets looking for gauze and bandages, as I ran next door to site 12 to see if the other woman was okay. I knocked on her door softly and called out, "ma'am are you okay?" After a few seconds, a small little lady answered the door. I could tell she had been crying. "Are you okay?" I asked again. Through her sniffles I heard her say in a soft voice, I could barely hear, "Yes, I'm okay. I saw everything. Is Dina okay?" she asked. "I'm not sure, her face is swollen terrible, she has some deep cuts on her wrist from the rope." I replied. "I used to be a nurse many, many years ago. I could look at her," she whispered. "I think that would help a lot. She's going to need all our help. I don't think she realizes her husband is gone yet," I said. "Oh, poor Don, he was a nice old man," she claimed.

"I'm D'Ann, I've seen you around but have never met you," I said. "I'm Polly, my husband is Jim." she replied. "I wish we would have met under different circumstances," she said, as we crossed the drive. Once inside, Polly looked over Dina's injuries. "I'm afraid it doesn't look good. She's in and out of consciousness. She is elderly, and her injuries are pretty severe. I'll stay here with her today, and maybe we can switch off tomorrow," she said. "Okay, just let us know if you need anything," Liz said. As we walked out the RV door.
Curt and Jim were walking up the sidewalk, completely drenched by sweat. "It's done," Curt said, looking at both of us. "Maybe we can have a brief service for him later this evening when it cools off a bit," Liz said. "Sounds good, hopefully Jay will be back soon," as worry crept into my head.

I picked up my gun I had left sitting by the chair they had tied Dina to and walked to my RV. I could hear my dogs whining and carrying on, so I opened the door, let them out of the bedroom and into the yard to pee.

The sun was going down behind the mountain and Jay wasn't back yet. After our brief service we had for Don, we had decided we needed to take turns and keep watch in case anyone tried again.

We had made a schedule to keep watch. Every half hour we were to check on the far west side, walking around the park and making sure no one came from that direction.

Since Jay was not home yet, I agreed to go first. Besides, I wanted to keep an eye out for him. Since there were now five of us, we did 5-hour shifts. Dina was still out of it, so Polly stayed with her. She didn't look well, and she had not been coherent enough to even tell her we buried her husband.

The days were so hot, but the cool desert nights were a welcome relief. "Didn't realize how much we enjoyed the AC till there was none," I thought. I sat on my patio with my rifle on one side and my pistol on the coffee table. The dogs seemed on alert most of the night, listening and watching. "Where could he be?" I asked the universe as I looked over the Vegas valley.

There were still flames across the valley, the smoke was still thick even up there on the side if the mountain. It was hard to breathe sometimes. I couldn't believe that everything was gone. My thoughts were, "surely there are stores open down there! It just can't be that everything has stopped." I didn't want to believe it. I didn't want to believe that it was everywhere. "Maybe it's just the Valley," I thought. "Maybe we will get on the other side of the mountains and our cell phones will work."

My 5-hour shift was ending. "Uneventful," I told curt as he took my place on watch. "Please wake me if you see or hear Jay," I begged Curt. "I will," he replied.

The dogs and I retreated inside. It was late, really late. The sun would come up in just a couple of hours.

"If he's not home by morning, I'm going to get on my 4-wheeler and go look for him," I thought.

Day 4 Jay

The RV dealerships were just a few blocks from the dispensary where Jay worked. They carry many RVs, from 5th Wheels, bumper pulls, to motor homes. What we needed was an older model motor home that didn't have all the electronic crap on it that wouldn't have been fried by the EMP.

Jay knew when he pulled in the lot, the older models were in the back area. The trade-ins. That's where, hopefully, he would find what he was looking for.

He rode down rows of RVs until he got to the motor homes. Nothing, nothing older than 2000. "Now what?" he thought. Thinking there was nothing there that would start, he headed towards the gun range. It was getting late, and he knew D'Ann would be worried sick.

After several blocks, a thought came to him. When he used to work for the tow truck company last year, they had towed an old motor home into the lot because it had been repossessed. "Maybe it's still there?" he thought. "It's not but a mile or so out of the way from the gun range."

He drove the ATV as fast as he could through the streets to the tow yard. Several times slamming on his breaks, which weren't too good anyway after riding down mountains in Colorado, to avoid hitting a stalled car or a person who ran out into the street to stop him.

He reached the tow yard and noticed someone had broken the gate off its hinges. He rode to the building that they had housed the RV in when he worked there. There was a padlock on the garage door. He got off his bike and searched for something to break the lock off with. In one of the old trucks, he had found a crowbar. Prying the lock, it broke off and he opened the door. Junk was everywhere. They used this building as a storage area for all the stuff they found in the cars and that went unclaimed.

Pushing his way through, making a path he could barely navigate himself; he made his way to the back. There it was. It looked to be in one piece. He made his way to the door; it was unlocked. He opened it and climbed inside. It, too, was full of junk. Boxes and bags of trash. He pushed them out of the way and made his way to the driver's seat. "Damn it! No keys," he cursed. Moving trash and searching the glove box, the cup holder and the visor, no sign of keys anywhere.

Not knowing how to hotwire a car, and with no YouTube available to walk him through it, he decided he would make his way out of the building and to the main office. If he remembered right, they used to keep all the keys in a key box hanging on the wall. He would check that first.

Jay checked his bike and the bags of "Green Gold" to make sure they were secure and then headed to the office. The office door was locked. But the door was half glass and all it would take was something hard to break it and open it. Looking around on the ground and in the office's front was a rock garden the owner of the tow company's wife had made years ago. He picked up a rock big enough to break the glass. He walked around to the side door and smashed the glass.

He reached his hand through an unlocked the door. Once inside, he remembered the key box was in the manager's office. His friend Sean had recently become the manager of the tow yard. As he walked towards the manager's office, he heard a noise. It sounded like a gun being cocked. He drew his pistol, which had still been in the back of his pants. Slowly, he walked into the office. The next thing he felt was a burning pain to the side of his head. Then everything went dark.
Jay blinked his eyes after a face came into view. His hand reached to the side of his head, and he could feel the fresh blood still seeping out of a cut that seemed to be about an inch long. "What the fuck!" Jay said as he tried to sit up.

"I'm so sorry. I had no idea it was you. What are you doing here?" Jay's friend, Sean, had asked. "Was trying to see if that old motor home was still here and if it would start," Jay said, holding his bloody head. "Trying to get back to Texas." "I am really sorry," Sean repeated. "What are you doing here still? Is your mom okay?" Jay asked. Sean lived across the valley from the tow yard. He had moved back in with his mom when his marriage went south. "I don't know. None of the vehicles will run and it's just too far to walk," he replied. "I didn't even think about that old thing in the storage building," Sean said. "Do you know where the keys might be for it?" Jay asked. "Let's look in the box," Sean replied.

As Jay got up from the floor, he was a little wobbly from the concussion he had probably just received. "Here they are. You want to go see if it will start?" Sean asked.

Sean threw the keys to Jay. Missing them, they fell to the floor. Jay bent over to pick them up and a rush of dizziness came over Jay. He went down on his knees. "Maybe you should lie down a bit," Sean said. As the room spun, Jay agreed and headed to the sofa in Sean's office, laid down and shut his eyes.

Jerking awake, Jay opened his eyes. He searched the room for Sean, but he was nowhere to be found. He struggled to his feet and headed to the front door, bracing himself on the walls as he walked.

The sun was setting behind the mountains. "How long was I out?" Reaching up, feeling the cut on his head. "Long enough for the cut to stop bleeding and crust over," he thought.

He headed slowly towards the storage building, then he stopped dead in his tracks. "My bike!" He said surprised, "it's gone," as his eyes searched the area for any sign of his bike or the bags. "Fuck, Sean must have taken it to go to get Andie or his mom," he cursed under his breath. Although he wouldn't have blamed him for wanting to get to his mom to make sure he was alright. He didn't understand why he didn't wake him.

Opening the door to the storage building, he heard noises, slowly he pulled his gun, ducking behind the mountain of boxes and trash he made his way to the RV. The noise was coming from inside the RV. Jay rounded the front of the RV to the side door. Almost being hit by a box, he saw Sean throwing crap out the door.

"You're up. How do you feel?" Sean asked. Shocked to see Sean, Jay just stood there, not saying anything. "Are you okay?" Sean asked again. "Yeah, I think so. Where is my 4-wheeler?" Jay asked. "Well, I saw what you had in all those bags, and I pushed it behind those cars out back, just in case someone came around," he answered. "I thought you took off on it," Jay said. "Nah, I wanted to see if this hunk of junk would start," Sean replied. "And?" Jay asked.

Sean jumped in the driver's seat, put the keys in and it started right up. It choked and coughed a little, but it was running. "We had some gas cans in the shop area. I filled it and your ATV." Sean commented. "Wholly crap, it runs," Jay said. "Yip, but I got some bad news. One tire is really low, and with no electricity, the air compressor won't work." Sean commented sadly.

"Sometimes motor homes have generators built in. Did you check?" Jay asked. "Nope, had no idea. Let's look," Sean replied, as he turned off the engine and headed towards the back of the RV.
Jay lifted the back door panel on the RV and, sure enough, it had a generator. "Get the air compressor and let's see if this tire will hold air," Jay said.

After putting air in the tire, they finished emptying the trash and boxes out of the RV. "Now we have to move all the crap out of the way just to get this baby out the door," Sean commented. "Yeah, that might take us a minute," Jay replied, rolling his eyes.

By the time they had finished moving stuff out of the way, the sun had gone down behind the mountain. It was getting dark. "I think you should stay the night here with me and head out in the morning. It's too dangerous to drive this at night," Sean said. "Your right, but D'Ann has got to be worried sick. I really need to get back to her," Jay replied. "I know, but it's just too dangerous," Sean rebutted.
"Sean was right," Jay thought, so he grabbed his bags and stuff off his ATV and put it in the motor home. "I know you're worried about your mom. Do you want me to drive you to your house in the morning

before I head out?" Jay asked. "No, I know you gotta bet back to D'Ann, but if I can use your ATV, I won't have to walk," Sean replied. "Of course, you can. I won't need it," Jay said. "Once you get to your moms, do you want us to pick you up on our way out of town? We are going to our deer lease in Texas. It's probably the best place anyone can be," Jay continued.

"I'm not sure. I don't know what my mom and Andie will want to do," Sean replied. "Well, I will not leave you here to fend for yourselves. We will come by your house and if you're still there, we will have plenty of room for all of you, plus we might need the gun power," Jay said. "Okay, that's a plan," Sean replied.

As they settled in for the night, all Jay could think about was D'Ann, hoping she was alright.

CHAPTER SEVEN
Tow Yard Intruders

Day 5: Jay

Jay and Sean had opted to sleep in the RV, which was still parked inside the storage building. Jay had stuffed his bags underneath the dinette seats for safe keeping. They searched the cabinets and storage places for anything that might be of use for the long haul to Texas. They found a few lanterns and matches, but most of the remaining stuff was trash. The Inside of the RV was covered in dust and dirt. It had been sitting in the building for almost 3 years, as far as Jay could remember.

Jay slept on the sofa, while Sean climbed up above the driver's seat onto the loft bed. Just as the sky was coming to life with color, Jay and Sean were both jolted awake by the sound of the garage door banging and clanging open.

Jay set up on the couch to look out the front windshield, as Sean swung his legs over the side of the bed and jumped down as quietly as he could. Hitting the floor, he immediately crouched down beside Jay. Jay and Sean had both kept their pistols on them as they slept. They both reached behind them and pulled them out. Because of the heat of the night and being shut up in the garage, they had slept with the RV door open. Sean eased his way to the open door with Jay right behind him. Even with the garage door open and the sun rising, it was still quite dim in the garage. Both men stopped when they got to the door. They heard whispering in the building but couldn't tell where it was exactly coming from.

"You go around the backside, and I'll go this way," Sean said, pointing towards the front of the RV. As quiet as could be, they both exited the RV. Jay turned right and headed around the back. Sean creeped slowly towards the front.

Jay had slowly and cautiously reached the front of the RV when he heard a child's scream. He froze. "Daddy, Daddy! Over there I saw a monster," a small child's voice cried. "Jenny, get her and stay put," Jay heard a man's voice say.

Sean had been standing in front of the RV. As Jay joined him, they walked cautiously towards the voices. Appearing around a stack of boxes, they saw the family. A man and woman looking to be in their thirties, a little girl with one arm around a teddy bear and the other arm wrapped tightly around the woman's arm. The woman's other arm held a toddler who appeared to be asleep on her shoulder.

The family stopped dead in their tracks as Jay and Sean appeared. Noticing their guns, the man raised his hands. Jay lowered his arm and put his gun to his side, and motioned Sean to do the same. "We are just looking for shelter," the man immediately said. "We were driving, and all of a sudden our car stopped. We've been walking all day trying to get to our home. Our kids are tired and hungry, and we're just trying to find a safe place out of the heat to rest," he continued. "There are some crazy ass people out there and we needed shelter. We thought since this place was behind a fence and seemed to be secure, we would stop and rest."

Sean put his gun away in the back of his jeans. "I've got some bottled water and some food in a vending machine in the office you can have," Sean said as he headed towards the open garage door.

The man turned and followed Sean out the door. "Stay here, with the kids. I'll be right back," the man commented to his wife. She stood there for a moment and watched him walk out the door.

Jay walked towards a sofa that had boxes and bags stacked on it. "Let me clean this off and you can sit down and rest," he said as he started removing the junk from the sofa.

The woman gently laid her toddler on the sofa, trying not to wake her. "How far do you live from here?" Jay asked the woman.
Not knowing if she should answer him, she looked away and told her other little girl to sit down on the sofa and rest.
"Not too far, just a little North of here," she finally said and then sat down next to the little girl holding the teddy bear.
The woman looked really nervous, so not to make her anymore uncomfortable, Jay walked towards the open door of the RV.
Sean and the man came back with arms full of water, cans of soda, and bags of chips.

Sitting down the goodies, he picked up the little girl and sat down on the sofa next to his wife. "Can I have some chips, Daddy?" the little girl asked. Opening and handing her a bag, he leaned back and rested his head.

Jay could tell the sun was almost completely up. "It has to be at least 6 am by now. I really need to get going," he thought to himself.
Jumping out of the RV he walked towards where the family and Sean were sitting. "Where exactly do you live from here? I'm headed north to my home and could drop you off," Jay said. "But I'm in a hurry and got to leave now."

The man immediately looked up at his wife, then at Jay. "We are up past Craig on Jones Ave," he said. "I can go right past there," Jay replied. No more did he say that, and the man jumped up with the little girl in his arms and motioned for his wife and baby to follow.

Once everyone was in the RV, Jay and Sean moved the last of the junk out of the way. Jay jumped into the driver's seat and started the motor home up. Slowly, he drove it out of the garage. In front of the gate, he jumped out.

Jay hugged and handed Sean his ATV keys and told him to take care of himself and that we would be at his house on Saturday morning, which was only 2 days away. Sean opened the gate, waving at the RV as Jay drove it out on to the street and headed north.

Day 5 D'Ann

I tried to sleep. My mind was racing, worrying and wondering why Jay had not made it home. He had been gone all day and all night. "It should have only taken him an hour or two to get to his work and let his coworkers out." I thought. All kinds of scenarios kept playing in my head.

I knew the route he was going to take to his work and the RV dealership he was going to go to. Looking out the blinds from the sofa "it will be light in about 30 minutes." I said, as I stood up from the sofa and stretched. "I can't sleep. I have to go see if I can find him," I said to myself.

I let the dogs out to do their business and opened all the windows. "It's going to be hot again today," I murmured to myself. I grabbed a backpack, stuffed it with several water bottles, granola bars, and my "little pink lady" into the main compartment. There was a box of bullets on the table. "I better not forget these," as I stuffed them in the side pocket.

I called the dogs back in, handed them a treat and told them to be good and try to stay quiet. Shutting the door behind me, I saw Curt on patrol, walking a few sites down from my site. He turned and walked toward me.

I took the cover off my ATV, "he will not stop me from searching for my husband," I thought to myself as I kept taking the cover off.

"What are you doing?" he said as he approached me. "Jay didn't come home last night. He's been gone almost 24 hours. I can't just sit here and do nothing," I replied as I gave him a determined look. "I don't think it's safe down there, and I don't think Jay would want you to put yourself in jeopardy like that," he said, "I don't really care, I'm going and that's that, but can I ask a huge favor of you?" I asked. "Will you take care of my dogs?" He looked at me and said nothing but nodded his head. "It shouldn't take me more the 5 hours to get to his work and back. But I have to look," I said, as I kick started my ATV.

Not waiting for a reply, I took off to the exit of the park and down the road towards the Valley.

Scanning ahead as far as I could see, looking for anything, I followed the route he would have taken to his work.

The streets were littered with cars and debris. Trash cans had been knocked, or blown over, trash laying everywhere. I passed the store that Jay had gotten supplies from and noticed it was more or less destroyed. Turning on to side streets, I saw burned-out houses. I slowed down and stopped, looking where a house had sat. I saw a burned Blackhawk helicopter sticking out the front of the "what used to be a really nice house."

"I wonder if that's the one I heard the morning this all happened?" thinking to myself. Most of the houses had burned to the ground in this neighborhood. The smell of something dead caught my nose.

I had grown up on a farm in Kansas and had seen my share of dead animals and knew that smell. I don't know if this was an animal or human, but I didn't want to stick around to find out. I continued down the street, looking for any signs of Jay or signs of life.

Nothing seemed to move. Occasionally, I would see a cat or a dog running across the street. But no people. I could tell that people had been there after the event happened, because people left their cars just sitting in the streets. Several times I had to ride up over the sidewalk just to get around some abandoned vehicles.

Turning down the next street, I noticed a school up ahead that seemed to have movement on its playground. As I got closer, I saw people. Some kids playing and a couple of adults sitting under a tree fanning themselves.

As I approached, they all stopped what they were doing and stared at me. I didn't know if I should stop or if they were going to storm my ATV and try to steal it.

I proceeded slowly. I reluctantly waved at the couple sitting under the tree, the waved back and didn't offer to get up, so I slowed and stopped right in front of them. "Hi," I said, putting my hand up in a slight wave. "Is this a shelter for anyone?" I asked. The lady sitting under the tree nodded her head yes. "It's about all we have left around here," she replied. "Is there any communication in there, any news on what happened, and is this just us or all over?" I asked. "No, no one knows anything," she said. "Okay, thank you for the information. I'm just looking for my husband that went missing yesterday," I said, as I looked towards the doors of the school, seeing that several more people were coming out, pointing and whispering at me. I suddenly felt unsafe, thinking that if I didn't get moving, I may get attacked and my 4-wheeler taken. I nodded my head at the couple and gave my ATV gas and sped off.

I saw block after block of homes burned. In the neighborhoods that weren't burnt, some of the houses were boarded up, most likely to keep people out. I saw a few homeless people in tents with their shopping carts. "These people were ahead of the game because they were homeless before the event happened," I thought.

Finally, after what seemed like a couple of hours, I reached Jay's work. I could see the back of the building was destroyed, and most of the rest of it had burned. I rode around as far as I could on the side. No sign of him, or his ATV, and no sign of any other employees. "I don't think he's here. I didn't see him on the streets either. Hopefully, he's at the RV dealership," I said, feeling defeated.

I headed to the dealership. "I probably should put the rest of my gas in my ATV." I definitely didn't want to run out. Arriving at the dealership, I saw no sign of him. I poured the last of my gas into my ATV, took a bottle of water and a granola bar out of my pack and headed back home.

I took a different route home, thinking Jay may have done the same thing. This was one of the busier streets, or at least would have been before the event. It also held a lot of shopping centers along the way. I may find a few more supplies. "I need dog food and treats for the dogs too," I told myself.

The first shopping center I arrived at to had a pet store, a gym, and a clothing store. I pulled into the parking lot, which seemed to still be full of cars. The pet store's windows had been busted out and the front doors stood wide open. "Well, I wonder if there is anything left?" I said. I didn't want to leave my ATV sitting out in the open in fear someone would take it, so I drove it right through the front doors.
Looking around in the store, I could tell there was still a lot left on the shelves. "I guess people aren't thinking of their pets," I comment, looking around. I found the dog food and treats that my dogs eat, shoving several packages into my backpack. And a huge 25lb bag on the back of my seat right behind me. Going down the toy aisle, I grabbed several squeaky toys and some collars.

I went down the aisle towards where they keep the puppies and kittens for sale, not knowing what I would do if there were some there. "None!" I was so glad. But as I headed towards the door, I noticed all the rodents, mice, rats, hamster, and reptiles still in their cages. "Ugh, I can't let them starve to death, but I am not taking them with me," I exclaimed. So, I got off my bike and started taking the lids off the tops of their cages. The smaller rodents that were in aquariums and wouldn't be able to crawl out, I tuned on their sides. Even the snakes and lizards. I took the lids off and then ran. Laughing as I got back on my bike and headed toward the door.

I really didn't think there was much else I needed at this shopping center, so I went back on the street towards home. I had little room on my bike for too many supplies. I had what used to be a milk crate bolted to my front and a big bag that held tents and other camping supplies I had emptied before I left on the back. "Man, I should have put the gas in the side-by-side and brought it," I said.

Approaching what I knew as a major shopping area, I remembered there was a huge hardware and lumber store just a couple of blocks up. I pulled into the lot and noticed that it, too, looked just like the pet store. The doors were wide open. I rode right in. Trying to go through a list in my head, I headed towards rope and bungee cords. Strapping on a couple of bags of charcoal and lighter fluid, thinking we would at least be able to cook, I rode up to the checkout stands. The cash registers were open and looked like someone had broken them into. At the checkout stand, I grabbed batteries and a gas siphoning kit. "This might come in very handy," thinking I better grab a few In case one breaks. I had little room for anything else. I had flashlights and boxes of lighters. I had grabbed what was left of tools, hammers, pliers, and screwdriver in my front basket. Taking one last look around, I noticed most all the electric tools had been taken. Shaking my head, I wondered what idiots would take those when there was no electricity.

I left the store and continued home. Approaching another shopping area, I noticed a couple of what looked like teenagers carrying TVs out of an appliance store. Suddenly they turned to the sound of my ATV. "Hey, stop!" they yelled, dropping the TVs and running towards me. "Oh shit," not thinking they were coming just to help me with my groceries. I took off. With the extra weight on my bike and all the debris in the road, my bike was hard to steer.

Although I had been riding an ATV for a few years, I was still not completely comfortable going too fast. Turning sharp trying to dodge cars and stuff in the road, I could see the teens were still coming after me. I finally reached a stretch of street that was clear, and I could open it up and speed ahead. Looking back, I could see they had given up. My heart was in my throat. I slowed down again once I knew I was far enough away from them.

Almost out of the shopping district area, I decided I would try to make one last stop. Thinking about Dina, I wanted to see if I could find some first aid supplies and maybe some medication, especially Jay's high blood pressure medication. "He's going to need some," I told myself. The last store was a major well-known pharmacy. I drove up to the doors, but the doors were not big enough for me to ride in. I drove around the side of the building to see if there was a place I could stash my ATV so no one would see it. It wasn't the best place, but some bushes on the side would camouflage it a little. "I have to hurry!" I said, getting off my bike and jogging towards the door. I was cautious as I went inside, thinking there might be people in here also wanting drugs. Looking around, the store was pretty torn up. Didn't look like there was a single thing left on the shelves.

I walked to the pain relief area and found several bottles of acetaminophen on the floor, stuffing them into a backpack I had found on the floor in the back-to-school supplies aisle. I turned down the next aisle to the antacids. "Yes, I need some of these," I said. Finding my favorite brand, I stuff as many as I could find into my bag. "Now to first aid," I said. The aisle looked like someone had thrown most everything on the floor. I dug through the piles and found bandages and first aid creams and grabbed them. Looking up towards the back where the pharmacy was, I noticed it was in even worse shape. Besides the products on the floor, someone had pushed the shelves over. "I'm going to have to climb over some of this," I thought. Having no clue how the pharmacy stocked things, I did not know where Jay's medication could be. Just looking at bottle after bottle that was on the floor, his particular medication was nowhere to be found.

I found some antibiotics that I thought might come in handy if we needed them, and after finding several bottles of my medication, I stuffed them all in my bag.

Knowing I had spent too much time looking for medication, I headed for the door. Then something caught my eye. What I saw couldn't have come at a better time. An entire row of chocolate. I ran back to the school supply Isle and grabbed another bag. Stuffing as much chocolate as I could into the bag, I thought to myself, "if I'm going to die, at least I'll have chocolate. It may melt, but it's still chocolate." Once I had stuffed every imaginable kind of chocolate, I could find I ran out the door to my ATV. "I gotta get this stuff home and see if Jay made it back," I said as I hit the gas.

Day 5 Jay

Jay could tell his blood pressure was up, the stress he was feeling was almost unbearable. He needed to smoke. But knew he couldn't risk the family he was taking home to find out what he had.

Knowing the family would most likely have little supplies and no way to get any, he asked if they would like to stop at a grocery store and get some supplies if there were any left.

The man looked at his wife. "We at least need to get some diapers and formula for the baby," she said.

Acknowledging what he heard, Jay pulled into the next grocery store they came upon.

"You stay here, with the kids, and keep the door locked," the man said to his wife. She nodded her head.

Jay and the man walked into the store. Jay had pulled his gun and was prepared if he needed to be. As far as they could tell, no one was in the store. Most of the food was gone, but Jay grabbed a shopping cart and piled whatever he could find into it. At least they were able to find several packages of diapers and cans of formula. On their way out, they grabbed sacks to put all the stuff in once they got back to the RV. No one spoke a word for the rest of the trip. Jay took his time winding around cars and keeping to side streets in hopes the RV didn't draw any attention.

As Jay turned the corner into the family's neighborhood, he noticed most of the houses had burned. "Turn left at the next street," the man said. "Third house on the right." But Jay knew if it was any sign of the houses he was seeing, it would not be a pleasant sight.

Jay turned left and stopped in front of the third house. They all stared out the window. Jay heard the woman cry. He looked back at them as the man reached for her and pulled her to him. She cried uncontrollably into his chest.

The man looked at Jay. "Thank you for giving us a ride. It would have taken days for us to walk this far," he said. "Are you guys going to be okay here?" Jay asked. "We will be fine," he replied, as he looked down at his wife. They both turned and picked up their sleeping girls and headed towards the RV door. The man picked up the sacks and opened the door. Jay helped set the diapers outside.

"Thank you," the woman said, looking at Jay as she exited the RV and started walking to their home that the fire had spared.

Their house was the first house in a line of houses that had not burned. Jay put the RV in drive and headed back towards home. Wondering how D'Ann was doing, he stepped on the gas. Eager to get home, and not paying attention to the road as he should be, he saw out of the corner of his eye movement coming fast through the last intersection before the road to the gun range. He slammed on his brakes and swerved, trying not to hit the ATV that had appeared out of nowhere. "What the hell!" he yelled as the ATV swerved the other way to avoid getting hit. He stopped and stared at the driver.

Day 5 D'Ann

Going faster than I should've been, I approached the intersection where I needed to turn north to head to the compound. At that exact time, a motorhome was entering the intersection. I swerved to keep from hitting it and slammed on my brakes.

Turning around to give the driver of the motorhome a "What the hell look?" I saw the familiar face I had been longing to see.

I jumped off my bike and started running towards the motorhome as Jay jumped out the driver's door and started running towards me.
We met halfway in between, flung our arms around each other, and held on. Neither one of us spoke a word.

As I lead the way into the park on my ATV, Jay followed me in the motorhome. As we reached our RV, Curt and Liz came running out to meet us. "You made it. You found a motor home!" Liz said with a huge smile on her face we hadn't seen since before this all started.
We all sat on the patio and filled each other in on what had taken place. "I'm sorry I wasn't here to help," Jay said with regret in his eyes. "I can take next watch."

Liz said she and Polly had been taking turns taking care of Dina, but Dina was in such terrible shape they didn't know how much longer she would last. "I'll go over and stay with her in the morning so you guys can take a break," I said.

Jay looked at me and said, "We need to get things together and put them in the motorhome. I noticed a lot of bad stuff going on in the city and I just don't think it's safe here anymore."

Curt told him about all the supplies we had stashed in the maintenance garage up by the clubhouse. "We can go up and get all that stuff first thing in the morning," Curt said. "Sounds good," Jay replied. "We have plenty of room in the motorhome."

"Do you think Polly and Jim will want to go with us now?" Liz asked, "we can ask them, are we going to have room for them?" Curt asked Jay, "plus if Dina makes it, we will definitely have to take her," he continued.

"I talked with Benny and Nadia, I told them we would check on them, we should try to get them to go with us. Nadia knows everything about survival, and all the supplies they have will come in handy," I continued.

"We might also pick up Sean, Andie, and his mother on our way out of town," Jay commented. "We will make it work. I'm not leaving anyone behind that wants to go," I replied with a don't argue with me look on my face.

The sun was setting behind the mountains, and the amount of sleep I hadn't gotten was showing on my face and in my eyes. "Why don't you go lay down and get some sleep? I'll stand guard tonight," Jay said as he got up out of his chair, bent over and kissed me on the forehead. "I'm exhausted, I think I will, see ya all in the morning," I said, as I rose and went up the steps to our RV. Curt and Liz said their goodnights and walked off towards their RV.

For the first time in a day or two, Jay sat for a few moments more and tried to relax. Then he remembered he had the perfect thing in the storage area of the motorhome to help him relax even more.

CHAPTER EIGHT
Rest in Peace

Day 6

The sun shining through the blinds and the sound of the RV door shutting brought me out of a deep sleep. I felt the bed move and didn't want to open my eyes. "Baby, you need to get up. We really need to get going," Jay whispered in my ear. I threw my arms around him and held him tight. I didn't want to let go. I snuggled my nose into the side of his neck and breathed in his smell. "Wish we could just stay like this forever," I whispered back.

After drinking a "Lukewarm Diet Coke," yuck. I ate a pop tart and headed to Dina's RV. I quietly knocked on the door, hoping not to disturb Dina. Polly opened the door. "How is she this morning?" I asked, climbing inside the RV. "Still about the same. She is still in and out but mainly out," she replied. "Go get some rest. I'll stay with her for a while, then Liz said she would come over," I said. "Oh, but I got a question. Jay found a motorhome and we will be leaving in the morning headed towards a safe compound in Texas. You and Jim are more than welcome to come with us, Dina also," as I nodded toward Dina laying on the sofa. "I think Jay will talk to Jim also, but I just wanted to let you know so you can think about it," I continued. "I will definitely talk to Jim about it," she replied as she stepped out of the RV.

I walked over and pulled up a stool next to Dina. Dina was a beautiful lady, her silver hair cut in a pixie, but matted to her head as she lay lifeless. Her breathing was shallow, and when I put my hand on her chest to feel her heart, it seemed to beat exceptionally slow.
I re-wrapped the bandages on her wrists, and then sat back and watched her chest go up and down.

Dozing off as I sat there, I suddenly heard her move. I opened my eyes and looked directly into her eyes. She wanted to talk, but the pain and the swelling of her jaw prevented her from opening her mouth. "How are you feeling? What can I get you?" I asked her. Tears filled her eyes as she looked around the room. She was looking for her husband, I could tell. I didn't want to be the one to tell her that her husband had passed away. I could tell the panic and fear was coming into her eyes and on her face. "Calm down, it's okay, you're okay," I said. She tried to rise, but as weak as she was, fell back down on the sofa. She sobbed loudly now. I placed my hand on her shoulder to calm her, but mainly to hold her down.

Her breathing had increased. It was almost like she was panting as panic gripped her full force. Then suddenly, her body stiffened up like she was having a seizure. "Dina, Dina!" I cried out to her. Her body released the seizure, her body relaxed on the sofa, and as I watched in horror, her chest stopped moving. I sat and watched for the longest time to see if her breathing would start again. But it didn't.
I walked out of the RV, saw Polly and Jim talking to Curt. They all looked over at me. I shook my head from side to side. They seemed to know what I meant. They met me halfway, and I told them it seemed she had had a heart attack and had passed away.
I continued home and noticed the motorhome was parked on the other side of our RV and knew Jay had moved it. I could see he was moving things around in the motorhome.

"Hi," I said as I stepped in the door, "Dina just passed," I told him. He looked down and said, "it was probably for the best. She wouldn't have made it too far on this trip. Now she can be buried next to her husband."

I helped Jay finish putting things away. The cabinets were full of water and canned goods, nonperishable snacks, and ammo, lot of ammo. But we knew we would still need more supplies along the way. It was over 1300 miles to the deer lease.

I grabbed sheets and pillows, even though it was hot as hell. I grabbed all the blankets, too. I picked up a laundry basket and headed to Dina and Ben's RV to grab anything I could find that would be of use on this trip.

Their RV was neat and tidy. Her cabinets were full of most everything we could use. I grabbed her blankets and pillows and all of her nice towels. While back in her bedroom area getting the last of her pillows, I noticed a picture frame on the desk that held a picture of her, Don, and three adults and what looked to be like several grandchildren. I took the picture to the dinette table. Alongside the refrigerator was a pad of paper. I found a pen and sat down to write a note.

To whom it may concern:
If you are the family of Don and Dina, and have come here to find them, I'm so sorry to inform you they both passed away. They were so brave during this time. You will find them buried in the park under a tree. We place a big rock as their headstone. I'm so sorry for your loss.

D'Ann site #6

I tucked it under the picture frame, picked up the supplies, and locked the door behind me. As I walked back to the motorhome, tears filled my eyes. "If this happened to my family, I hope someone would leave a note and let me know what happened," I thought.

After putting the rest of the supplies away, I slumped down on the sofa and, with my face in my hands, I wept. I knew we had a long road ahead of us and it would not be easy. I just hope we make it in one piece, I thought.

The rest of the day, we moved stuff from Curt and Liz's RV to the motorhome. We grilled the rest of the meat that had just thawed out. We all sat and enjoyed our last meal before we had to leave the next morning.

I walked over to Polly and Jim's house and asked them to join us. We had a ton of meat we had to cook and needed to eat. They accepted and brought over the last of their vegetables they had in a cooler.
As the summer sky turned orange, the wind was like a blow dryer. But I knew when the sun went down it would cool off, and it did. The wind died down a little, but you could still smell the smoke from the valley. We all sat around complaining how full we were, but we knew this could very well be the last good meal we would have until we got to Texas.

Jay turned to Jim and asked, "have you decided if you're going to Texas with us?" Jim looked at his wife, "we don't want to go all the way to Texas, but if you could get us as close as you can to Colorado, we have a son in the Colorado Springs area, we might be able to get to him," he said.

Jay stared down at the ground. I could tell he was thinking and process what Jim had just said.

I got up and went into the motorhome and brought out a cake that I had gotten the day before the event. We had been so busy with everything we had not even touched it. I sat it on the picnic table and told everyone to help themselves.

"I think if you go with us, there are several small towns and farms along the way. We might find an old car or truck we can get started and you can take it to your sons," Jay said, looking at Jim.

Jim shook his head. "Okay, we will go with you. Polly, we need to go get our stuff ready," as he got up and stuck out his hand to help his wife up. "We have little," Polly said. "I hope to come back here when all of this is over."

Since the motorhome had a generator, we could wrap up the leftover meat and put it in the fridge.

Curt had decided he would take night watch so Jay could take the first shift driving in the morning.

Since we had emptied our RV, we decided we would sleep in the motorhome. After letting the dogs out to, we climbed in the motorhome and laid down in the bed.

The motorhome had a musty old smell to it, but we knew this was our new home for a while. It had a nice size kitchen, a king-size bed in the bedroom, and in the hallway were two bunks. The bed over the driver's seat and the sofa and dinette also made-up beds. We had plenty of room. For everyone.

I laid there with all kinds of thoughts going through my head. Jay lying next to me breathing deeply. I knew he was asleep. Not being able to sleep, I quietly got up. It was now dark outside, so I grabbed a flashlight and opened the door. The night air was cooling down, the desert was quiet. Only the sound of gunshot down in the valley could be heard, but because we lived on a gun range and heard gunshots all the time, I wasn't alarmed. Till I thought about it for a minute, those gun shots weren't supposed to be happening though.

I opened the door to our RV that we were sadly leaving and climbed in. I opened the windows to let the small breeze blow in and sat down on the couch.

Leaning back and closing my eyes, memories of when we first bought the RV and our time in Colorado and Texas came flooding in. "It's all over," I whispered to myself.

Almost dozing off, I heard a faint engine. It didn't sound like an ATV. After opening my eyes, I set up. I walked over to the door, opened it, and climbed down. I looked around trying to find Curt, who was on patrol. After walking around a couple RVs, I saw his flashlight heading towards the entrance to the park.

I ran back to the motorhome and gently shook Jay. "Jay, someone's coming up the road. Curt is out there, but I have no idea who or how many there are."

Jay got up and grabbed his rifle, which was lying on the floor beside the bed. I followed him and grabbed my revolver out of my bag.
"No, stay here and be quiet," Jay commanded. "No, I want to come. I'll stay back and watch, but I'm not staying here," I replied.
We both jogged towards where Curt was hiding near some bushes at the entrance to the park. Since the electricity was off, the security gate was in the open position.

We waited and watched as an old military Jeep came driving up the road. Jay stepped out and blocked the drive with his gun in hand. The Jeep stopped.

"Sir, put your gun on the ground," a man yelled at him. As Curt and I ducted further behind the bush. Jay held his gun and didn't budge. "What can we do for you? This is a private area."

We could see a soldier jump out of the Jeep and walk towards Jay. He also had a gun. A big gun. "We know this is a gun range and we need to collect all the guns and ammo that are stored here," the soldier said, coming to a stop in front of Jay.

"These are privately owned guns here," Jay said. "They have initiated martial law. We are taking what we need to protect the citizens that are left in this city," the soldier interrupted.

Jay knew he would not win any argument with this man, and he knew martial law was bad news.

"It's really dark up at the clubhouse and would be best if you came back in the morning. We could help and direct you to all of them," Jay lied.

The soldier was young and not a very tall man. Looking Jay over and knowing there were only him and another soldier, he replied, "we are only scouting tonight. We will be back at daylight and will expect you to cooperate."

"Yes, sir," Jay said as the soldier jumped back into the Jeep and drove back towards the valley.

Curt and I appeared from behind the bush. "We need to go. We need to leave now before they get back," Jay said with a pissed off tone of voice.

We hurried back to our RVs. I ran over and knocked on Jim and Polly's door. They had not been in bed yet, still packing. I told them what had happened, and that we needed to leave within the hour.
It was close to midnight when we finished putting everything in the motorhome. "Let's go potty one more time, kids," I said to my four dogs.

Loaded, we all said goodbye to the homes we had lived in and drove out of the RV park.

We knew it was going to be difficult to maneuver the streets in the dark and dangerous, so just a few blocks ahead were one of the local casinos. We all agreed that it might be the safest place to pull up behind the building and sleep the rest of the night, and in the morning, we would head to Benny's house.

We parked close to the exit and by a block fence that backed up to the interstate, so we only had to watch if someone approached from the front of the motorhome. There were no other cars parked in that area, so we felt pretty safe, but still decided someone needed to keep watch. Every once in a while, we could hear a motor running. Sometimes it sounded like a motorcycle or ATV, but we also heard what sounded like a car or a truck driving by on the interstate.

Curt stayed up and kept watch, sitting right outside the RV door. The rest of us slept, Jay and I in the bedroom, Liz crawled up on the loft bed above the driver's seat. And Polly and Jim pulled out the sofa, which was made into a full-size bed.

Curt could tell the sun was getting ready to rise as he walked around the area to stay awake.

CHAPTER NINE
Leaving Las Vegas

Day 7

"Good morning," Jay said, startling Curt. "Jeez, you scared me," Curt replied. "Everything good?" Jay asked, "Yeah, but it wouldn't hurt to get going," Curt said.

After looking everything over on the motorhome, making sure that tire was still holding air. Driving out of the drive, Jay headed east to Bobby's house.

Feeling the motorhome moving, I sat up and looked out the window. The sun was bright. Hurting my eyes, I laid back down. I just can't believe the turn our lives had taken. Thing we're going the best they had gone in years, and now it was gone.

I could feel the motorhome making sharp turns left to right. Nauseated, I decided I better get out of bed and see what was going on out the front windows.

Bobby's house was just a few miles from where we were. The streets were dotted with cars here and there. As we drove by businesses, we noticed most had their windows broken out and trash seemed to spill out all over. Every once in a while, we would see people coming out of a business carrying arms full of stuff.

We made it to Benny and Nadia's home, parked right out in front. "I'll go see what they want to do," Jay said. "I'm coming with," I added. By the time we had got to their front door, the door opened, and Benny motioned us to come in and gave a wave to the others waiting in the RV. Nadia came out of the bedroom and sat next to me on their sofa. "So, are you going to go with us?" I asked her. "We have Liz, Curt, Polly and Jim and we are picking up Sean, Andie, and Sean's mom. You remember them?" I asked. "Yeah, the couple that came over and played pool a couple of weeks ago?" Nadia commented.

Nadia looked at Benny and asked, "Well, what do you want to do? We thought about it, and all our family is in New Mexico. If you can drop us off on the way, we would love to go. Do you have room in that rattle trap for all our supplies?" Benny asked. "We will make room," Jay replied with a smile on his face. "Good, let's get hauling stuff out," Benny said.

Everyone piled out of the motorhome and started hauling thing from the house. We stuffed every single nook and grannie with Nadia's supplies. "Do we have room for my survival books" she asked. "I'll find room. We will definitely need them," I replied.

When the motorhome could not possibly hold another thing, we all climbed aboard and settled in. "So, how are the roads? We haven't ventured out since this all stated," Benny asked. "Just keep your eye peeled for anything," Jay answered.

Jay drove, Benny rode shotgun, while Jim, Polly and Nadia sat on the sofa, and Liz and I sat at the dinette table. Since Curt had been on patrol all night, he slipped into one of the bunks to take a nap. The four dogs slept on the bed with the door shut. We didn't want to take any chance of Diamond biting anyone.

We had made our way to the interstate. "I thought we might try going this way, maybe fewer people. If it's not good, then I'll get off and we will take the back streets to Sean's," Jay commented.

The interstate had several cars and trucks scattered about. The event had happened in the early morning, so rush hour traffic had not yet begun. As Jay weaved in and out of cars, I studied the cars as we went by. There were a few crashes, but no people around. In some places, it looked like a parking lot, but we were able to drive on the shoulder and get around.

Sean's house was about thirteen miles from where we had gotten on the interstate, then a couple miles off the highway through several neighborhoods.

Taking the interstate took off a lot of time, then if we would have taken the back roads. Although it took us a little out of the way to go around the airport, it seemed a lot faster, and no people were around. As we went around the curve, approaching the exit to the airport. "Oh my God, what the hell?" Jay said as he slowed down. Up ahead was a gigantic pile of debris. We could see metal and plastic. There was still smoke streaming up in several places. As we got closer, we knew exactly what it was, being this close to the airport and right on the flight path. We knew it was an airplane that had gone down. There was no getting through this enormous mess. We pulled up as close as we could get and noticed movement coming from the area. I grabbed Jay's binoculars and could see what looked to be people in hazmat suits, moving debris. "I think we should turn around and go back to the first exit and see if we can get around this. There are people there in hazmat suites. Looks like military, so I'm sure they don't need our help," I said, looking at Jay.

"Your probably right, nothing we can do for those people now," as Jay turned the motorhome around and headed the other way.
We reached the exit as a motorcycle approached. I got up out of the seat and ran to the back bedroom and grabbed my revolver that was

lying on the floor next to the bed. Benny had his rifle in his lap as I returned to the seat.

It was only a lone rider on the bike, as he slowed down as if wanting to talk to us. Jay rolled down his window as the man rode up next to us. "How's it going?" Jay asked. "Where you headed?" the man on the bike asked. He looked to be about in his late thirties, with a pretty good 5 o'clock shadow going. "Just trying to get across town. Trying to get around this mess," Jay continued. "If you get off here and go up to Rainbow, you can get around it," the man said. "Thank you," Jay said as he rolled up his window, not wanting to talk anymore. I could tell Jay was getting nervous sitting there and didn't want to waste any more time.

We continued to the exit and headed toward Rainbow like the guy had said. The man on the motorcycle continued down the highway towards the plane crash.

As we drove on the side streets and back roads, we saw more and more people just out walking about. We could see makeshift tents and camps set up along the street. As we drove by, people stopped what they were doing and stared at us.

I was getting really nervous, thinking these people might storm us and try to take our stuff. I sat, being very observant with my revolver in my hand.

"Man, I don't like this. We need to hurry and get out of town. It's just a matter of time before we run into people that want what we got," Jay said. "We are just going to stop at Sean's house long enough to pick them up, and then we are out of here," He continued.

I pulled out the map and laid it out on the dinette table. "I really don't see any other way out of Las Vegas but to take the interstate. At least till we get to Kingman, Arizona," I said, looking at the map. "I think you're right; we should take Highway 93 and maybe Interstate 40,"

Liz agreed, pointing to the route on the map. "We should probably top the gas tanks off before we leave town. There is nothing between here and Kingman," Jay commented. "We can siphon some gas out of cars. I think there is a shopping center right by Sean's house. Let's pick up about 5 more 20-gallon gas cans and some straps and strap them on top," Jay said. "That's going to take a while to siphon that much gas," Curt replied. "I know, but we're going to need it," Jay replied.

We continued to weave around vehicles and debris till we finally got to Sean's street.

Sean's house was a small two story at the end of a dead-end street. Driving through his neighborhood, you would have thought nothing had happened. Cars were parked in driveways, or along the street, the houses all looked normal, no houses on fire or even burnt. Windows and doors still seemed to be intact. No trash or debris in the streets or in the yards. It just seemed normal, but we knew different.

We pulled into Sean's driveway. Not seeing his mom's car was a little concerning. The garage door was open and there was no sign of anyone there.

Jay jumped out of the RV. "Everyone stay here. I'm going to look around," he said. "Nope, I'm going with you," as I opened the door and jumped out, my revolver in my hand.

Jay looked mad, but I didn't care. I would not sit there and wonder if he was going to be okay. "Come on, then," he growled and started walking through the garage to the door.

I followed him, looking around to see if I could see anything unusual. All of a sudden he stopped. The back door to the yard was open. As I approached, I could see what he was looking at. The ATV was parked in the backyard next to the house.

We both looked at each other and knew that Sean had at least made it home. Jay tried to turn the handle on the entry door that led into the kitchen. Locked. He motioned for me to exit out the back door into the backyard. I knew there were patio doors in the back of the house, because of a BBQ we had attended here just a couple months ago.

As we walked towards the doors, we could see the glass was shattered all over the ground. I looked at Jay with a shocked and horrified face. Holding his finger up to his lips, I knew he wanted me to be quiet. He tip toed through the glass, trying to make as little noise as possible, and entered the house. He stuck his arm out the door and motioned me to follow him in.

As quietly as we could, we slowly walked through the kitchen, which opened up into the living room and dining room area. As I walked around the huge center island looking towards the dining room, I gasped.

The sound made Jay turn and look at me. I pointed towards the dining room table. It was covered in bloody towels. There were paper towels covered in blood all over the floor.

I stood there staring at the horrifying scene in front of me, as Jay, now with more urgency, ran towards the stairs. Taking them two by two, he disappeared into the bedroom.

All I could do was stand there. I heard his footsteps running above me from room to room. "No one's here," he called out as he ran back down the stairs.

"What could have happened?" I said, still staring at the mess. Jay went into the living room, searching for any answers he could find. "I don't know," he replied. "Jay," I whispered as I pointed to the kitchen and the patio doors. The sound of footsteps on the broken glass had us both scared.

I ran as quickly as I could across the room to where Jay was standing. He pulled his pistol out of the back of his pants. "Jay!" Sean's voice sounded as he and Andie came through the patio door. Jay and I both exhaled the breath we had both been holding. "Damn it man, that's twice now, shit," Jay replied as he walked towards Sean, and they hugged. "Oh my God, Sean, what happened here? We were so scared," I asked, taking my turn to hug him and Andie.

"As I was coming home yesterday, I came upon my mom's car. She had crashed it a couple blocks over, her leg was severely cut and broken. I got her here to the house, but we couldn't stop the bleeding," he said. "I rode the 4-wheeler over to the hospital to see if there was anyone there. They've made a makeshift emergency room out in front. So, an old jeep they made into an ambulance came back here, and we got her over there. She had lost a lot of blood. But she's going to be okay, she's outside by the motorhome, they gave her crutches, but she can hardly move," he continued. "Well, are you coming with us?" Jay asked. "Yes, but do you have room for my brother? He should be here in about 5 minutes. He rode his bicycle to see if he could get mom some more pain pills at the CVS on the corner," he asked. "Of course, we won't leave anyone. It's crowded, but we will make room," Jay replied.

"Let's get your mom settled in the motorhome and get your stuff. Again, we don't have a lot of room, so just the essentials," Jay said as they walked out of the house.

I helped Andie pack some clothes for Sean's mom and grabbed her jewelry box and a shoebox full of pictures and memory keepsakes she wanted.

Sean's brother Dre showed up just in time to help carry the last of Sean's guns out to the motorhome.

We took a last look around and walked out the front door, locking it behind us.

Sean's mom Vickie was lying on the bed. I made a little makeshift bed on the floor next to the bed for the dogs. I slowly introduced Diamond to Vickie in hopes she wouldn't bite, but much to my surprise, Diamond must have sensed Vickie was hurting, because she jumped up on the bed and curled up right next to her.

We had grabbed a couple of lawn chairs from the garage and set them up next to the door and in the kitchen, there was no room to walk, but at least we all had a place to sit.

Back on the road, we knew there was a small shopping center close to Sean's house. "We will see if we can get a couple more gas cans and siphon some gas out of the cars in the parking lot," Jay said as we drove to the shopping center.

We passed a few people walking around. They seemed to still be in shock, walking around looking like zombies. Some were pushing shopping carts with what looked like all their worldly possessions. Others had nothing, just wandering around.

We got to the shopping center. The building was still intact, but most all the store doors were busted open. We weren't sure if we would find any gas cans, but we had to look.

To the south, near the end of the parking lot, a few people looked like they had set up a sort of tent city. They strung tarps that were probably taken from the store up along the fence and a couple of cars.
Jay pulled the motorhome right up next to the doors. "Me, Sean, and Liz will go in and see if there are any gas cans left. You stay here and be looking out for us," Curt said as they headed out the door.

Jay and Benny jumped out of the motorhome and stood watch, while the rest of us waited inside. About 10 minutes went by when Liz came out the doors with 3-25gallon gas cans. She handed them to Jay, then reached into her back pocket and pulled out three siphoning kits.

I came out of the motorhome and brought back the other siphoning kits I had gotten the other day. I handed one to Polly, Jim, and Dre. "Let's hurry and try to get as much as we can," I said, heading toward a group of cars in the parking lot.

Jay stayed back at the door waiting for Curt and Sean, making sure we were all secure by watching the parking lot and any movement coming our way.

The first car I came to had a locked door on their gas cap. "Ugh, this will not be easy," I grumbled. I went to the second car, same thing. Thinking this might be true about all of them, I walked back towards the store. "I need a screwdriver or a crowbar to open these gas tank doors," I said to Jay as I walked by him into the store.

A couple of minutes later I returned with a complete tool set and prying open the doors I siphoned gas out of the cars.

Curt had come out with four more cans and Sean had an arm full of heavy-duty bungee cords and some tie down straps. It seemed to take 2-3cars just to get enough gas to fill one tank and with only about ten cars in the lot, we only filled three cans.

Benny and Jay strapped the gas cans on the roof of the motorhome as Liz and I went back into the store and grabbed cases of water and snack food that were at the checkout stand. Settled back in the motorhome, we drove out of the parking lot.

We had all agreed we would take the interstate to get out of town and then head on highway 93 to Kingman, AZ, but before we left town completely, we would need to find more cars and fill up the motorhome and gas cans.

Winding our way back to the interstate took about an hour, and it was getting late in the afternoon approaching evening. The sky was clear, and it felt like it had gotten over one hundred again today. The A/C in the motorhome didn't work very well, so we had all the windows open.

Closing my eyes and letting the hot air blow in my face, I had a wonderful thought. Lake Mead was on the way to Kingman. We could cool off in the lake and spend the night. It had been several days since I had had a shower and I'm sure the rest of the crew hadn't had one for a few days.

Popping my head up, I looked at Jay in the mirror that was mounted above his head. "Hey, I just had a great idea, the lake is just a few miles out of town, I don't know about you, but I could use a swim to wash this crime off and cool off, and we could spend the night there." "Come on, there might be gas at the marina also," I pleaded. Looking in the mirror, he looked at the other passengers, "what do ya all think?" he asked.

"I don't see why not," Curt replied, looking around at the others as they nodded their heads yes and shrugged their shoulders.
The road to the lake was pretty clear, a car here and there, but again because it was so early in the morning when the event happened, there weren't many people out at the lake.

We approached the entrance to the state park that surrounded the lake. The gate was closed, and no one was around. Benny hopped out and held the arm to the gate up while Jay drove through. We continued to the marina area. From a distance, we could see a couple of trucks with boat trailers in the parking lot but no people around.

We parked and got out of the motor home, while Nadia and Andie stayed with Vickie. The doors to the Marina store were locked and still intact. No one had vandalized it, yet. The sign on the door said the hours were from 8am to 10pm, so we figured the store had not opened and no one had come to work yet when the event happened.
Jay, Sean, and Bobby walked towards the boat gas filling station to see if they could get the pumps working. Bobby and Sean, being the mechanics, thought they could rig up the pumps well enough to get some gas.

After about 20 minutes, they had it pumping by hooking up some marine batteries to the pumps. They filled all the gas cans and filled up the motorhome.

Everyone was exhausted. It had been a long, hot day. We drove the motorhome to the boat ramp and parked next to the water, hoping a pleasant breeze would come off the lake and keep it cool so we could all get a good night sleep.

Vickie was in a deep medicated sleep, so we felt best to let her sleep. The rest of the girls grabbed towels, and I grabbed some shampoo, and we headed to the boat ramp and water.

The water was clear and cold, which felt so good in this heat. I watched as the guys walked towards the motorhome, climbed up on the roof and brought down the BBQ grill.

After rinsing my hair in the water, I got out, wrapped the towel around me and stood looking out at the water. The other ladies followed me out. "We should go see what we can fix for dinner. "I'm starving," thinking back to when we last ate.

Jay lit the fire, while Polly and I got the meat that we had cooked the day before and wrapped it in foil to reheat on the fire. Nadia grabbed some of her canned veggies and a pan and put it on the grill.
I think we were ready for the next leg of our trip. Kingman was the next town, and it was one hundred miles away.

The inside of the motorhome was cooling down since the sun went down and a breeze was blowing off the lake. Knowing that Vickie was still in a deep sleep on our bed, I grabbed a reclining lawn chair and pillow and set it up outside. Jay followed suit and joined me. We would take turns keeping watch while we slept outside.

CHAPTER TEN
The Road to Kingman

Day 8

As the sky brightened up, I stretched in my chair. "You should jump in and wash, never know when the next time we will be able to bathe," I said to Jay as he got up from his chair and stretched as well.

"I'll go get you the shampoo and let the dogs out to potty," I said as I got up and headed to the motorhome. I let the dogs run. I knew they wouldn't go far. Walking towards Jay with shampoo and a towel, I saw him take off all his clothes and walk in the water. Shaking my head, I knew he would do that. It didn't seem to bother him there were other people still sleeping and could see him. "Really, Jay?" I asked. I threw him the shampoo and laid the towel on the chair and hurried back into the motorhome to get him some clean clothes.

The sun was coming over the mountains and lit the sky completely now. As I walked back towards the water, I noticed something floating just a few feet from Jay. "What is that?" I said as I pointed to the right of Jay. Jay stood up in the water and walked towards it, then stopped. "It's a body!" Jay exclaimed as he started backing up and headed towards me.

"Look!" I screamed, as I pointed out further in the water, "there's more," I continued. I handed Jay the towel as he walked out of the water. We stood there looking out over the water. Not only were we seeing several bodies floating, but debris also started washing up on the shoreline.

"We need to get everyone up and get out of here. What do you think happened?" I asked. "I don't know, but we better get out of here."
The rest of the group were getting up and coming outside. We showed them what was going on. We all stood there looking out over the water. "Wow, that's crazy, let's get breakfast cooking and get on the road," Jay commented to everyone.

"How's your mom Sean? Is she awake? Is she in pain?" I asked. "I slept with her last night, and she didn't move much," Andie replied. "She should probably stay in that bed and rest a couple more days, then we need to get her up and start walking on that leg," Nadia commented. Nadia had trained to be a nurse a few years back, but never really worked as one. But we knew her knowledge would be a great help.

Liz and Polly had started the grill and made a big batch of pancakes, as Dre and Andie ran up to the marina store and brought back some syrup and found some semi melted butter in the cooler.

"Man, that was good and filling," I said as I put my paper plate in the trash bag. I hollered for the dogs which had been lying in the motorhome's shade. "Did you guys go potty?" I asked as I pet Diamond on the head and picked up Tator. I snuggled his neck and gave him a hug. "You are just a Yote," I told him as I put him down, then picked up Lil Man, who was begging for me to pick him up. "Here's my wolf," I told him and made him snuggle with me. I had nicknamed Tator "a Yote," which was short for "coyote," and Lil Man "my wolf." I put Lil' Man down and looked at Brooklyn, aka Brooky, but knew she hated to be picked up and snuggled, so I bent down and ruffled her hair on her head. "Let's got, get inside," I commanded as all four dogs jumped in the motorhome. I thought I better get them a treat while I could still get to them before everyone else got in.

Soon everyone was inside and ready to go. We drove out of the park and headed back towards the interstate that took us over the Hoover dam and to Arizona.

Crossing over the dam, I heard Jay say, "Oh my God, look!" as he pointed out the window.

We all moved to that side of the motorhome to look out the windows. Several hundred yards out into the lake was a huge airplane halfway under water, debris and luggage and what looked like bodies floating all around the area.

I gasped and put my hand to my mouth. "Oh jeez, I feel so bad," as tears welled up in my eyes. We all went back to our seats and rode in silence.

The highway to Kingman was one hundred miles long, no homes, no services, only desert and a roadside park halfway between Kingman and Las Vegas. We saw several big eighteen wheelers stranded on the road, sometimes having to maneuver around them. But saw no people. Not wanting to push the old motorhome too hard, Jay stayed around fifty mph. It would probably take us several hours more than normal to get there. We had decided when we got to the roadside park we would stop and let it rest for a while.

About twenty miles from the roadside park, we saw more abandoned cars in the roadway, which worried us. "Where are these people?" Approaching the roadside park, we could see makeshift tents and shelter. Several people walking around. Because the highway was just a 4-lane road with no median, there was only a roadside park on one side of the road, our side.

We all got nervous. "We better not stop. We will probably get takin' over by these people. They probably have no food and are desperate,"

Benny said. "I know it doesn't look good. I'm going to stay as far left as I can. Everyone grab a gun and be ready," Jay replied.

As we got to the exit to the park, people noticed us and started running out towards the road. "If Jay steps on it, we might get past before they reach the highway," I thought.

Jay had the pedal all the way to the floor. "If they get to this side of the highway, I'm not stopping. I may have to hit them," he exclaimed. "Don't stop whatever you do," Jim cried.

I watched as several of the people made it to the road just as we went by. One was waving a rifle in the air, showing us, he wanted us to stop. "Shit, gun!" I yelled, as Curt hurried and slid open the window above the sofa, stuck his rifle out and fired a shot right above the man's head. All the people stopped in their tracks and ducked. As we whizzed by. Jay could see in the side-view mirror the man was taking aim at the motorhome. "Get down, he's going to shoot the back!" he yelled, as he looked in the mirror. We didn't hear the shot go off, but we saw a little puff of smoke come off the rifle, and the sound of the bullet hitting the motorhome. "Everybody okay, no one hit?" Jay asked. Everyone got up from the floor and returned to their seats. "Yeah, we are all good."

We had gotten about five miles down the road when Jay saw a dirt road going off to the west. "I'm going to pull over here and check to see what was hit," Jay said as he pulled off the road.

Jay stopped the motorhome and him, Sean and Benny jumped out and walked around to the back. "There!" Sean said as he pointed up at the gas cans. They could see gas pouring out of the cans from a hole. Jay climbed up the ladder to check it out.

He untied all the cans and started handing them down. "Hurry and pour what you can into the gas tank before we lose all the gas," he said, handing them down. Every single can had a hole and gas was pouring out. "Well shit, we're going to be in trouble. We're going to have to find some more cans and gas," he said.

They filled the tank up on the motor home and still had gas left, which was still pouring out of the hole. Jay grabbed a roll of duct tape and made a plug, trying to tape the holes closed. It at least slowed the leak down. They poured what gas they saved into two gas cans that had holes near the top. In all, they saved about twenty gallons.

Jay put the cans back on the roof and tied them down. They returned to the motorhome as Jay headed back out on the road. We still had about fifty miles to go. The first fifty miles took over 2 hours. It was now close to noon.

Liz made sandwiches, the best she could, with little room to maneuver as we continued to go down the road. "We should be at Kingman by 3pm," Jay said. "I hope we can make it to I40 without too much trouble," he continued.

As we approached the city limits of Kingman, we spotted a car dealership, and all of at once said "gas!" As we all laughed out loud. Jay pulled the RV into the parking lot. It didn't look like anyone was around and the doors and glass were all intact, so we figured it was secure. Jay, Curt and Jim went around to the service area as Sean, and I took the dogs out to potty. We heard breaking glass, and we stopped in our tracks, wondering what had just happened. About that time Jim yelled, "we're okay, just had to break the door to get in." We gave each other a look and continued on with the four dogs.

Jay, Curt, and Jim entered the service area and scouted for gas can in hope they would find some full ones. Curt yelled out, "I found some, but they're brand new, no gas in them. I guess we need to see if there is a gas pump, or we need to siphon the gas out of the cars out front," Jay replied.

Not finding a gas pump, each guy took three cans and gave Dre and Sean 2 cans each. As I put the dogs back in the motorhome. They spread out each with a siphoning kit and began filling the cans. After they had filled the cans, they emptied several cans into the RV and now it was full again, and then returned to fill the cans back up.

It took about 2 hours for them to finish filling the cans and strapping them on to the RV. "Since it's getting late, should we stay the night here? It seems safe," I asked. "Kingman is not that big. I would like to get through it and on the other side before dark if we can, then find a place we can stay," Jay replied.

Everyone seemed to agree, so we loaded up and headed back on the road. We didn't get too far when we came to a roadblock blocking the entire four lanes of the street. Someone had moved cars and pushed them together so no one could get through. We slowly approached the cars. Two men with guns stepped out from behind the cars.

We all held our breath as Jay came to a stop and rolled down his window. One man approached. "Can we get through?" Jay asked. "We're not letting no one in," the man replied. "Then how can we get around? We're on our way to Texas," Jay said, knowing there were no other roads that would take us around the city. Benny, Sean, Curt, and Jim, both slowly and quietly without being noticed, grabbed their rifles and told us ladies to get towards the back of the RV. I grabbed the dogs and ushered them towards the bedroom.

"I don't know what to tell ya, but you're not getting through here," the man repeated, more sternly this time. Jay sat there for a minute and then replied, "what about a trade? I'll give you something you can either keep or trade yourself, and you will let us pass," as Jay reached down under his seat and brought out a baggie of marijuana and held it up to the man.

Curious, the man looked at it. "This is all I have left, but I'm willing to trade it for passage," Jay lied, knowing he had thousands of dollars' worth hidden in the RV.

As the man took the baggie from Jay's hand, he motioned to his partner to come over and look at it, Jay looked up in the rear-view mirror at the guys and whispered, "if this don't work be ready to shoot," They nodded their head and sat ready.

The other man approached the RV. Both men examined the bag, opened it, and smelled it. "That's some good shit right there," the man's partner said. He looked up at Jay and said, "what if we just take it, and still don't let you pass?" as he glared at Jay. "Well, then we might have a problem. See, there are two of you and I have four guns pointed right at your heads. So, one way or another, we will get through." The men looked towards the back window and saw the muzzle of a gun pointed right at them.

"Okay, okay, we will move the car so you can pass, and we will take this bag of weed," the man said. "Good idea," Jay replied.
The two men walked over to one car and pushed it out of the way. Jay did not hesitate and drove right through. "Shit, that was a close one. I'm still shaking," Jay said with a shaky voice. "Girls, find us a way out of this town that is not on the main roads. I don't want to do that again," he said.

Liz grabbed the map and spread it out on the table as we looked for an easy way out of Kingman. Looking at the map, we saw that highway 66 would take us out of town, but it was going out of the way to the north. It would eventually come back and met interstate 40. It passes through a couple of small towns.

The city of Kingman looked a little better off than Las Vegas did, but it was a much smaller town. We still had to dodge vehicles and debris on the roads, and we saw several people on ATVs and older model cars. We saw several groups of people gathered around schools and churches. But fearing they would overtake our RV; we drove right past them and didn't stop.

Within a few minutes, we had reached the outside of Kingman and I40. Again, we could see they blocked the road just a few feet before the interstate. Jay slowed down and came to a stop. "Now what?" he asked. "I guess we will see if they will let us leave town," Curt replied. Jay put the RV in motion as we approached the roadblock. Again, two men stood guard with automatic weapons. One held up his hand, motioning us to stop. Jay came to a stop and rolled down the window. "Good evening, sir," Jay said. "We are leaving town and would like to take I40. Do you know if it's clear?" The man approached the open window. "You can leave town, but you cannot come back in," he exclaimed. "From what we've heard, I40 is clear until you get almost to Flagstaff. There is a bridge that was hit by an airplane and is non passable, surrounded by cliffs no way you can get around it," he continued. "You will have to exit a few miles up on Highway 93 or Highway 89 at Ash Fork and head towards the South," the man yelled to the other guard to open the roadblock so we could leave.

As Jay gave the old RV gas, again we all sat back and breathed a little sigh of relief. We entered I40 and headed east. The road was again littered with cars and big trucks. As we passed most of the trucks, we could see they had already been looted. We weaved in and out of stalled vehicles. The further from town we got, the fewer cars we saw. Now we were seeing a few bodies scattered along the road, mostly what looked to be older people. We guessed they most likely died of heat strokes or heart attacks from walking so far in the heat.

It was going to be dark soon, so we decided the next road or area we could pull off and hide the RV would be a good place to stop for the night.

Just up a few more miles, Jay saw a dirt road that turned off and into the trees. He turned on to the road and found an area that could not be seen from the highway and could see anyone that might come up the road.

As the men set up camp, I decided I would Let diamond out to take a walk. Suddenly, she heard something in the bushes not too far from us. Her ears perked up, and I noticed the hair on the back of her neck stood straight up. The low, deep growl I heard coming from her throat meant she was serious.

Suddenly, she took off running deep into the woods. She didn't listen when I yelled for her to stop. I took off running after her, knowing there was no way my fat, short legs could even come close to catching her. I could still hear her barking as I stood, catching my breath. I could tell it wasn't getting any further away. "She must have stopped," I whispered in my out of breath voice. "Maybe it went up a tree, whatever it was, or she has it cornered somehow," thinking to myself. I continued towards the sound of her barking as fast as I could without tripping on the branches and rocks.

As I approached the area, I could see she indeed had something up a tree. I yelled for her to come to me, but her eyes never left the figure in the tree. I slowly approached her and grabbed her collar. Still growling and fixated on the upper branches. I looked up and the hair on the back of my neck stood up, matching Diamond's.

Jay looked towards the trees where he had seen D'Ann run to get the dog. "D'Ann!" he yelled. After a few brief moments, he yelled again and approached the edge of the trees. Liz came out to join him. "I'm sure she will be right back, but she better hurry. It's getting dark," she said as Jay stepped closer into the trees. "Maybe I should go look for her?" he questioned. "Give her a few more minutes. I'm sure she's on her way back."

Jay nodded his head in agreement and headed back to the RV to grab a flashlight and his gun just in case he would have to go search for her. It seemed like forever had passed when he decided it was time to go look for her. The others wandered back outside and started gathering firewood to make a fire.

In the tree just a few branches up was a mountain lion baring his teeth at us. "Oh, shit," I whispered. I grabbed the back of Diamond's collar and started backing up, never taking my eye off the big cat in the tree. Diamond was still growling as we slowly backed away. Then it happened. The cat, with all its teeth showing and growling right back at us, jumped out of the tree just feet from where we had backed up to. I reached to my back and pulled out my pistol. I knew I would have to hit that cat right square between the eyes to kill it or it would attack us. Diamond started going crazy. Barking and growling, I could barely hold on to her. She was a big dog, all seventy pounds. The cat slowly and cautiously started towards us. My heart was beating hard and fast. I knew the cat could pounce at any second. Suddenly, Diamond broke free from my grip. The cat was about twenty yards away and Diamond was closing in. Then, from behind me, came a deafening sound. The shot struck the cat in the chest just as it was getting ready to attack Diamond. I watched the cat collapse and fall to the ground. Dead. I turned around to see where the shot had come from, and Jay was standing there with his AR. I stood there in shock and cried. Jay ran over and pulled Diamond off the dead cat and headed back towards me. "It's okay baby," he said as he took me in his arms. "It's over, let's get back to the RV. It's dark and I don't want to run into anything else." Still crying and shaking, we headed back towards the RV.

As we came out of the woods to the clearing, Liz and Polly came running towards us. "Is everything okay? We heard a shot," Liz said. "Yeah, it was a mountain lion. They both almost got eaten," Jay replied. "Take D'Ann over and sit her down and get her some water. She's just in shock. I'm going to put Diamond up."

I sat by the fire and sipped on my water, as I finally calmed down. I was now exhausted and ready to lie down. Liz and Polly helped me to the RV, as the guys were figuring out who would get the first watch. I snuck into the bedroom where Vickie was sleeping and lay down on the floor beside the bed, not wanting to close my eyes. Jay came in and handed me a piece of chocolate. "Here, eat this. It will help you sleep," he whispered. I took the edible and popped it in my mouth and let the chocolate melt. I moved over close to the wall, and he crawled in beside me and held me close. The chocolate did its trick.

The chocolate hit me hard and fast, and in what seemed like minutes, I was asleep. Between the chocolate and the sheer exhaustion, I never felt the RV start up or felt it moving. Morning had come too fast.

CHAPTER ELEVEN
There's THC in That

Day 9

Before I could even open my eyes, I smelled it, cooking bacon. Liz and Polly were cooking the last of the bacon on the propane stove as we rolled down the highway.

I sat up, and took deep breaths through my nose, taking in the wonderful smell of the bacon, knowing this would probably be the last time I would get to smell it, at least till we got to Texas and could shoot a wild hog.

I got up and joined the rest in the front of the RV. Not a word was spoken as we all ate a piece of bacon, savoring it slowly.

After breakfast, Liz and I pulled out the map and started mapping our way to Texas. The route we were taking would take us through several small towns. Not knowing what to expect. We just knew we needed to restock on a few items and hoped we would find a place and not have any trouble.

Back on I40, the road had been as it was yesterday, fewer, and fewer cars and only bodies alongside of the road. It had only been 9 days since our world was turned upside down. The days were hot and long. People wouldn't be able to survive much longer without food and water, and in this heat.

A couple hours had passed, and we had only gotten about eighty miles, but we didn't want to push the RV too hard, so we kept the speed around forty-five mph. We started noticing a few more cars and trucks on the highway, again weaving in and around. Sean had started out driving and as we approached a sign, he yelled out. "Seligman is coming up in about fifteen miles. We need to get in position in case there are people ahead."

Jay was sitting with a shotgun and already had his AR in his lap. Jim had his rifle and was sitting by the window right behind Sean. Benny and Curt sat at the table, and each had a shotgun loaded and ready, and I was in the bedroom looking out the back window with gun in hand, making sure nothing came up behind us.

As we approached the exit of the tiny town, we saw no movement. The guys had filled up the RV's gas tank that morning and knew we had enough gas to last us until we could get to Ash Fork to turn off. From the highway, we could tell there wasn't much as far as stores and houses in this town. We continued driving east, right past it. Whatever and whoever was there, we didn't want to find out. We drove about five more miles, then Sean pulled over. There were no vehicles insight. "This looks like a good place to stop and walk the dogs and make some lunch. Let's see if we can get mom up and walking today," Sean said as he turned off the RV.

I grabbed the leashes and took the dogs outside, not wanting a repeat of the night before I kept a tight grip on Diamond. The other ladies made sandwiches with the last of the lunch meat and bread. "We definitely are going to need to get some more supplies soon," Polly commented. "Hopefully we can find some in Ash Fork," Jim replied. Sean and Andie helped Vickie get to her feet and gently walk her to the front of the motor home. She slowly sat on the sofa and let out a big breath of air. "You still in pain, mama"? Sean asked. "It's not too bad right now," she replied. "I sure could use a shower, though," she continued. "Hopefully soon we can find a place and all of us can take showers. It's smelling pretty bad in here," Sean replied with a smile on his face.

The men put the last of the gas in the tank and looked over the motorhome. "So far, so good," Jay said. "We might just keep an eye out for another older motorhome, just in case this one quits," he continued.

It would probably take us about two hours to get to Ash Fork, where we would turn off because of the road being closed up ahead.

Liz, Polly, Nadia, and I sat at the table making a list of supplies we had and what we needed, if we could find them.

The sun was high in the sky, and it was getting almost unbearably hot in the RV. We had all the windows open, but the breeze was just hot. We knew once we turned off at Ash Fork, the elevation was higher and lots of trees it would cool down a little.

I closed my eyes and leaned back against the wall. Thoughts of our family were going through my head, wondering if they were safe. If they were going to be as lucky as us as to finding the RV and friends to help us get to the deer lease.

Jay's family and my son Jordan and his family would have to navigate through the city of Houston to get there. After seeing what Las Vegas was doing, I knew it was going to be difficult, if not impossible, for them. I had always told my son if he could not get him and his family out of Houston, then try to get to Nate's house. They only lived ten miles apart.

My thoughts went to my oldest son, Thian, and his family. It had been last summer since we saw them and got to spend time with the grandkids. We had gone to visit them on one of our off weekends from the RV park. He had purchased ten acres down a dirt road on the side of a mountain and had just completed a small 2-bedroom cabin next to the river outside of Durango, Colorado. They lived completely off the grid, had solar panels for electricity, and a water system that collected rainwater and snow and filtered it for drinking water. He hunted and fished for meat as Kris grew an amazing garden for vegetables. If anyone would be ok through all this, it was him. He had been preparing for this all his life. He too knew if he could make it to Texas, he should get to the deer lease. But I knew if he couldn't, he would be okay.

My youngest son Jordan would be thirty-three this year, him and Ashlyn worked so hard to build their dog rescue. Although I told them to get to the deer lease, deep down in my heart, I knew they wouldn't be able to leave all the dogs to fend for themselves. I had told Jordan repeatedly to stock up on prepper type supplies. They lived only fifteen miles from the Gulf of Mexico, and hurricanes were always a threat. Praying that after the last hurricane that came through there, they learned a lesson, and at least started prepping for times like this. I shook my head and smiled. "Probably not," I thought to myself. Jordan was a scrapper, though. He wouldn't let anything happen, and he had a couple guns and knew how to protect himself and Ashlyn.

My mom, and my youngest brother and his family only lived a couple hours from the deer lease. I knew my brother had older cars he was restoring in my dad's old garage. I'm pretty sure one of them would run and be able to get his family and mom to the deer lease. I prayed they would already be there waiting for us when we got there. As the thoughts faded, my mind started drifting to sleep.

I startled awake as I felt the RV come to an abrupt stop. "Look alive people," Sean yelled as he rolled down his window. "We got a military vehicle approaching." Jay, Benny, and Sean jumped out of the RV with guns in hand. They walked to the front of the RV as the old Jeep approached. We could see there were two men sitting in the front and looked like one in the back.

"Hello there," Sean said to the men as their Jeep came to a stop and they jumped out. "Where are you coming from?" one man asked. "Las Vegas," Sean replied. "What's it like there?" the driver asked, looking at Jay's AR sticking out the window. "It's bad. Buildings are burning, people are looting and robbing each other," Jay exclaimed. "We're headed to the air force base there," the man from the passenger seat said. "How is the highway getting there? Any trouble?" he asked. "There's a roadblock in Kingman, but I'm sure they will let you through," Sean replied. "How about going east? How's that?" Sean asked. "The road is completely blocked before you get to Flagstaff. No way to get through. Where are you folks headed?" the passenger asked. "Texas," Jay replied.

"Any word about what's going on? Has this affected the entire country or the world?" Jay asked. "We just came from the Air-force base in Phoenix. We hear rumors it was an asteroid that hit the Pacific Ocean near Hawaii, but we don't know how far the shockwave reached. It's all rumors though, that's all we know," replied the driver. "We better be going if we want to get to Vegas before dark," he said. "Oh, one thing though," the driver said. "Be careful and on alert, not all military and law enforcement are on the right side of this," as he jumped in the old Jeep and started down the highway. "Side of what?" Jay yelled back at them as he turned to face Sean and Benny. "Wonder what he's talking about. They know more than what they said." Jay continued. "Let's get out of here and see if we can find some more gas and supplies," Sean said as they headed back to the motorhome.

The town of Ash Fork was not too far away. Everyone got into position as we exited the interstate. The town was small. A gas station sat at the exit. As we pulled in, we noticed the door and windows were smashed, the gas pumps ripped from their bases. We didn't see any people, so we stopped in front to look to see if we could get any supplies. Jay went in first with his AR ready, followed by Benny, then

Curt and Jim, both with their pistols. After looking around and checking the back, they decided it was all clear. The shelves were basically empty, a few things scattered on the ground. In the back room was a big freezer. Even though he knew things would be spoiled, Curt opened the door.

The ungodly smell was more than he could take. He ran for the front door, but before he could reach it, his stomach was already heaving. Jim was right behind him but made it out the door before spilling his guts on the pavement. Polly and Liz, who had been standing watch outside, ran to their sides. "What the hell happened in there?" Liz asked.

About that time, Benny and Jay came out the door holding their shirts over their noses. "Let's get out of here, try another store," Benny said. "What is it?" Liz asked. Benny looked at Jay and replied, "probably the owner and his wife, shot dead and in the freezer. They were already decaying," Benny continued. "Come on, let's go try the next place."

The gas station was at the exit of the interstate but was still about a half mile or so from town. The town seemed to be big enough for a small grocery store, another gas station that had a tire shop attached, and what looked like a small church. There only seemed to be a few houses along the main highway. As we drove slowly through town, several people came out of their houses to see what the engine noise was. We pulled into the grocery store and could see several people standing at the door, some with guns. The store looked in one piece, no broken windows or doors. Sean stopped the RV, turned around and gave us a look, a look we knew to be in our positions and be ready. "Stay, Sean, keep the motor running. Let me go talk to them," Jay said. Sean nodded and kept one hand on the wheel and one on his rifle.

Jay jumped out, but left his AR in the RV. We knew he had a pistol in the back of his pants. As he walked to the front of the store, he put his hands up in the air. "We aren't here to cause any trouble, just needed some supplies and then we will be on our way," he said as he stopped at the door. "We have nothing to spare," one man said. "Just go on and get out of here," he yelled, looking nervously at the RV. As one man lowered his gun and pointed it right at Jay, my heart started beating out of my chest, "Come on Jay, let's go," I whispered to myself. "Okay, we will leave, no problem, how about gas? Is there any gas we could barter for, a trade?" Jay asked. One man standing in the back stepped forward, "I own the gas station, what do you have to trade?" as he started walking towards Jay and the RV. Jay saw the other men that were standing in the doorway look at him with interest. "Can we go to your station and talk?" Jay asked. The man looked back at his buddies and motioned them to stay as he walked across the street to the gas station. Jay jumped back in the RV and pointed to the station. Sean followed his command and drove slowly out of the parking lot and across the street. We watched the men standing in the grocery store's doorway. They didn't make a move, instead they all turned around and went back inside.

The owner of the station motioned Sean to pull alongside a tanker truck that had been ready to unload his fuel when the EMP hit. Jay jumped out and approached the owner. He had a small bag in his hand. The station owner looked at Jay and asked, "Okay, what do you got to trade?" Jay held out the small baggie. The owner looked at it with caution and then took the baggies from Jay's hand. He opened it and smelled it. "This is Marijuana!" The owner looked up at Jay. "This shit is illegal here, and I don't smoke," as he closed the bag and threw it back to Jay. "I don't think so," he said. "What else you got?" he asked. Jay looked down at the bag. "We don't have anything else. Even if you don't smoke it, trust me, you can trade it for what you need. It's better than money. All we need is enough gas to fill our cans and we will be on our way," Jay said as he held the bag out towards the man. The man looked at the baggie for what seemed forever. He shook his head no but reached for the baggie. "I will fill your cans up and that's it, then be gone," he said as he headed for the tanker truck.

Benny jumped out of the RV and helped Jay get the gas cans down from the roof. I was staring out the window towards a small white house that sits right behind the station. A woman coming out the door of the house caught my eye; she was walking with a cane and didn't seem to move very fast. I could tell see was an older woman and was in a lot of pain by the way she moved. She sat down slowly in a rocking chair on the porch.

I watched for a few more moments and then grabbed a package of chocolates and a jar of THC cream and motioned to Nadia to come with me. I approached the owner and asked who the woman was and was she was in pain. The owner looked at me when his eyes watered. "That's my wife," he said. "She has severe arthritis in her back. The pharmacy in the grocery store ran out of her pain pills a couple of days ago. She's in so much pain," he continued. "I have something for her that might help," I said, "and Nadia here is a nurse. Maybe we can help," I continued. I handed him the package of chocolate and a jar of cream. "The chocolate will help her sleep and spread the cream on her back. I can look at her and see if there is anything I can do to help," Nadia added. The old man looks at us with caution in his eyes. "Please let us see if we can help her," I asked. The old man nodded reluctantly. Nadia and I walked over to the old lady. "Hi, I'm D'Ann and this is Nadia," I said as we approached the porch. "Your husband said you have no more pain medication," I commented. "I have a couple of things that might help, and Nadia here is a nurse. Maybe she can look and see if you can give you some relief," I explained. "I'm Connie," the elderly lady said with labored breath. "Come in," she said as she struggled to get out of her chair and walk into her house. "I can rub this cream on your back. It will help with the pain and here is some chocolate that has THC in it. It will help you sleep," I commented. The lady laid down on her sofa so Nadia could examine her back and rub the cream on her. I sat the chocolate on the coffee table and watched Nadia. "I don't know how long it will last, but it should give you some relief." The lady looked at me with tears in her eyes, "I don't know how to thank you?" she said, choked up. "Just lay here and let it soak in. I hope it helps," Nadia said as she stood up and we walked to the door.

As we walked over to where Jay and Benny were putting the last of the gas cans back on the roof of the RV, the owner was standing nearby. "I just hope it helps," I said. Without a word, the owner walked over and picked up the hose that was attached to the tanker truck and walked to the RV, took off the gas cap, and started pumping the gas into our tank. When the RV was full, he came to where we were standing, watching him. "Thank you, I hope this gets you to where you're going," as he held out his hand to shake both of them. We all jumped back in the RV as Sean started the engine and drove out of the drive.

We continued to drive south on AZ 89 trying to get close to Prescott, Arizona, before it got too late in the day. We passed through a couple of small towns, but there were only houses and maybe a small gas station. But we didn't want to take a chance of trouble, so we kept driving, looking for a safe place to camp for the night. The road was a two-lane blacktop, not in the best of shape, but the best thing was there were hardly any cars or trucks stranded along the way. We had passed a couple of forest service roads and decided we would pull over on the next one we saw. Even if it wasn't that late, we could use the rest after the day we had and let the RV rest a little too. We turned on the next road we found, followed it around the hill and it seemed to wind back around so we ended up on top of the hill. We could see the road and if anyone came towards us. "Let's camp here for the night," Jay said. "Get some good rest. We will go through several little towns tomorrow, so we need to be well rested. No telling what we will run into."

The men decided they would look for some firewood so we could build a fire as Liz and Polly started preparing food to cook. Again, not wanting a repeat of Diamond getting away, I put a leash on her as the other dogs followed along. We walked along the road that we had just driven in on. My mind kept wandering back to the events that we had just gone through. Thinking of all my friends and family, wondering how and what they were doing right now. Have they found a vehicle that worked in order to get them to the deer lease? If they didn't, there's no way they could make it on foot. My son Jordan and most of Jay's family were five hours away from the deer lease.

CHAPTER TWELVE

The Storm is coming

Day 10

The morning air was finally cool, being in the forest and on top of a hill. The birds were singing, a sound I hadn't heard in a long time. They sang as if the world had not just blown up. Jay and I finally got to sleep in the bedroom last night, of course, with all four dogs. Vickie was moving around a lot better last night and had slept on the lower bunk bed, as Dre slept on the top bunk. Being the youngest of all of us, Sean and Andie slept on the floor, while Curt and Liz laid out the dinette table and Polly and Jim pulled out the sofa. The last couple Benny and Nadia crawled up on the bed above the driver's chair.

Jay, Jim, and Curt had taken watch throughout the night, each taking turns, as it was a quiet night. I lay in bed looking at the ceiling, not wanting to get up. I could feel that others were stirring as the motorhome jiggled around. We didn't take time to put the jacks down to steady it in case we had to make a quick getaway.

I wasn't sure what time it was, and it seemed still rather dim outside. I finally got the strength to get up and look out the bedroom window. No wonder it was dim outside. Heavy clouds blocked out the sun. I could see sprinkles on the windows. "I think it's going to rain." I turned to Jay, who was opening his eyes. "We better get off this road then before it rains to bad, and the road gets muddy," Jay said. He jumped out of bed and put his 3-day-old shirt back on. It smelled terrible, but then all of us were smelling terrible. "I hope we can find a river or stream along the way. Maybe we can bathe in it," I said, as Jay opened the bedroom door. Sean and Andie were sitting in the chairs at the front of the motorhome, and Curt and Liz had put the dinette back the way it was supposed to be. Polly had folded in the sofa, and was still laying on the sofa, while Jim had taken the last watch. Dre and Vickie were still sound asleep.

Jay stepped outside behind a tree to pee, as I stepped into the bathroom and used the toilet. We tried not to use the toilet that much, and usually the men went outside. But I could tell we needed to dump the tank. We all had agreed not to use the water in the sink or shower. I looked in the mirror and pulled my brush out of the drawer and brushed my hair, which was sticking up like it does every morning. But the sweat and dirt that was building up in my hair was disgusting.

As I opened the door to the bathroom, Liz was waiting her turn. She hugged me. "How did you sleep?" she asked as she went inside. "Good," I said. Walking to the kitchen. I opened the fridge and took out a cool, not cold, bottle of water. But it was better than a hot can of Diet Coke. "If anything is good about all this, it's I've quit drinking Diet Coke," I said out loud but mainly to myself.

"We really need to get going, at least get off this road before it rains, and we get stuck," Jay announced. "Can everyone be ready in 10 minutes"? he asked. "Yeah, yes, okay," came from everyone. Curt opened the door and climbed into the motorhome. "It's so nice outside, but it's going to rain soon," he said, shutting the door behind him. "You want me to drive?" Curt asked as he looked from Jay to Sean. Both shrugged their shoulders and nodded their head in agreement. Everyone took their seats as we headed back down the hill.

We had just gotten back on Highway 89 when the rain started. Curt turned on the windshield wipers, they swiped across the windshield but there was no rubber on the wiper. The metal to glass noise got everyone's attention. He turned them off quickly. "Hey guys, the windshield wipers are not working," he exclaimed. "it's not raining too hard yet, I can still see, but if it comes down any harder it's going to be dangerous," he said.

"Well, let's keep going. If you think it's getting too bad, let us know," Jay replied. "We aren't too far from Prescott. I'm sure they have an auto parts store or something," he added.

Curt kept driving. He drove slower than usual but could see out the window so far. We all sat quietly and nervously in our seats just looking at each other. "I see a sign, 5 more miles to Prescott," Curt yelled out. "Okay everyone, be alert. This town is a lot bigger than the last little towns we went through, which means more people, more trouble," Jay announced.

"When we get to Prescott, we are looking for Highway 69. It will take us to Interstate 17," Liz yelled to Curt. "Okay," he replied, "I'll help watch for the turnoff and for an auto parts store," Jay said as he was sitting in the shotgun seat.

As we reached the outskirts of town. The rain let up. We opened the windows back up to our relief. It had become quite stuffy inside, and the windows had fogged up. The rain cooled air was a welcome relief. The streets had standing water in some areas. We had just missed a downpour. The streets were quiet. No one was out and about, very few cars in the streets. We passed a couple of gas stations which had been boarded up. "There is Highway 69 turn off," Jay said, pointing to the left. As we headed northeast on Highway 69, the business area of town was just ahead. "There's a Wal-Mart up here on the right," Jay pointed ahead.

We pulled into the drive, and towards the front doors, the doors were all boarded up. "I don't think we better attempt it," Jim said from the sofa. "Maybe there will be a smaller auto parts store further up. That might be easier," he continued.

Curt drove through the parking lot, and back out to the street. The rain had completely stopped, but we could see the sky ahead and it was getting darker with storms. As we passed a major intersection and wormed our way through the stalled cars, Sean noticed down a side street an auto supply store. "Stop!" Sean yelled. "Turn left. There's a store right over there."

Curt turned sharply not to miss the street. The map and a bottle of water flew off the table and onto the floor. "Sorry," Curt said as he pulled into the drive of the parts store. The doors were boarded up, but there was glass on the ground around the door. "It looks like someone has already broken in even though it's boarded up," Curt said. "Let me go see if the board is loose and if I can get in," Sean said. "Cover me Jay," he said. Sean and Jay got out of the motorhome.

Benny followed and took the windshield wiper off the motor home. Sean and Jay walked up to the door and noticed, sure enough, the board was hardly hanging on. Someone had already been in the store. Sean eased the board open enough he could squeeze in. Benny arrived at the door with windshield wiper in hand, as Jay moved the board out of the way for him to enter. Sean and Benny proceeded to the wiper area quietly in case there was someone in the back. Benny searched for the correct wiper blade, but the correct one was gone. "Maybe they have some in the back?" Sean whispered to Benny. As they turned to walk towards the back, they heard a bang come from that area. Both Sean and Benny pulled their handguns they always carried out of their holsters. They walked slowly towards the back. BANG! Another bang came from the same area, peaking around the corner. Sean saw no movement. He motioned for Benny to go around the other way and come up the other aisle. BANG! Sean looked to the left from where the bang came from and could see through the shelves the back door was open and was swinging in the wind. Sean let out his breath he was holding. "Benny, it's just the back door swinging open and shut." He yelled out. Benny came around the corner and saw the extra wipers on the lower shelf near the back wall. They found the correct one and grabbed several and started towards the front. "Do you think we might need anything else?" Benny asked Sean as they walked towards the door. "I have no clue, hopefully the motorhome will last till we get where we are going. It's doing great so far," as Sean knocked on the wooden counter. They walked out behind the wood as it startled Jay. "I heard some banging in there. I was almost going to come in. What was it" Jay asked. "The back door swinging in the wind," Benny answered.

Benny and Sean put on the new wipers. We all watched them glide nicely across the windshield when Curt turned them on. "Let's get out of here," Jay said as they all returned to their seats.

Curt put the motorhome in drive and headed back to the highway. "Anyone hungry yet?" Liz Asked, "I can make some peanut butter and jelly sandwiches really quick," she added. Everyone agreed they would take one. "This will be the last of our bread, till we can stock up," she commented.

"There is a campground about fifty miles north of town. Maybe we can camp there, dump the tank, and maybe it will have a little store with some bread," I said as I was looking at the map.

"We'll see. We need to make sure there are friendlies there and not trouble," Jay replied.

The rain started coming down again, and the wind was picking up. Curt seemed to have a little trouble driving. The motorhome seemed to sway a lot more because of the wind and hitting standing water.

We could tell that Curt was getting a little nervous driving. His hands gripped the steering wheel, making his knuckles turn white. I looked around and no one else was really paying attention to him. Most everyone had their eyes closed or reading one of Nadia's books. I got up and moved slowly up towards the front, trying to stay steading on my feet as the RV swayed from side to side. I tapped Jay on the right side of his shoulder and whispered in his ear. "I think Curt is having a hard time," I said as Jay, who had been looking out the passenger window, turned and looked at Curt. Sweat was beaded up all over his forehead and running down the side of his face. "Are you okay?" Jay asked, concerned. But he didn't seem to hear him. "Curt," as Jay reached out and touched his arm. Curt turned towards Jay. Jay could tell by the look on his face he was not okay. "Why don't you stop and let me take over? You're probably tired," Jay said. At this point, everyone was watching Jay and Curt. "Oh, okay, yeah that might be a good idea," Curt replied, as he slowed down to a stop. "Why don't you go lay down on our bed in the back, just tell the dogs to get on the floor?" Jay said. Curt got up out of the chair, and headed towards the back, Liz got up and helped him to the bedroom.

Jay slipped behind the wheel as I squeezed into the passenger seat. "I hope he's going to be okay," I said. "Yeah, me too," Jay replied. "Should I go check on him?" Nadia asked. "Nah, just let him rest," Benny added.

Jay put the RV in drive as we continued down the highway. The weather was getting really nasty, and we all seemed to pay attention to it now.

As we approached a small town, we could see there was a gas station on one side and a roadside café with a 10-room motel on the other. Nothing much else in town. There were a couple of cars sitting at the café and one car sitting near the motel.

Jay pulled into the drive. "What are you doing?" I asked. "Seeing if anyone is around, maybe stay here till the storm passes," Jay replied. He pulled up and parked between the café and motel. Sean and Benny headed toward the door as Jay got out on the driver's side. Jim moved to the front to stand watch.

The doors to the café were unlocked. They walked in. No one was in there. It looked like people had been in there since everything had happened, but they must have left. Benny walked to the kitchen area to make sure it was empty. As Jay walked to check the restrooms. "Empty," they both said as they met the others in the dining area.

"We need to go check the motel office," as they all went out the doors. We watched them from the RV walk across the parking lot to the motel office. Again, the doors were not locked. We watched them disappear inside the office.

Benny walked behind the counter and into the office. No one, he thought. He noticed a board on the back wall with ten room keys. All ten keys were hanging there.

"I don't think anyone is here. Even the room keys are all here," Benny commented. "I wonder if anyone is in the rooms?" Sean asked, "I doubt it. All the keys are here," Benny replied. "This old hotel. They hand out those keys when someone rents a room," he continued.

"Jay," Benny said, "wonder if the water is still on. We each could take a room and shower and change our clothes," he continued. "The wives would love it."

Jay shook his head. "We should check out the rooms first, and we need to hide the RV, but I don't see why we can't at least get showers and wait out this storm," he said.

Benny grabbed the keys, and they headed out the door. As they came out the door, the rest of us had stepped out of the motor home. "What's going on?" I asked as we walked towards the guys. "We are hoping the rooms are empty and the water is on, so we can take showers and wait out the storm," Jay replied. "Oh my God, a shower, yes please," I said excitedly.

"Wait here everyone, while we go check all the rooms," Benny commanded. One by one, they opened the doors, while one of them went in and checked to make sure the room was clear. "There's water, but it's not hot," Benny said, coming out of the first room. "Don't know how long it will last so, everyone needs to take quick showers," he continued. He handed Liz and Curt the first key and Liz helped him into the room. Curt still did not look well, but we figured he just needed a nice shower and rest.

Vickie and Dre got the next key, Jim and Polly went to room three, Sean and Andie took room four, and Benny and Nadia went into five. Jay handed me the key to room six and told me to go shower and he would stay outside and monitor everything, then he would take a shower when someone else can take watch.

I grabbed some clean clothes from the motorhome for me and Jay, as everyone else did as well. The water was freezing but felt so good. I washed my hair at least five times, making sure all the dirt was out. "Nice and clean, and smelling fresh," I said, getting out of the shower. The bed was still made and on the dresser were two bottles of water, coffee pouches, and sugar packets. I gathered my dirty clothes in my arms, grabbed the water, coffee, and sugar, and carried them to the motorhome. The rain had stopped, and the sky was clearing. I met Nadia and Sean coming from their room, looking fresh and clean. "I wonder if we should grab some bedding and towels from the rooms," I asked them. "We might need them," Nadia responded.

After everyone was nice and clean, we all went back into our rooms and grabbed blankets, pillows, and towels. Plus, everyone's water, coffee, and sugar packets.

Jay had come out of the room all clean shaven and smelling fresh. "Nice," I said when I saw him. He smiled, and we walked to the motorhome together.

"We need to go see if there are any supplies and food in the café," he said to me. As the others gathered the items from their rooms, Jay and I walked to the café.

We walked back to the kitchen and saw several loaves of bread, some flour and sugar sacks, and several other items we could use. We carried what we could and took it to the motorhome. A couple others went in and grabbed the rest of the items that had not spoiled.

"I know it's still early, but do you think we should stay the night here? It seems to be safe," I asked Jay. "I want to take a consensus from everyone on what they want to do," he replied. We all gathered at the front of the motorhome, "do you all want to stay here for the night or keep going?" Jay asked the group. They all looked and mumbled to each other. "I think we are pretty safe here. We could stay, get some good rest," Vickie spoke up. "We're going to take a vote," Jay said. "All in favor. Raise your hand." It was unanimous we would stay. "We should still keep watch, just in case," Jay said. "I'll take first watch," he continued. The rest of the men made a schedule, except for Curt, whom was still not feeling well. "Go rest everyone," Jay commanded, as he took a lawn chair out of the motorhome and set it up against the motel wall so he could see the entire parking area.

I grabbed another chair and set it up next to him. "So, how are you holding up?" I asked, looking at him. "I'm okay, kind of worried about Curt. He didn't look good at all earlier today." He added. "I know. It kind of scared me, him and Liz, and Polly and Jim are a lot older than the rest of us. This trip is probably pretty hard on them," I said. "It's hard on all of us, but probably more so on them," I added.

We sat in silence and looked out across the parking lot and all the trees surrounding us. "It's so pretty here, all the trees and green," I said. "I miss it so much." Off to the north, you could still see the lightning flashing every once in a while, as the sky became dark from the night. But right above us, the moon had come out from behind the clouds.

The locust started making their music, and the crickets chimed in. It was like music to sleep to. It had been so long since I had heard those sounds. It was so relaxing, as I drifted off to sleep.

I felt Jay's hand grab my arm, which startled me awake. "Shhh," he whispered and pointed to the other side of the café. A tall figure and a shorter figure were standing in the dark. Jay moved slightly, so his AR was ready in case there was trouble.

The figures seem to just be standing there looking our way, not moving. The standoff seemed to last forever. Finally, Jay couldn't take it anymore and decided to find out who they were and what they wanted.

He slowly got out of the chair and walked towards them. Suddenly, the figures backed into the shadows and went around the building.

I grabbed my pistol out of my back and walked about ten feet behind Jay. By the time we reached the corner of the building, and peaked around the corner, they were nowhere to be seen. Jay continued to walk around the back of the building, as I stood and watched the front, and towards the motorhome and motel rooms where our friends were most likely asleep by now.

Jay cautiously walked around the area behind the building, trying to be as quiet as he could. But the moon was disappearing behind some more clouds, and the forest in the back was so dark he couldn't see anything.

He went back to the motorhome and just kept an eye out. He joined me at the corner of the building, and we walked back to our chairs. "Obviously they don't want trouble, or they wouldn't have left and hid," he said, still holding his gun ready for anything.

I got up and went into the motorhome, to let the dogs out to go potty and hurrying them back in. Giving them each a treat and a snuggle, "you guys stay in here tonight and be quiet," I said, patting them all on their heads. Finding the instant coffee, I put a small pot of water on the gas stove and heated it up. Carrying the cup and handing it to Jay, "here you might need this," I said, "thank you baby," he replied.

We sat for a couple more hours, watching the corner of the café and trying to see in and around all the shadows when the moon came out. But the night was pitch black, so we listened for any movement we could hear, which was quite difficult sometimes when the night bugs sang loudly.

We heard one of the motel doors open and Benny and Nadia came walking out with their rifles in hand. "You guys better go get some sleep. We got this," Benny said. "We saw some figures way over there on the other side of the café, but we checked it out and they were gone," Jay said. "They probably went into the forest back there. It's so dark out," I added. "Okay, don't worry. I will keep a close eye out and if there is any trouble, I will let you know," Benny added.

Jay and I got up and headed to our room. Once inside, we laid on the bed, which had no bedding because we had already packed it in the motorhome. But we didn't care, we were exhausted. The minute our heads hit the bed; we were asleep.

CHAPTER THIRTEEN
The Smell of Death

Day 11

A knock at the door had us jump and almost put us on the floor. "Jay, D'Ann, you awake?" a voice came from the other side of the door. "Um, we are now," I said under my breath while I got up and opened the door.

Nadia was standing there with two cups of coffee. "It's time we got going. Everyone is already in the motorhome. We knew you were up late, so we let you sleep in," she said, handing us the coffee. I raised my hand to show I didn't want any coffee. "Thank you so much, but I don't really drink coffee," I said. She withdrew the cup and took a sip herself. "It's okay, I need it anyway," as she smiled.

"Any trouble last night? Did you see the people we saw?" Jay asked as we walked out and shut the door behind us. "No, didn't see or hear anything, but it was so dark," she said.

Joining the others at the motorhome, Jay motioned to Benny to the front of the motorhome. "We should take one last look around, make sure no one is here," Jay whispered. "Let me grab the dogs and we will take them to go potty and look around," he said. "Don't tell the others what I saw last night. No need to worry them. We are leaving, and it's over now," he continued.

Jay and Benny took the dogs and made one last look around, deciding it was all clear, got back in the motorhome. Sean was in the driver's seat as Jay took the passenger seat. Sean looked down at the gas gauge. "Maybe we should put the last of the gas in the tank. Don't know how much further we have to go before we find more," he said.

Jay and Benny got back out of the motorhome and met Sean at the rear of the RV. Sean crawled on top of the RV and handed down the gas cans as Benny and Jay poured them into the gas tank. They still had two full cans. That wouldn't fit, so they put them back up and secured them. "Tank is full," Sean said, looking at the gas gauge. "We are going to need more, so keep a lookout for some vehicles," he added.

Sean pulled out onto the highway. As we all settled in. Looking around, I noticed Curt and Liz were not there, assuming they were in the bedroom. "How's Curt?" I turned to Nadia and asked. "Not good, not sure what is going on. He's really weak, has no appetite, and is just lethargic," she said. "I hope he pulls through this," I added.

The motorhome was slowing down, as we approached an older truck on the side of the road with a man and a woman standing beside it. What looked to be a child, about 7 or 8, standing behind the man.

Sean came to a stop and rolled down his window, as Jim and Benny sat on the sofa window, guns drawn out of sight of the family. "Hey," Sean said out the window. The man and woman were dirty from head to toe and looked distraught. "Everything okay," Sean asked. The man, not moving any closer, said, "we ran out of gas. We have hardly any food left and no water. We saw vehicle lights yesterday, so last night we walked up to the buildings up there," as he pointed towards the motel and café. "But we saw a man with a gun, and got scared, so we came back here," he said. They stood there quietly looking at us, as we looked out the windows at them. Sean turned to the group and said, "what do you think? We have two cans of gas left, and since we took most all the food and water from the café, we can spare a little, huh?" he asked. "I agree. I think we should give them the gas, we can find more, and some food and water." I spoke up. "Yeah, me too," Polly added, "and tell them they can take shelter in the motel for a while," Andie commented.

"We have a bit of gas you can have, and some food and water," Sean said as he got out of the motorhome. "There is a motel up the road. You can shower and take shelter in," he added.

Jay and Benny helped get the gas cans and poured them into the truck. We put together some food and bottled water in a bag. I took the bag and handed it to the woman. "Thank you so much, we just didn't know what we were going to do," she said as she handed her daughter a bottled water and a package of crackers. The little girl grabbed it immediately, opening the package and stuffing it in her mouth. "We haven't eaten anything since yesterday. We had to ration what we had," she added. "There is still some food left in that café up there by the motel. No one else is around there, so go eat it and take care," I said as I sent back to the motorhome.

The guys made sure the old truck started as the family waved and drove off. "Our good deed of the day," Sean said as the guys jumped back in, and we took off down the road.

The road signs up ahead read "Flagstaff 75 miles." The road was winding and hilly, so the motorhome was not getting as good a gas mileage as it had. The way we had it packed was probably only 4-5 miles a gallon, anyway. We hadn't come across many vehicles, but when we did, we stopped and siphoned the gas out and put it in the motorhome.

Polly, Nadia, Andie, and I sat at the dinette table studying the map. "Flagstaff is a pretty big town," Nadia commented. "But people were friendly the last time we were there," she added. We all looked up and towards the back of the motorhome as screaming for help could be heard. Nadia was the first to jump up and run to the bedroom. She opened the door and saw Liz sitting on the bed next to Curt. "Something's wrong," she cried. "I don't think he's breathing," Nadia leaned down and put her ear to his mouth and felt his chest to see if she could feel it. "Someone come help me, we need to do CPR," as Benny jumped up and ran to the back.

The rest of us sat in silence and shock. Vickie got up and helped guide Liz out of the bedroom. She sat on the sofa next to her, trying to comfort her. It seemed like time was standing still. "Sean, step on it. Let's get to Flagstaff and see if there is some kind of hospital," Jay commanded. Sean gave the motorhome as much gas as he could, as we sped down the highway.

The temperature gauge on the dashboard was creeping towards the red. "Jay, look," as Sean pointed to it. "Damn it, man, not now," Jay cried. We were still fifteen miles from Flagstaff. When steam started rolling out from under the hood. "You better pull over," Jay said. As Sean came to a stop. Jay, Sean, and Dre got out of the motorhome and opened the hood. Steam rolled out and the smell of antifreeze filled their noses. "Shit, Shit Shit!" Jay cussed. "It looks like we blew a hose or something," Dre said. "Hopefully it didn't crack the block or worse," Sean added. "What are we going to do" Dre asked. "Go check on Curt and the others, see what's going on," Jay asked Dre. Dre turned and climbed into the motorhome. As he was about to ask, Benny came out of the bedroom with a horrid look on his face. He looked at me and then at Polly. He shook his head no.

We all knew what that meant. Liz was sitting on the sofa with her face in her hands and had not seen Benny. She heard the bedroom door close and saw Benny and Nadia standing here. Nadia hurried to Liz's side. And grabbed her and took her in for a hug. "I'm so, so sorry Liz.

We couldn't get him to breathe again. We tried and tried, but it just didn't work." Liz started sobbing uncontrollably as Nadia and Vickie held her tight. I could feel the tears running down my face. I grabbed the Kleenex box and passed it around. Liz calmed down, she look up at us and spoke, she looked at Benny and Nadia, "Thank you for trying, but I kind of knew it was the end, Curt was diagnosed with stage 4 cancer last winter and was only given a couple months to live we thought we would make it home to our kids but obviously that will not happen now. I need to go say goodbye," she said as she walked to the bedroom.

Dre stepped out of the motorhome and told Sean and Jay what had happened. "That's sad," Jay said. "We should probably bury him here underneath the trees," Sean added. "Yeah, get the shovels out. We will figure this out later," Jay said.

Sean, Jay, and Bobby, with Dre at Curt's feet, helped carry him out of the motorhome. Liz wanted him wrapped in one of the soft blankets from the motel before they put him in the grave. The men covered him up with the dirt they had dug out of the hole. And Andie and I had made a makeshift cross out of branches, and Dre carved Curt's name.

We stood around the grave as Jim read a passage from his bible. Polly and Vickie helped Liz back to the motorhome and settled her down in one of the bunks.

"What are we going to do about the motorhome?" I asked Jay in a worried voice. "Is it a hose or what?" I continued. "I don't know yet. We need to get under it and see what's going on," he replied. "Okay, well, I'm going to take the dogs out for a while. They've been cooped up too long. They need some exercise," I said.

The others had pulled out lawn chairs and set them around. Someone had pulled out the grill, as Polly and Andie wrapped potatoes in foil.

I grabbed Diamond's leash and walked her and the three little ones up the road. They seemed so happy just to be out playing in the sunshine. It was a beautiful day. The sun was shining, and it was nice and cool still. The trees surrounding us were so green and tall. I missed the country so much since moving to Las Vegas, where it was brown and dry. Las Vegas had been in the worst drought it had ever been in. Lake Mead was drying up. Because of the water levels dropping several feet a week, long buried secrets were appearing. Boats that had sunk years ago resurfaced. They were finding the human remains of people that had drowned, and their bodies never recovered. Even finding a body in a barrel. They reported it was probably put there back in the seventies by the clothes it had on. The housing market was booming, people were moving to Vegas so fast there was little housing available. No wonder the water was disappearing. Besides no rain, more people were using it, I thought.

With my mind wondering, I didn't realize I had walked so far, I could no longer see the motorhome. "Come on kids, let's head back," as I turned around and headed back. By the time I had gotten to the motorhome, the dogs were panting. I left them outside and grabbed their bowl and a bottle of water.

I walked around to the front where the guys were standing around, looking at the engine. "So, what's the verdict?" I asked. "Well, it was a hole in the hose, we put duct take around it, and added water to the radiator," Jay said, "now to see if it can get us there." Jay said. "Everyone get in. If it holds, we need to leave immediately," he continued. I looked over towards the area where we had buried Curt and saw Liz and Vickie standing over his grave. It looked like they had picked some wildflowers and put them on top. I walked towards them and gently hollered, "It's time to go now." Liz and Vickie both looked up at me, as Liz kissed her hand and bent down and put her hand on the freshly dug dirt. "I will love you forever," she said, then stood up, and we all walked hand in hand back to the motorhome.

All inside, Jay started the motorhome. So far, so good, I thought. He put it in drive and watched the temperature gauge. We made it to the edge of town when a loud noise and grinding and smoke came rolling out of the hood. The motorhome stop at a jerk, as several items on the countertop fell to the floor. The dogs started barking, and people screamed. "Well, I think that is that for this," Jay said as he put it in park and shut the clanking engine off. "Oh my God, what are we going to do now" Andie cried. "Well, I don't think we can fix this. We are going to have to find something else," Sean replied.

We had made it to the edge of town. Still in the suburbs, if flagstaff had a suburb. Nice homes dotted the streets, cars were still in the drives and a couple stalled in the streets. It looked just like every other town we had gone through. We still had seen no people, but it had been 10 days already. If people didn't have supplies, it was a bet that they didn't make it. Maybe starved or was so dehydrated they died.

Jay and Sean turned around in their chairs. "I guess we need to decide what to do from here. Do we look for another motorhome, or find separate vehicles if we can?" Jay asked. "I vote we try to stay together at least till we get to New Mexico," I said. "If we can find a motorhome that will run, don't you all think it would be best?" as I looked around at everyone. "I do," Nadia agreed, as Andie and Sean shook their heads, showing a yes vote. "Are we all in agreement, then?" Jay asked. Everyone agreed. "Now, I guess we need to split up into three groups. Sean and Andie, Benny, and Nadia, and me and D'Ann, will spread out and look for another RV. Dre and Jim stay here with the ladies and protect our stuff," Jay said. "Diamond will help."

The three couples each packed a backpack with water and food. "You guys go down that way, he pointed east," as he directed Benny and Nadia to go. "Sean and Andie go that way," as he pointed west. "D'Ann and I will continue north on this road toward town. It's already getting late in the day," he said. "Just try to be back here before midnight. Everyone got ammo?" Jay asked. They all nodded, and we set out on our way.

It had been a long time since I had walked so much, after getting sick, walking hurt. But I was determined to pull my weight, literally. Jay and I walked at least a mile when we noticed more businesses. Some boarded up, some broke in to and thrashed. There was an odor in the streets, the smell of death. Up ahead, we could see Walmart. "Maybe we could get a bicycle or something, make it a little easier and faster," I said, complaining from the pain I was feeling in my hips. "I just don't know how long I can keep walking. I'm really sorry, I don't mean to hold you up." "It's okay, baby, come here and we can sit and rest for a bit," Jay said, sounding concerned.

We took another 15-20 minutes to get to the store. It looked like they had boarded up the doors and windows, so we checked out the garden center doors. Jay pushed the gates of the garden center open enough for us to squeeze through. The garden center doors were still in tacked and not boarded up, so Jay pushed the doors open. "Dang, those are heavy," he said, all out of breath. As we walked through the garden center, we could tell people had been in there. Stuff was off the shelves and thrown all around.

Since this was a smaller town, this Walmart was an older Walmart, not a super Walmart, it didn't have the grocery side. We walked to the bicycle department, and to our amazement, not only were there bikes, but there was a three wheeled bike with a large basket on the back. "Oh, there," as I pointed to it. "That will help a lot," I said.

Jay looked around and found a really nice mountain bike. As we pushed them towards the door, we threw stuff we thought we might need into my basket. Out of the store, I mounted the bike. "Thank God it has three wheels. It's been so long since I rode a bike I would probably fall over," I said, giggling.

We rode the bikes out of the parking lot and down the street. The sun was going down behind the mountains in the distance. "I don't think we are going to find anything in this area," Jay said. "I hope someone else had better luck. We better head back," he continued, "it shouldn't take us long to get back on these," I replied.

As we approached the motorhome, we could see that everyone had returned and was standing out in front of the motorhome, but there was no other vehicle in sight.

"No luck?" Jay asked as he brought his bike to a stop. They shook their heads no. I came to a stop and got off the bike. "Oh My God, my ass hurts," I laughed, as I walked like I had been riding a horse for days. "We got some more charcoal and stuff, so we might make some more potatoes and heat some other canned food."

"It looks like we are going to have to spend the night here and try again in the morning," Benny said. "Should we go check out one of these houses, see if it's empty, and move all our stuff into it so it's safe?" Sean asked, looking around. "That sounds like a good idea. See if anyone is in this one right here. It will be convenient to empty the motorhome since it's so close." Benny said.

Benny, Jay, and Sean walked up the drive to the house. As they walked by the garage, they could see through the window there was a pretty new SUV parked inside. They walked up to the front door and peaked in the side windows along the door. They saw no movement. Jay tried the handle. It was unlocked. He slowly opened the door, and they prepared to go in, but the smell from inside hit them all three in the face as they backed up, gagging. Sean leaned over into the bushes in the front and vomited. "I don't think we want this one," Benny said, holding his shirt over his nose. Jay slapped Sean on the back and said, "let's go to this big one here on the corner," as they walked towards the big two-story house.

There wasn't a car in the drive, and the garage had no windows, so they snuck to one of the enormous picture windows, which they assumed was the living room. Jay went first, as Benny and Sean followed right behind him. He peaked in the window and through the curtains saw no movement. "Go around to the back," he pointed to Sean and then around the side of the house. "I'll go this way and see if I can see anything in the side windows," Benny commented. Jay squatted under the window, peaking in, watching for any movement at all. Sean quietly slipped into the backyard.

It was an oasis, a large swimming pool, an outdoor kitchen and patio furniture all under a cover. He slowly tip toed to the sliding glass door and peaked around the corner into the gigantic kitchen and dining room. Sean saw no movement either, trying the sliding glass doors, but they were locked. He then saw the garage door a little way down and walked towards it. He turned the knob. "Yes," he said as the door opened.

 There was no vehicle in the garage, but what he saw made his eyes light up. Two 4-wheelers over in the corner. He had the urge to run over to them, but knew he better check the house to make sure it was empty.

The garage door went into the hallway, where he could see the front door. He looked around to see if anyone was there and walked to the front door and opened it. "I haven't checked out the house yet to see if it's clear," he whispered. Jay held the door open as Benny came back around the front of the garage. They entered the house. "At least it doesn't smell," Sean whispered.

Jay pointed to a hallway that led to some doors. With guns drawn, they walked slowly to them, each taking a room. They entered. Jay had entered a teenager's bedroom. He could tell it was a teen girl's room by the posters hanging on the wall, and the pictures of friends on her mirror. The room was neat. He looked behind the door, under the bed, and in the closet. "Clear," he thought.

Sean had entered the hall bathroom. It was small, with only a sink and a toilet. He backed out and walked towards where Benny was about to enter another room. Benny turned the knob and slowly walked in. It seemed to be an office. A large desk sat in the middle of the room. He peaked behind the door and headed over to what seemed to be a closet door. Sean and Jay appeared in the room, and as Benny opened the door, Jay stood to the side and pointed his gun into the closet. "Clear. Head upstairs," he whispered.

The sun was fading fast in the sky and getting dark. The inside of the house was also getting dark. "I'm going to run out and get a flashlight," Sean said, heading to the door. "Wait here till I get back," he turned and looked at Benny and Jay.

Within minutes, he was back with an old flashlight, but it worked. They slowly creeped up the stairs. At the top of the stairs was a landing that looked down over the family room. And several doors lined the area. All but one was open. They again each headed towards a door.

Checking the rooms, making sure no one was there. Then they all met at the closed door. "Okay, this is the last one. I'm going to open it. You two be ready," Jay said. He reached for the door handle. Locked. "It has to be locked from the inside," Jay whispered.

They all stood to the side. Jay gently knocked. Nothing, no sound, came from the room. He knocked again. "Is anyone there? We are not here to hurt you. We just need a place to sleep for the night. Nothing. If you don't open the door, we are going to bust it down," Benny said a little louder. Jay gave him a mean look. Benny shrugged his shoulders, and mouth, "What?" Suddenly, a noise came from inside, like a shower curtain opening and a shampoo bottle falling into the tub. "We know someone is in there. Open the door. We promise not to hurt you." Jay yelled. A few minutes passed, and then they heard the click of the lock and the door handle turn.

The door opened just a crack. Benny pushed the door open, and a girl jumped back. Tears ran down her face. "Please don't hurt me," she begged. "Are you here by yourself?" Jay asked. "Yes, my parents went to workdays ago and never came back." She replied. "You've been here all this time by yourself?" Sean asked. She nodded her head yes. "How old are you?" Sean asked. "I'm fifteen. I'll be sixteen at the end of the month." She replied. "Come on out, we will not hurt you. We were just traveling through, and our RV broke down. We needed a place to stay," Jay calmly said. Our wives are in the RV. "Have you eaten anything lately?" Jay asked. "I've had a little, I've had to get into the neighbor's houses to find more food," she replied, "except a couple house down that way," as she pointed. "Smells terrible. I didn't go in," she said. "We have some food we will share," Jay said as he pointed down the stairs towards the front door. "I'm going to get our stuff and bring it in," Jay added as they all walked down the stairs and out the door. "What is your name?" Benny asked. "I'm Casey," she replied, "I'm Benny, this is Jay, and that is Sean over there," as he nodded toward Sean.

The guys walked out towards the motorhome. We had just finished getting the last of the groceries out of the motorhome and sat them on the sidewalk. "This is Casey," Benny announced to everyone. "She is willing to let us stay in her home," he continued as he looked at her.

It took almost an hour to get everything but mine and Jay's clothing out of the motorhome, and into the house. I put the dogs in the backyard and watched them for a minute to make sure they would be okay. But the first thing that happened was Tator, being the rebellious one, walked right over to the pool and fell right in. "Oh my God!" As I ran to the edge of the pool. He was dog paddling to the edge but was too short to get up the side. I reached down and grabbed him by the back of his neck and pulled him out. "Tator, what the hell are you doing?" I scolded him as I put him down. Water flew everywhere as he shook. "Stay out of the pool," I said sternly, but with a slight smile on my face. I walked back into the house, as everyone had finished bringing the last few items in. They piled all the stuff up in the dining room that was next to the front door. No need to move it anywhere else when, hopefully, we would move it back into another RV.

Jay grabbed my hand and pulled me towards the front door. "I have to get me stuff out of the motorhome, without everyone seeing it," he whispered to me as we walked to the motorhome. "How?" I asked. "We gotta get our clothes. Do we have any room in our bags?" he asked. "I don't know. I guess I can make room," I replied. "Put it in a pillowcase and when I carry the bedding out, it will look like sheets and blankets," I suggested. The marijuana was sealed in smell proof bags when it was checked into the dispensary, so there was no chance of them smelling it. "That might work," he said, as I could see the wheels turning in his head.

I grabbed a couple of pillowcases as we pulled it out of its hidden location. Wrapped it in towels and stuffed it in the pillowcases. He had so much stuff it took three pillowcases stuffed full. I then wrapped each pillowcase with a blanket, and we carried it into the house. No one paid any attention to us as we put them in the corner next to our clothes. We piled the dog's stuff on top of them so no one would mistakenly take those particular blankets.

Polly and Liz had gone around and lit candles and lanterns throughout the kitchen and family room and prepared some potatoes and some of Nadia's canned meat. She had canned brisket and ground beef in several canning jars. "We would eat good tonight," we thought.

The guys were out on the back patio, tending to the grill, while Andie and I looked around the house. There was one bedroom downstairs and three upstairs, including a huge master bedroom with a master suite. "Oh, man, look at this shower," I said. As a noise from behind us startled us. "This is my parent's room," she said as she started to cry. We walked over to her and sat her on the bed. "We understand, honey," Andie said with her arm around her shoulders. "What happened?" she asked, looking up at me. "Girl, I don't know. All I know is that everything stopped working. Phones, electric, cars, everything electronic," I replied. "My parents went to work and never came back," she cried. "Where do they work?" I asked. "They both worked at the factory outside of town. My mom is a secretary, and my dad works in the warehouse," she replied. "How far is that?" I asked, wondering if it was close enough for her parents to walk home. "It's like thirty miles from here. It takes them about 45 minutes to get to and from work," she said, as she cried harder. "Look, when we find another RV, we will go right by your parents. Maybe they are still there and just can't get a ride home. Only the old cars work now," I said, as we tried to comfort her. "Would that be okay?" we asked. "Yes, I think I would like to find them," she said as she sniffled. I reached for the tissue that was on the nightstand and handed it to her.

We helped her down the stairs and into the family room. Polly had just walked through the sliding glass doors from the back patio. "There you are. Dinner is ready, outside," she said. "Come on Casey, you must be starving," I said as I directed her towards the patio doors. The back yard was all lit up with torches and lanterns. "This is nice," I commented as we stepped outside.

We all ate until we were stuffed, commenting on how good it was. "We better turn in. We got a long day ahead of us, looking for another RV," Jay said. "My grandma and grandpa have an RV. It's like that one outside your drive. It's pretty old," Casey said, as everyone stopped what they were doing. "Where do your grandparents live? Is it close?" Jay asked and walked towards her. "They just live a couple streets down. I walked over there, but they weren't home either. I think my mom had told me they had flown to California to see my aunt and uncle," she continued. "Can you show us in the morning where they live?" Jay asked. "Sure, I even know where the keys are, but are you sure it will turn on if none of the other cars are working?" she asked with a puzzled look on her face. "I hope so Casey, I really hope so," Jay replied.

CHAPTER FOURTEEN
Good-Bye Mom and Dad

Day 14

Jay and I had taken the floor in the dining room with our dogs and let the others have the sofas and beds. But it was actually to sleep next to his stash.

Jay was up just as the sun was coming up. Lighting the BBQ pit again, he put water on to boil for coffee. The smell of coffee drifted throughout the house. One by one, the group started to wake up. The ones that slept upstairs came down. I didn't want to get up. My body told me I was too old to sleep on the floor. I stretched and tried to get up, but the pain was too much. I sat on the floor and grimaced in pain.

Nadia had walked over to one of her tubs and noticed the look on my face. "You okay?" she asked. "Not really. This floor has done a number on me. I'm hurting," I replied. Going to the next tub, she opened it and found some Tylenol 3 with codeine. "Here, take one of these. It will help. It might make you drowsy, but until they get back to the RV, there's nothing you need to do. Let me help you up to the couch," she said, reaching down and extending her arm.

It took a bit, but I was able to get off the floor, limped my way to the sofa and plopped down on it. "Jay!" I yelled into the kitchen where he was putting sweet n low in his coffee. "Can you let the dogs out to go potty?" I asked. "Can I?" Casey came bouncing out of her room. "The big dog and the little, tiny dog slept with me last night," she giggled. "That's Diamond," as I pointed to the big dog. "That's Tator," pointing toward him. "The other two are Lil' Man, he's the white one, and Brooklyn she is the other." I replied. "Go head, if Diamond was nice to you and slept with you last night, there shouldn't be any trouble," I added.

I laid back on the sofa to relax and let the meds kick in. Jay came over, leaned down, and kissed my forehead. "As soon as Benny and Sean are ready, we are going to go to Casey's grandparents and see if we can get their RV running. Relax. You've been doing too much lately. You need to let your body rest," he said as he turned to Nadia, "make sure she stays right there." he said. "I will," she replied.

As soon as Sean came down from upstairs, the three guys and Casey took off to go to her grandparents' house. "I've been up and down these streets and I don't know where anyone went. It's like they disappeared," she commented as they walked past all the houses.

After about 15 minutes, they turned down a street, and she pointed. "There, it's the third house, straight ahead." The pace quickened as they got excited to see if the RV would run or not.

She took out her key and opened the front door. They all walked in and towards the kitchen. Looking around, they could tell it was definitely a grandparent's house. The décor looked like it was from the nineties. "It smells like old people," Jay thought. Casey reached up to the key hook by the back door and grabbed a set of keys. She turned and handed them to Jay. "It's out here under the cover," she said as they walked out the back door.

They walked out into the yard, and towards the back was a big diesel pusher bus. Jay looked at Sean and they both kind of deflated. "It might be too new," Jay said to Sean. "I don't know. Guess we gotta try," Sean replied. Jay unlocked the side door, and the three walked inside as Casey stood outside, watching. The inside was huge, the slides were still in, but even with the sides, there was plenty of room. "This would be perfect," Benny commented. "If it will start," Jay shot back. Jay jumped in the driver's seat, put the key in the ignition. Nothing, not a single noise or light. He tried it again, switching it off and on. He hit the steering wheel with both hands. "Damn it," he yelled out. "Check out the engine and see if maybe the batteries were fried by the shock wave," Sean said, as he went out the door to the area where the engine was. He opened the door and looked for the batteries. "No battery!" he yelled out. "What, no battery?" Jay yelled back. "Nope!" Sean replied. "Well, no wonder it wouldn't start," Jay said. "Maybe if we got a new battery, it would start," he continued. "Where are you going to get a battery?" Casey said, walking around the side of the bus. Jay thought for a moment. "There is an auto parts store right by the Walmart down the street. I think we should go back to get the 3-wheeler bike and go get one," he said. "That just might work," Sean said, and they shut the door, locked it, and walked back towards the house. "Casey, do you want to grab some of your grandparents' pictures and stuff? You may not be coming back here again," Jay said as they walked through the house. Casey looked puzzled as they walked, "Look, we don't know what is going to happen in the future, the electric and stuff may never come back on, I don't mean to scare you, but we can't leave you here by yourself, you will die. We will try our best to get to your parents. But if your grandparents are in California, I don't think they will ever make it back here. You should get what you need to get and say goodbye to the place," Jay continued. Casey looked around, and with sad eyes, she agreed. "Benny will stay and help you if you want to stay here and do that until we get back. We are going to go get a battery, you pack up what you want, and we will be right back," Jay said. "Okay, I will," she replied.

It only took the two of them to return to the house in under twelve minutes. Jay went straight to the garage where they had parked the bicycles. As Sean went in and explained to the group what was going on. "Say a little prayer that all we need is a battery," Sean said as he walked into the garage and helped Jay manual open the garage door.

Since we only had two bicycles, Jay decided they would be the ones to go, since Jay knew where the Walmart was and how to get in, and Sean would be his backup. "Jay look, what about taking those?" as he pointed to the 4-wheelers. They both got a smile on their face and walked over to them. Keys were in the ignition. "Okay, see if they will start," Sean said. Jay checked the gas tanks. They were both full. He hopped on one and Sean on the other. They would have to kick start it, but it would be wonderful if they started. Jay looked at Sean and they both turned on the ignition and stood up and came down on the kick starter. Both rumbled but didn't start. They tried again. Sean's roared to life. With a big smile on his face, he drove it out of the garage. It took Jay three more times before he got his running. They both sped down the drive and out onto the street. It would only take them a few minutes to get to Walmart and back to Grandma's house now.

They arrived at the auto parts store. As Sean went in and grabbed a couple of batteries, as Jay stood watch. Then, stopping at Walmart, Sean followed Jay through the gates and through the garden center doors. Jay looked surprised to see the doors were wide open, then remembering when he and D'Ann had ridden the bikes out, they didn't close them. He rode his 4-wheeler right in and to the automotive area. Jay grabbed a couple other things he thought they might need, while Sean went over to the RV area, and grabbed some black tank deodorizer and couple other items just in case. He strapped them on, and they quickly rode out the doors and back out to the street.

Jay looked back at Sean with a big grin on his face. "That was easier than I thought it would be," he said. They sped through the street to grandma's house. Parking in the driveway, Jay and Sean unstrapped the batteries and carried them through the house to the backyard.

Benny and Casey joined them as they installed the batteries. Sean shut the door and looked at Jay. "Okay, go try it," he said with a hopeful look on his face. As Jay walked to the bus and sat in the seat, he said a little prayer. He put the keys in the ignition, looked up at Heaven, and turned the key. The bus roared to life, "Yes, yes, yes!" he said and looked to Heaven. "Thank you, thank you."

Sean and Benny ran to the big gate and opened it as Jay drove the huge bus out and on to the street. He let it run as he got out and checked the tires and made sure everything was okay. He went towards the back and opened the door to the generator. It looked brand new. He hit the manual start button, and it purred. Driving down the street will keep the batteries charged and the generator ready to use.

Sean and Benny helped Casey carry two tubs to the bus. Jay opened one of the basement doors on the bus and put them in. Then he opened the other doors to the basement. "Damn, that is a lot of room. We should be able to get most everything in the basement storage area."

Benny and Sean opened the garage door and pushed the 4-wheelers in the garage. After locking up the house, they all hopped on the bus and headed to the house to load everything up.

Jay and Sean were smiling from ear to ear as they parked the bus right out in front of the house. "Better get going," they said excitedly as they walked in the front door. Several of the others looked out the front windows and started clapping. "Great job, guys," Jim commented. "Let's get it loaded," Benny said.

Jay walked over to where I was still sitting on the sofa. "Stay right here till we are ready. I'll get everything," he said as he kissed me. "Thank you, baby. The meds have kicked in. I'm feeling much better now," I replied.

It didn't take long for everyone to load the bus up. The bus was over 40ft long, with a bedroom and a bunk room with four bunks. The living room area had two full size sofa beds, and the dinette converted to a bed as well. The living room also had two recliners and the drivers and passenger seats turned completely around and faced the living room and reclined. Even though it was an older bus, they kept it in perfect condition. When the two-opposing slide in the living room where extended, the living room was huge, over 16 ft from one side to the other.

"Before anyone puts their stuff in the bus, Jay and I wanted to draw who is getting the bedroom and the big king size bed." I said. But before we could draw names, they all said in unison, "You guys get the bedroom," as they looked at us and our four dogs. "Are you sure?" Jay and I looked at each other and then at the group. "Yes, yes," they said. "Vickie and I will take the bottom bunks, the kids, Dre, and Casey, can have the top bunks," Liz said. "The rest of you can fight over who gets what, sofa." She laughed. "I don't need a bed," Casey said. "We know, but you can put your clothes and stuff up there till we get to your parents," Jay said.

We showed the dogs the bedroom where they would stay most of the time. It seemed twice as big as the other one, and when the slides were out, it was huge. Jay brought our stuff into our bedroom and found a great place under the bed for the pillowcases. I jumped on the king-size bed and spread eagle. But it didn't last long as the dogs jumped up on the bed, crowding me out. Jay reached down and picked Brooklyn up and put her on the bed. She was too fat to jump up by herself.

Sean, Benny, and Jim put the gas cans in one of the basement doors. The roof was too tall and not made for things to be put up there. Jay then joined them as they went over to the old motorhome and double checked everything was out. "We will go check the house one more time and lock it up," Andie and Nadia said.

After about 15 minutes, everyone was back on the bus and ready to go. I came out of the bedroom and sat at the surround around dinette table. "Six people could sit at this table," I thought as I sat there. "Everyone ready?" Jay asked as he started it up. Benny had slipped into the passenger seat and Sean sat right behind Jay in one recliner.

"Can you drive this big ass thing, Jay?" Sean asked. "It is a beast," Jay replied.

The bus rode so smooth and quiet. It didn't even seem like we were moving. "Can I have everyone's attention?" Jay yelled to the group. Everyone stopped talking and gave Jay their attention. "We are going to get back on I40 and head east. About thirty miles is the factory that Casey's parent work at. Keep an eye out for people walking or a group of people in case they walked from the factory." Everyone shook their heads. I lifted the shade at the dinette table as Nadia lifted both shades over the sofas and the kitchen window.

We all watched as the houses went by and businesses started appearing. "Should we get some gas in the can before we leave town?" Liz asked. Jay shook his head. "Yeah, this is a diesel, so we will most likely have to look for pickup trucks and big 18 wheelers," Jay replied.

"Well, look," Jim said, pointing out the front windshield, "There's a truck dealership right up there," he said smiling. "Okay, let's go see what we can find," Jay said as he slowed to pull into the dealership.

All the men grabbed the gas cans and siphoning kits and went hunting for diesel. Nadia and I took the dogs for a last walk before we got on the highway.

We walked Diamond in and out of the vehicles as the three little ones followed. Suddenly, Diamond started growling. The hair on the back of her neck stood up. "Grab Tator!" I yelled at Nadia. She bent down and picked him up. I knew Lil' Man and Brooklyn would listen to me and stay put if I told them. I looked towards the area Diamond was growling. I could see a church across the street and down a little way, which had lots of people standing outside. "Look Nadia," as I nodded my head towards the church. "Wow, people, seems to be a lot over there," she commented. "I don't think they have noticed us or the bus yet," I said. "It might be dangerous if they see the bus," I added. "We should head back to the bus and see what they want to do," I said as we turned and quickly walked back.

The men were loading the bus with the gas cans. Nadia took the dogs into the bus, as I told the men what we had seen. "I don't think they saw the bus. Should a couple of us walk Casey over there and see if her parents are there?" I asked. "I guess we could," Jay replied. "Maybe a couple of women and Casey should go. We might not be taken as a threat. You guys can stay back a way and cover us." I added.

I walked around the bus and hollered in the door for Casey and Nadia to come. I explained what we were going to do as we walked towards the church.

The church was enormous. As we walked up, the people outside really paid us no mind. We walked into the church. The main room had all the pews removed, and they lined makeshift beds up in rows. Women, children, and men sat around, some playing cards, others reading books, while others slept. Over to the right was a table with a big sign saying "registration, please sign in." I pointed at the table. "I'm going to go see if Casey's mom and dad are listed."

We walked up to the table, as a woman came out of the room right behind the table. "Hi, can I help you?" she asked. "Do you need help?" she continued. "I'm looking for my parents, Tammy and Ryan Brown," Casey said. "They worked at the trailer factory out on east 40," she continued. The woman looked up at her and then at me. "Umm, let me check," as she looked at her list of people. "Are you related to her?" the woman asked as she looked at me, then to Casey. "No, just trying to help her find her mom and dad," I replied. "I don't see anyone by those names," she said. "Is this the only shelter?" I asked, "Yes, there is a hospital set up at the high school. The other hospital burned down when all this happened," she replied. Casey looked at me with fear in her eyes. "I'm sure they aren't there. They're fine," I reassured Casey. "Where is the high school?" I asked. "I will show you," Casey interrupted. We thanked the woman and walked out. Again, no one paid any attention to us.

The men that were waiting and watching joined us as we walked back to the bus. "We need to go to the high school," I said to Jay. "They turned it into a hospital," I added as Jay looked at me with concern in his eyes. "Okay, let's go look," he said. Casey tried to smile, but the concern was too much for her as a tear rolled down her cheek.

Casey explained how to get to the high school. It wasn't too far out of the way. When we got there, I told Casey to wait outside and I would go in and see if they were there, "if they are I will come and get you," I told her. "Okay," she said as we walked from the bus. This time, several people standing outside the doors watched as we walked up. They seemed very interested in the bus. I kept my head down and didn't make eye contact. "Stay right here. I need to get in and out quick," I told her.

As I walked in, I noticed they set the first few classrooms up as hospital rooms, with over ten patients in each room. A handwritten sign with an arrow pointing to the check-in desk. I walked up to the desk. No one seemed to be around. I stood there for a few minutes before a man in scrubs walked out of a room. "Can I help you?" he asked. "I'm looking to see if my sister and her husband are here. I can't find them," I lied. "What are their names?" he asked. "Tammy and Ryan Brown," I replied. He pulled out a notebook with names written on it. He skimmed the pages and looked up at me. "I don't see their names listed. Are they local?" he asked. "Yeah, they were at work at the factory outside of town," I replied. "The trailer factory?" he asked. "Yeah that's it," I said. "I'm sorry to tell you that the entire factory went up in flames. An airplane just taking off from the airport crashed into the buildings and it exploded on impact. No survivors," he said. "Oh my God," I said as my hand covered my mouth. "I'm so sorry for your loss, ma'am," he said.

I shook my head and turned to walk out the door when I saw Casey standing right behind me. She had heard everything. "No, no, that can't be true," she cried. "I'm sorry," turning back to the man, "they are her parents," I said. Casey, sobbing and screaming no, turned and ran out the doors. I followed her as fast as my sore legs would go. Once she got to the grass, she collapsed, crying uncontrollably.

Several people were watching. I bent down and tried to comfort her. "Casey, come on, we have to get out of here before those people storm the bus. We will go to the factory and make sure what he was saying is true," I said, and I helped her up off the ground. Holding my arm around her, I got her to the bus as soon as I could. Benny helped me get her on the bus, as the crowd at the school doors started walking towards the bus. "Hurry, get in," Jay yelled. "They're coming." As I crawled up the steps and shut the door.

Casey ran to the back and shut the door to the bunk room. I followed her and asked Nadia to join me. We opened the door and saw that she had crawled up on the top bunk and had buried her face in her pillow. Dre was in the bunk across the room reading a book. He looked up and gave me a "what's going on look." "Dre, can you excuse us for a moment so we can talk to Casey?" I asked. "Sure," he said as he jumped down from the bunk and walked out of the room.

"Casey, we will find out for sure what happened. But if what he said is right, we will not leave you alone. Do you have any other family close by?" I asked. She didn't answer, she just sobbed. "Come on, leave her alone till we know 100%" Nadia said, "Casey honey, if you need anything just let us know, we are here for you," she continued.

We walked out and sat down in the living room. I explained to everyone what the man had told me, and that Casey heard everything.

"Well, the factory is on our way. We will stop and see what's going on," Jay commented.

We found our way to Interstate 40, winding through neighborhoods and around cars. Several cars were blocking the entrance ramp to I 40. Jay eased the big bus over to the shoulder. "I think we can get through," he said, eyeing the edge of the road. He drove slowly, coming within inches of the cars and the edge of the shoulder where a guard rail kept cars from driving over the side.

It was nice driving on the interstate. We could drive the speed limit, only slowing down to maneuver around big semis. We had made it within a few miles when we saw smoke coming from ahead of us. "Look," Jay said as we all looked out the front window. "I figured we are getting close to the factory. There is an exit up about five miles," Jay said. About that time, Casey came out of the bunk room. "Take the next exit," she commanded as I scooted over, and she sat on the sofa beside me. I put my arm around her. "No matter what we find, it's going to be okay. Everything will be okay," I said, trying to comfort her. The exit was up ahead, Jay slowed down and exited to the frontage road. As we topped the hill, we could see it, the factory with an airplane sticking out of the biggest building. The building had been burned to the ground, several buildings around it had also burned. Casey put her hand to her mouth as if a scream wanted to come out. Jay slowed as the driveway to the factory was ahead. He turned and drove to the only building on the property that hadn't burned. He came to a stop and put the bus in park. Turning to Sean and Benny, "We need to go see if there are any survivors," he said.

They walked to the building's front but found no one. "We are going to have to search in the rubble of the buildings," he said. They walked out and headed around to the side of the buildings. They stood there and looked at the rest of the property. All the other buildings were destroyed. They started walking back around to the other buildings, when they saw Casey running from the bus. "That's my mom and dad's car," she pointed over to the parking lot. "They worked in those buildings over there, the ones that are burnt." She said as she cried. "What do your parents look like?" he asked. "We will go see if we find them," Casey reached in her back pocket and pulled out a picture of all three of them and handed it to Jay. "Benny stay here with her, Sean come with me," he said.

They both walked to the area where she had said her parents worked. Moving a few pieces out of the way they looked around, burnt bodies were everywhere. The scene was grizzly. It reminded Jay of going to the dispensary after the incident. They walked towards the office area of the building. And they saw a woman sitting behind a desk. A large beam had fallen from the ceiling and had struck her in the chest. Jay looked at the picture and then at the woman. "It's her!" he said and bowed his head and prayed. "Over here, Jay," Sean yelled. "Is that him?" He pointed to the area where a bunch of rubble had fallen. Jay showed the picture to Sean. "God, it's him," Sean said. "Should we let Casey come in and say goodbye? They are decomposing and smell. No way can we get them out to bury them." Sean continued. They turned and walked out of the burned-out rubble. Casey and Benny were standing at the edge. "Well, did you find them?" Casey begged. Jay looked at Sean, "honey, I'm sorry, yes they are both in there and both deceased, I'm so so sorry," Jay said as Casey broke down and cried dropping to her knees.

Jay bent down to make her get up. "Casey, listen to me, Casey, do you want to go in and tell them goodbye? They are under heavy pieces of building, and we cannot get them out to properly bury them. Their bodies are not in good shape. CASEY? what do you want to do?" Casey looked up, sobbing, "yes, I want to go in and say goodbye." she cried. "Okay, come on, I'll help you." Jay held her as they walked into the building. "This will not be easy, but you can do this. We are here right beside you," He continued.

Stepping over debris, they arrived at her mom's desk. Casey stepped over to her mom, visibly shaking. She put her hand on her mom's head and stroked her hair. "Mama, I'm so sorry this happened to you. I love you more than you know," she looked down at her hand and noticed her mom's wedding ring. "Do you think we can get this off?" she turned and asked Jay and Sean. "Yes, I'll get it off," Sean said. Then she unclasped the necklace that was around her neck, remembering that her dad had given it to her mom for her birthday last year. She rarely took it off.

Casey was able to open the desk drawer and pulled out her mom's purse. "I want this too," she said. "Yes, of course," Jay said. Casey kissed the top of her mom's head and turned around and followed Jay to her dad. Again, as Casey approached her dad, tears started falling. Her dad was buried pretty good under the rubble, but she could bend down and touch his head. "Oh, daddy, I love you so much," tears streamed down her face. "What am I going to do?" she cried. "I'm so scared," she kneeled as close to him as she could, but she still couldn't reach him, so she kissed her palm and placed it on his cheek. Jay couldn't take it anymore. He turned around so she wouldn't see him cry.

He backed away from her to give her more time with him. She visibly sobbed as her hand held his cheek. "At least you and mama are together, and I know you will watch over me," she cried. "Mr. Jay and Mr. Sean and their families will take care of me now. They've said I can go to Texas with them," she said. "I love you, daddy, and I will always be your little girl," as she kissed her palm and placed it on his forehead. She got up and turned towards Jay. Jay was drying his tear on his shirt. He reached out and held her. "I'm so sorry, Casey, our family will take care of you now."

They walked out, stepping over all the debris. They met Sean outside of the crumbled building. He held his closed hand out to her. She reached for his hand as he opened it, and her mom's wedding ring was lying there. She picked it up and held it in her hand. "Thank you so much," as she looked up at Sean and he reached out and hugged her. "Time to go," Jay said as they walked towards the bus.

Jay climbed into the driver's seat as Sean and Casey sat on the sofa. "Honey, we are so sorry for your loss," Nadia said. "As crazy as everything is right now, they are in a much better place. They will be watching over you," she continued. "They will be your guardian angels," Andie added.

I moved up and sat behind Jay and reached my arms around the chair and gave him a hug. He was upset and had been crying. I whispered in his ear, "I love you. I know that was so hard." Jay said nothing, he just put his hand on my arms. "Everyone inside?" he asked. I turned around and looked around. "Yes, we are all here." Jay turned the key on, put it in drive and we drove out of the parking lot.

It was late afternoon by now. "Holbrook is just about one hundred miles up the road. I think this is where we should find a vehicle and head off towards Colorado," Jim stated. Jay looked at Benny who was in the passenger seat, "I guess keep a lookout for an older vehicle," he said. "We should also find some diesel and fill this and the gas cans up again," Benny continued. "Winslow is a small town. Hopefully, we can find what we want and get out fast. It's just up here about fifty miles," Jay said.

The day had been so draining and tiring that Jay and Sean realized they hadn't eaten all day. "D'Ann, can you make me a sandwich or something? I haven't eaten all day," Jay asked. "Yes, of course," as I got up and made my way to the kitchen and made him a peanut butter and jelly sandwich, grabbed a bag of chips and a cold bottle of water. I handed him the water. "Wow, it's cold," he said. "Yes, the fridge works," I said excitedly. "Hey Jay, why don't you let me drive? You and Sean need to get some rest, then you can take over and drive," Benny said. "Okay, give me about an hour, we will be in Winslow, then I'll let you drive after what we just went through. I don't think I could close my eyes," Jay responded. "Well, I'm going to go lay down on the floor in the bunk room," Sean interjected. "Take my bunk," Vickie said. Sean and Andie went to the bunk room and shut the door. Casey curled up in the sofa's corner and cried herself to sleep. Everyone settled down for the ride.

This part of the interstate was littered with more vehicles than before. Big trucks made it very congested. All the swerving in and out was making me car sick. "You got anything for car sickness, Nadia?" I asked. "I think so. Let me grab my little emergency bag," she replied as she got up and went to the hall closet/pantry. When she came back, she handed me a little bottle of Dramamine. "Thank you, don't know how much more of this weaving in and out my stomach can take," as I open the bottle.

We reached Winslow in just over an hour; the sun was setting low in the sky, and we figured we only had a good hour, if that, to find a vehicle that might work for Jim and Polly before it got dark.

The moment we got off the interstate, we could tell it was a terrible idea to stop here. Right next to the main road going into town was a small airport. We could tell by the destruction of several airplanes that they had missed the runway. The road was completely blocked. It looked like a war zone, like the ones you see on TV. The buildings were burnt, vehicles were burnt. We couldn't go much further; Jay stopped the bus and we all just stared out the windows at the destruction.

"There's another exit further down on the interstate, maybe we should try it," Jay said, as he put the bus in reverse and turned it around. We got back on the highway, and about five miles down was another exit. We could tell this end of town fared a lot better than the other end of town.

"Look up, there is a used car dealership. Maybe we will get lucky," Benny pointed out. Jay eased the big bus towards the dealership. There wasn't enough room to pull in, so he just stopped it in the middle of the street, not like anyone was going to be coming down it.

Benny, Jim, and Jay got out and walked around the lot. Near the back, they came across several older models. "Let me see if there are any keys inside," Sean said as he came up behind the guys. Sean and Jay walked over to the office. The glass was still intact, and the doors were locked. "Go around the side and see if there is a smaller glass door. I hate to break this huge door and make a lot of noise." Sean said as they walked around the side.

Several of us that were still on the bus decided to step outside and stretch, as I took the dogs out for their break. Standing around making small talk, we heard glass break. We whipped our heads toward the sound, and just stood there looking at each other. Then we noticed Sean opening the front door. He waved to us standing outside, showing us, everything was good. Benny and Jim joined Jay and Sean inside and looked for keys. In an office right inside the door, a room with a big board and all the keys were labeled and hanging there.

Sean fumbled through them and found the oldest vehicles he could find. Threw a couple of sets of keys to Jim and a couple to Benny. "Now let's go find these vehicles and see if they start," Sean said as they all walked out the door. The first vehicle Sean came to was a 1991 Dodge Caravan. It wasn't the prettiest, but this was what my mom called "a fly-by-night" kind of dealership. The kind where you didn't have to have good credit. In fact, the sign said, "No Credit Needed,"

Sean opened the door, put the key in the ignition, and the van started right up. The men heard the engine start and looked over at the van. "Here ya go," Sean said with a smile on his face. Benny walked over to Jay. "Maybe we should find something also, since we will be splitting off from you guys a little further down the road," he said. Jay shook his head but looked down at the ground. "I'm going to be sorry to see you go. Sure, you don't want to go all the way to Texas with us?" Jay asked. "I would, but I have to go check on my great-grand son and other family members. Who knows, maybe we will grab them and head your way," Benny replied. "You know you're always welcome," Jay said as he hugged Benny. The other men looked over at Jay and Benny, hugging. "What's going on?" Sean said, walking towards the two. "Benny's going to look for a vehicle as well. They will be splitting off from us a little further down the road, but this might be the only chance we get to find something that runs," Jay replied.

They had one row left, after they had tried several other vehicles with no success. The last row was trucks. The first two they tried didn't turn over, then the third one, which seemed to be a rust bucket. Started right up. "Okay, I guess this is it," Benny said.

"Okay, let's drive them over by the service shop and go over them and make sure they are ready to go," Jay said.

We watched the men drive a van and a truck around the corner of the building and lost sight of them. "Their over there at the service center," Nadia said as she walked away to see where they went.

The sun was gone now, and darkness rolled in. It was pitch black outside because the moon hadn't come out. The only light was coming from the light in the bus that was being run off the batteries. I put the dogs on the bus and sat down on the curb. Nadia and Andie came and sat beside me. "It looks like one of those vehicles is for you," as I looked at Nadia. "Probably, we will turn south about the Arizona, New Mexico border down to his family," Nadia said. "I'm going to miss you, girl," as I put my hand on her knee. "I know, it may be the last time we see each other, depending on what happens," she said with tears in her eyes. "You guys can always come to Texas. I gave you directions on how to get there," I said. "Maybe," she replied.

"Do you hear that?" Andie asked as she stood up. Nadia and I stood up and looked in the direction Andie was looking. "I don't hear anything," I said. We listened for a few more seconds. Faint off in the distance, we could hear an engine. The sound was still very faint but getting louder. "Hurry, run go tell the guys," As I looked at Andie. "We need to get inside," as Nadia and I climbed the steps. "Hurry, shut the lights off, and shut the windows, someone's coming up the road," I said as I grabbed Jay's AR. "Casey, take the dogs to the bedroom and try to keep them quiet," I said. "The rest of you, grab a gun and be ready."

We sat and waited as the engine came closer, then we heard the squeak of the brakes. Dre was peeking out the blinds. "They're right here. There are three men. They got guns," he whispered. They're coming around to the door. At that instant, there was a bang at the door. "Hey, get out here. We don't appreciate people coming to our town and stealing our stuff," an old man yelled. "Get out here now, all of you, or we will start breaking windows," he continued. "Shit, what do we do?" I whispered to the others. No one said a word. The look on their faces was enough.

Dre stepped forward, being the only male on the bus. "Let me go first," he said as he opened the door. I was right behind him but stayed at the top of the stairs. The men grabbed Dre and threw him to the ground, as one of the men held him down. I put the AR behind the seat, so it wasn't seen, and stepped down the stairs. The other man grabbed me and held my arm. "Who else is in there?" he yelled. Polly and Nadia walked to the door. They put their hands up and came down the stairs.

I looked at the bedroom window and could see Casey peeking out of the shade. Vickie and Liz had been lying down in the bunk room. "Hopefully they were hearing everything that was going on and stayed put." I prayed. Then the worst happened. Diamond and the dogs started growling and barking. "Those are my dogs. I locked them in the bedroom, so they won't get out," I said with a shaky voice. "Where are the men? Someone told us you were stealing cars," the old man said. "I don't know they are over there," as I nodded my head towards the dealership. "Well, we don't take kindly to strangers coming into our town and thinking they can just take anything they want," he said. "Maybe we will just take something from them," as he grabbed Nadia. Nadia started squirming. "Get your hands off of me," she yelled. Nadia was small, she was right at five foot tall, but she was solid muscle.

The old man picked her up and threw her over his shoulder like she was a sack of flower. I pulled my arm loose from the man that was holding me. "Let her go!" I screamed as I grabbed his arm. The man that I had just escaped from grabbed me around the waist and threw me to the ground. I didn't move. My body was in so much pain from hitting the ground I just lay there and sobbed. "And stay there, bitch," the man said, and he put his heavy boot on my back. Between the pain and the heaviness of his boot, I couldn't catch my breath. Trying to suck in air and let sobs out, things around me went dark.

Nadia fought and wiggled till he finally sat her down. He pushed her to the ground as she landed on her butt. "Stay there," the old man said to her. Nadia sat there, but she was hatching a plan.

"Look lady, you are old, and we don't want to hurt you, so sit down and be quiet and you won't get hurt," the old man said to Polly. Polly sat on the ground and cried.

"James, go in there and shut them dogs up," the old man said to the man standing over me. "What about her?" he said, looking down at me. "I don't think she's going anywhere," he replied.

"That dog is mean. I wouldn't go in there," Dre struggled to say. "Well, I got something that's meaner," and James pulled out his pistol.

As the guy holding Dre down relaxed a little, Dre rolled over and kicked him in the balls. The guy went down. Just as Dre was getting up off the ground. The old man hit him right between the eyes with the butt of his rifle. Dre went down like a limp rag doll.

I struggled to open my eyes. The weight on my back was gone, but the pain in my hips was unbearable. I didn't move, but listened to what was going on around me.

"James don't worry about them dogs. We need to go find those men," the old man yelled as James had climbed to the top of the stairs, and then turned around.

My face was against the ground, but as I heard one of them step near me, I closed my eyes and stayed still. "Bernie, you pussy get up off the ground and come tie this one and the old lady up." As the old man threw some rope, he had pulled out of his back pocket on the ground next to Bernie. Bernie struggled to get up, cupping his private parts. "Mother Fucker," he said as he kicked Dre in the stomach. But Dre didn't move. He picked up the rope and slowly walked over to Polly and tied her hands behind her back, helped her up and moved her to the steps of the bus, then tied her hands to the steps. "You stay here, so you don't get hurt," Bernie said.

He then went over to Nadia, she willingly put her hands behind her back. He tied her up, but was distracted by Dre moaning, to see that she had slipped her knife out of her pocket and held it in her closed hand. He lifted her up and moved her over by Polly and did the same thing, tied her to the steps.

"Hurry up," the old man yelled at Bernie. "What about her?" he said, looking at me, as I laid still as could be. "Don't worry about her, I don't think she's going anywhere," the old man replied as they all three started walking towards the service area.

Andie had reached the men just as they were getting ready to leave. "Sean, Sean," she yelled, all out of breath. "What?" he replied. "Someone's coming," she said, as the men all ran to the corner of the building.

It was too late they were already there. They watched as Dre stepped out of the RV and was thrown to the ground. They all drew their guns and ran to the first line of vehicles. "Don't shoot, you might hit one of the girls," Jay whispered. "Let's just get close enough to hear what's going on," he said. "Stay hidden," he continued. "Stay here," Sean said to Andie, as she crouched down on the ground.

The men weaved in and out of cars, sneaking as quietly as they could. By the time they got close enough, they could see Dre and I were on the ground out cold, and Polly and Nadia were tied to the stairs. Jay and Benny were moving together as Jim and Sean stayed together. "Oh my God, what has happened?" Jay said as he saw me lying on the ground not moving. He wanted to bust right in there, but Benny held his arm. "Wait, think for a minute, we can't just bust in there guns a blazing, we might hit one of them." Benny said. "I know, but I got to get to D'Ann" he said as anger was building up inside him. "Look, they are headed this way," Benny said. Jay looked over at Sean, which was several cars down, and made a "wait" sign with his hands.

The three men walked towards the service area, holding their guns in front of them. Jay could tell they each had rifles. But all the guys had on them were handguns. They waited until the three men passed them. Then they attacked. Jay and Benny grabbed the old man from the back, before he knew what hit him. Threw him to the ground as Benny held his pistol to the man's neck, and Jay lunged for Bernie. Bernie turned to see what the commotion was just as Jay punched him in the face. Bernie, being startled, dropped his rifle. In the meantime, Sean jumped James and hit him on the back of his head with the butt of his pistol, as Jim ran over to help Jay. As Bernie bent down to pick up his rifle, Jay came back at him and kicked him in his ass. He went flying and landed on his face. Jim ran over to him and his pistol at him.

"Andie," Sean yelled, go get that duct tape back there on that truck we were working on. Andie took off running, grabbed the tape and threw it at Sean.

They taped the three men's hands and feet and put a piece of tape around their mouths. Then drug the men to the service area and put them in the bathroom. Sean and Jay push a big toolbox on wheels in front of the door and set the break. "Jim and Benny, get your vehicles and get out of here," Jay yelled as he started running towards the bus.

By the time Jay had reached the bus, Nadia had cut her ropes that tied her hands, cut Polly loose and was helping me to my feet. Polly was checking on Dre, who was in a sitting position. Jay came running up to my side. "Are you okay?" he asked. "I need to get inside and sit down," I said, crying from the pain. He helped me up the stairs and sat me on the sofa. Casey, Liz, Vickie and the four dogs came running out of the bedroom. Casey sat down beside me. "Oh my God, we were so scared, we didn't know what to do," she cried. "You guys did perfectly, exactly what you needed to do," I said. The dogs were still upset, barking and growling. "Please put them back in the bedroom and help Nadia get Polly inside." I asked as Casey got up and hurried them back into the bedroom. Vickie stood at the doorway and watched as Sean and Jay helped Dre onto the bus and back to the bottom bunk. He was in and out of consciousness. "He's got a severe concussion, I'm sure," Nadia said as she brought a wet cloth for his head. She handed it to Vickie. "You okay?" Nadia asked, looking at Vickie, "Yes, we just stayed hidden," she said. "That's the best thing you could have done," Nadia replied.

Benny and Jim parked their vehicles and went to see if they could assist anyone. "We need to get out of this town," Jay said, heading to the driver's seat. "We will find gas and diesel elsewhere and decompress, but for now we need to get out of here," he continued.

Jim and Benny jumped in their vehicles and followed as Jay put the bus in drive, turned the thing around and drove straight to the interstate.

Once they got about ten miles out of town, Jay pulled the bus over. "I think we need to find a place and just stay for the night,." he said. "We agree!" Sean and the rest of us agreed. Sean jumped out and ran back and told Benny and Jim the plan. "We'll follow you," they said.
As Jay searched for a secure place to pull over and sleep.

CHAPTER FIFTEEN
Splitting up

Day 13

I was still asleep when I felt the bus move. I opened my eyes and noticed it was still dark outside. Jay wasn't in bed, but I could feel the dogs around me. Quietly getting out of bed, opening the door, and limping down the hall. Usually, I would see one of the sofa beds pulled out with Jim and Polly asleep on one side and Benny and Nadia on the other. But neither one was pulled out. Liz was asleep on the dinette. I saw Jay driving, and no one in the passenger seat. I made my way up and sat down in the empty seat. "What time is it?" I asked, rubbing the sleep out of my eyes. "It's about 5am," he said. "Where are the other couples?" I asked. They are behind us in their vehicles. We all woke early and thought we would get on the road. "We need to find some diesel and gas, and some more supplies. Nadia and Benny will take most of their stuff with them," he said. "Yeah, I'm really going to miss them," I said. "Well, Benny said they might pack up their family and come to Texas," he responded. "That would be great. I would love it if they did," I replied. We are only about twenty miles from Holbrook, where Jim and Polly will head to Colorado, so we need to help them find more supplies as well," Jay added.

We rode in silence as the sun was coming up in front of us. I rolled down the window to let the fresh air in. We didn't have to run the A/C at night here in Arizona. The nights were nice and cool with the windows open, plus we could hear if there were noises outside.

"There's a sign up ahead," I said, breaking the silence. "Five miles to Holbrook," it read. "That billboard we just passed said there was a truck stop at the next exit in three miles," I said. "Okay, stay alert. Let me know if you see movement up ahead," Jay said. I nodded my head in agreement.

We took the next exit and headed to the truck stop. We drove past several 18-wheeler trucks that were in the parking lot and parked about 100 ft from the convenience store entrance. "Stay here, I'm going to go check it out," Jay said as he opened his door and got out. I ran back to the bedroom and put my shoes on. I could tell the dogs wanted to go out. "Wait, just a minute let daddy see if it's okay," I said to them, like they understood.

I saw Benny and Jim walk by the bus windows and met up with Jay. The doors to the store were standing wide open. When they entered the store, to the right was a café. To the left was the store and ahead were the bathrooms, showers, lounge area, and laundry. The three went in cautiously to look around. "Hello?" Jay yelled. A voice came from the lounge area. "Hello," as a man and a woman walked out of the room. "Man, it's nice to see someone," the man said. "We've been stuck here for days," he continued. "That's my truck out there," as he pointed to an 18-wheeler parked out front on the street. "After the incident, we could keep driving whenever one else seemed to stop. But a couple miles down the road, the truck started acting up. We coasted in here," he said. "We were trying to get to our family in Colorado," the woman added. "Oh, where's my manners, I am Brian, and this is my wife Betty," holding out his hand to Jay. "I'm Jay, this is Benny, and that is Jim over there," Jay said as Jim was walking over to the store area. "We just need to find some diesel and gas, then we will be on our way," Jay said. "Which way are you going?" Brian looked at his wife and then at Jay. "We are headed to Texas," Jay replied. "Oh," Betty said, looking defeated. "We were hoping we might get a ride, but we need to go to Colorado," she said.

Jay looked at Benny but said nothing. Benny knew exactly what Jay was thinking but said nothing as well. "I can show you what trucks you can get diesel from. Come on," Brian said as he headed to the front door. "Jim, come on, we are going to fill up the vehicles and gas cans," Benny hollered to Jim. As they were walking out the door, Benny and Jim walked several feet back. "This couple needs a ride to Colorado Jim, what do you think?" Benny whispered to Jim. "Do you think we can trust them?" Jim asked. "I don't know, but at least you would have help if anything happens," Benny replied. "True!" Jim said. "Let me talk to Polly and see if she would be comfortable with them riding along," he continued as they walked faster to catch up with the others.

"Nadia, Andie, we need to go get some supplies," I said as I watched Jay, and the guys walk over to the trucks with the couple. In the store, there were still plenty of canned goods, toilet paper, and other supplies. They grabbed grocery bags and filled them up. "We may need all this when you take your supplies with you," I said, looking at Nadia. "I'll leave you a few things to get by," she smiled. "Thanks, we appreciate it," I replied, smiling back.

Polly and Vickie were gathering some supplies from the bus for Polly and Jim to take with them. Casey and Liz had taken the dogs out to let them run in the parking lot and played fetch with Diamond.

Sean had joined the guys, helping them carry the cans to their vehicles. The guys filled the bus up with diesel and all the cans. Benny had grabbed a couple more gas cans from the store and gave Jim four and kept four for himself. There were a few cars in the parking lot, but it was enough to top off both their tanks and fill their gas cans. Jim strapped his on top of his Van, while Benny put his in the back of the truck.

"Come over here and look at this," Brian said with a big grin on his face. The guys walked toward a big 18-wheeler with "Wal-Mart" written on the trailer. They walked to the back as Brian opened the doors. They all stood there with their mouths open in amazement. In the truck were stacks and stacks of groceries. "I know not all of it will fit, but we can stuff as much as we can in the bus and vehicles," Brian said. "Wow!" is all they could say. "D'Ann, girls come here look at this," Jay yelled across the parking lot, as we were carrying sacks over to the bus. We handed the sacks to Polly and Vickie and walked over to where they were standing. "Oh my God!" Nadia said. "Well, just don't stand there. Get some of this stuff loaded," she said with a smile on her face.

As Jay and Sean jumped up in the back of the truck, Jim pulled Brian aside. "Look, you didn't have to show us this. You could have kept it to yourselves, but you didn't. Me and my wife are headed to Colorado. I would be honored to give you folks a ride," he said. "Thank you, thank you," he said, shaking Jim's hand. "Betty," he yelled over to her, "This fine man is going to get us home," he said, as Betty walked towards them. "Oh, bless you," she replied.

We had stuffed as much as we could in all three vehicles. Once we were as full as we could get them, we all stood outside, saying our goodbyes to Jim and Polly. "You guys take care of yourselves, and each other," I said to Polly, "We will, and you too," as she hugged me. They went around to everyone, hugging and saying goodbye. We stood there and waved as we watched the four of them drive off. "And then there were 10," I said. "I have lunch just about done," Liz said as she got onto the bus. Liz had put some beans in the crock pot and added some Ham that Nadia had canned. "I just popped cornbread in the oven, should be done," she added, as we all walked to the bus. The smell was incredible as we walked in. "I'm starving," Jay said. Liz handed out bowls of beans and a piece of cornbread to everyone. Not a word was spoken as we all stuffed our mouths full.

"Before we take off, there are showers in the station. Does anyone want to take a shower? The water will be cold though?" Jay asked the group. "Yes, yes," were the voices replying. "Okay, well everyone go so we can get on the road," Jay commanded.

Thirty minutes later, everyone had taken a quick shower, except for Dre, who was still laying down. But feeling much better. Liz and Nadia cleaned the kitchen as I took the dogs out for one last potty break.

Nadia and Andie were at the dinette looking at the map. "We need to take Highway 180/191 south to Springerville. That's where we will go south as you guys go east," Nadia said. "It looks to be about an hour and a half from here."

Jay had jumped in the truck with Benny as Sean drove the bus. We all got back on the interstate and saw the 180/191 exit about five miles down the road. "Good, we won't have to drive through town," Sean said as he took the exit. Highway 180/191 was a two-lane road headed south.

Several vehicles had stalled in the middle of the road, making it tricky for Sean to maneuver the big bus through, but being a tow truck driver, it was a piece of cake for him. The further away from town we got, the less traffic there was. A couple times Sean would yell out here comes a vehicle as a car or truck would approach and drive right past us like nothing was going on. One time we passed a field of cattle and saw a man on a tractor with hay feeding the cattle. Seeing these sights, it was like nothing had happened. Life seemed normal until we saw a crashed airplane in a field or cars littering the highway. And then we would see the occasional dead body alongside the road, then we knew it was not normal.

We made it to Springerville in just under 2 hours. Springerville was a small town of approximately 2000 people. As we drove through it, again things seemed normal. People were sitting on their front porch and stared as we drove by. We looked at them as weirdly as they looked at us, wondering which one of us was the unusual ones.

We reached where highway 180/191 and Highway 60 met. Benny and Nadia would take 180/191 south and we would continue to Highway 60 east and make our way across New Mexico into Texas. There was a little church at the intersection with people all around it. They watched as we turned the corner. Not wanting to be overrun by them, we continued down the street to an area where there were no people watching and pulled into a parking lot.

We helped Benny and Nadia gather their supplies and transferred them to the bed of their truck, then covered it with a tarp. The tears started flowing when we had to tell them goodbye. "Please try to come to Texas," I whispered in Nadia's ear as we hugged. She shook her head as tears rolled down her cheek. I then hugged Benny. "Take care of my girl," I told him. "Will do," he replied. It was déjà vu as we stood there, and watched Benny and Nadia drive off in their truck.

"Time to go," Jay said as we all climbed back into the bus. Sean turned back on to the street and headed the way we came and then turned east on to Highway 60. We all settled in as the road to Texas was going to be a long one. But first, to make it through New Mexico.

The view out the window as we went down the highway was beautiful, with mountains all around us. Although parts looked like desert, similar to Vegas, most of it was green with trees. The road was deserted, not a single vehicle broke down or was sitting on the highway. It only took us 45 minutes to reach the next town. Quemado, New Mexico, was a one-horse town. Literally, as we entered the city limits, a statue of a horse stood off the side of the road with a sign. "One horse Town." We slowed, taking in the beauty of the small town.

We passed a tire shop, a small market, and the post office, and then we were out of town.

Liz and Andie studied the map again. "About another hour, hour and a half. We will come to Interstate 25. Then will need to go south to exit Highway 380," Andie said. "We pass through a couple smaller towns before we get there," she added.

I sat back and reclined in the chair behind Jay. Looking out the bus door window, watching the outside pass by. My mind wondered. Before I knew it, I was thinking about my son Jordan down in Texas. "How were they going to get to the deer lease?" I thought. "If I have to go get them, I will. Houston is a large area. I'm sure there were many people that survived. No telling what kind of shape they were in." It had been almost 2 weeks since the incident happened. Tears filled my eyes. "Two weeks! If they weren't prepared, how in the world are they surviving? We have seen so many dead bodies along the way that didn't make it cause they starved or didn't have any water. What if they couldn't find more food or water?" I couldn't hold it in anymore. My tears wouldn't stop. Eventually, I drifted off to sleep.

"Mom, mom!" I was being shaken awake. "Wake up, mom, we gotta go," I heard him say. "What, what?" as I tried to open my eyes. There were flames all around me. The place was burning, people were screaming. But I couldn't move, my seatbelt was stuck. "Help, help, I can't get the seatbelt off." But no one heard me over all the screams. "Hurry mom, get up," I heard the voice. "I can't, I'm stuck, help me," I screamed. As the flames got closer, I could feel the heat surrounding me. It was burning my feet and legs. "Help me please," I pleaded. No one came. I looked around me and all I saw were bodies lying everywhere. They were burning. I started screaming and screaming. The pain was too much.

"D'Ann, D'Ann wake up, you're having a nightmare," I eventually heard Jay's voice, as he was shaking me. My eyes opened, and I saw Jay and Andie standing over me. "It's okay, D'Ann, you were dreaming," as tears filled my eyes. "It was horrible we were burning to death," I muttered through my sobs. Jay bent down and held me. "It's okay, you are safe. I won't let anything happen to you," he said. I sat for a few minutes to gather myself and reassure myself it was not real.

"Look alive, people. We got a roadblock ahead," Sean shouted. "Crap, not again," Jay replied. "And we are 2 men down," he added. Jay grabbed his AR, which was just behind his seat. "Casey, go to the bedroom and let Vickie and Dre know to stay down and be quiet, then go to our bedroom and keep the dogs busy so they are quiet," Jay commanded. Casey did as she was told. Liz and I grabbed rifles, and we took our place on the sofa. We closed the windows and blinds and shut off all the lights.

The bus slowed down as two men held up their hand so Sean would stop. Sean and Jay stared at the two men, which both had ARs. As one man approached Sean, Sean rolled down his window. "This road is blocked. You can't come through here, no outsiders," the man said as he walked up to the window. "We are just passing through. We promise we won't stop," Sean reassured. "Yeah, well, that's what the last people said when we let them through, and now we have four dead citizens," the man replied. "I swear to you sir, we have women and children in here and don't mean you any harm," Sean said. "Look, we can pay you with some supplies if you just let us through," Jay announced. "What if they take it all?" I hissed to Jay. The man walked back to the other man and seemed to have a conversation with him. Then he came back to Sean's window. "We will let you pass, and we can use the supplies, but we will follow you out of town. One wrong move and you're all dead, you hear me?" the man said. "Okay, but we will give you the supplies on the other side of town," Jay yelled from the other side of the cab. "Fair enough," the man said. "We will follow you to the other roadblock and when you give us the supplies, we will let you out," he said. He waved to the other man to move the barricades. "Go on through, we'll be right behind you," he said, as Sean put it in drive and eased it through.

Town was only about two miles long, lined with older homes, a market, and a school. We got to the other barricade and Sean stopped the bus. Two men stood there looking kind of confused, wondering where we came from. The first man drove around us and parked his truck. "We are letting them pass. They are paying us with some supplies," he said. "Help them load em in the back of the truck." Jay jumped out of the bus and opened the smallest of the basement storages that we had stuffed full of groceries from the Wal-Mart truck. "You can have all this. We will try to find some more on our way. If you have the means to make it up to Holbrook, there is a Wal-Mart truck up there full of supplies. We took only what we could fit." Jay said as he watched the men load up the truck. "All we have left is what is in our small kitchen, and that needs to get us by till we find some more," Jay lied. "There are eight of us, but we can get by with what's left," Jay tried to convince the men so they wouldn't be greedy and want everything. "Well, there are about 150 people left in this town and our food supply is getting low," one of the other men said. "We haven't ventured out of the city limits in fear of what's out there," he continued. "Well, there hasn't been a lot of traffic that we have seen on our way here, but I bet if you have the means to get to the interstate, you will find tractor trailers with a lot of supplies in them," Jay said. "Well, thank you for your kindness," the man said as he motioned to the men to move the barricades. "I pray you have safe travels," he continued. "Thank you," Sean and Jay said in unison. Jay jumped back on the bus as Sean put it in drive and drove out of the town. "Wow, that was a close one," I said, putting the rifle down and letting out a big breath.

It was completely dark now. The road was pitch black except where the headlight shone. "I know we want to get to Texas, but maybe we should not drive at night. It could be dangerous," Sean said, looking over at Jay. "I guess so, but where do you want to stay?" Jay asked. "I've seen a few farmhouses. Before it gets too dark, maybe we can see if one is empty and hide in the driveway," Sean replied. "Okay, girls keep your eyes open for a mailbox or driveway," Jay said, just as Sean blurted out, "Here's one right here," as he slowed the bus down almost too fast. He pulled into the drive. The drive was longer than he thought as he approached the house. It was a small two-story farmhouse, just like the ones I knew in Kansas where I grew up. We could see no light coming from inside. Sean turned off the headlights and then the engine. Jay grabbed a flashlight and his AR. He and Sean exited the bus. They snuck up to the porch and to the front door. Jay tried to peek in the window, but it was just too dark to see. Sean tried the doorknob, it was unlocked. He opened the door and for the third time, the smell of death had him retching. Jay shined a flashlight into the small living room and in the rocking chair was a decomposing body of an elderly woman, and on the sofa was a man equally decomposed.

Jay backed out of the house and shut the door. Shown the flashlight and went around the side of the house. There was a drive that went to the back of the house towards the barn. "I think we can back it in here," Sean said, startling Jay. "Mother Fucker, you scared the piss out of me, AGAIN!" he shouted. They both laughed and headed back to the bus. There was just enough room for Sean to turn the bus around and back it up in front of the barn. After parking, I took the dogs out for a quick potty break. "I think we should take turns taking watch, just in case," Jay said. "I can take first watch. I had a great nap earlier and I'm not tired at all," Liz said. "Are you sure?" Jay asked. Liz gave Jay a look that made him smile. "Okay, but if you need me, you wake me up, understand?" he asked. "Yes, I will," Liz said. I put the three little dogs on the bus and put Diamond on a long chain. "Here, she will help you and keep you company," I said, chaining Diamond to the steps. Liz took out one of the lawn chairs from the basement storage and sat it in front of the door. With a rifle and a flashlight and Diamond by her side, she settled in. "Wake me up in a couple hours and I'll take watch," Sean said. "Will do," she replied.

17 Days to Texas

CHAPTER SIXTEEN
My Diamy

Day 14

I jumped awake. "What the hell was that?" I mumbled, all out of breath. There it was again. My heart was beating fast. I looked around the bedroom. Jay was gone and so were all the dogs. I swung my legs out of bed and slipped on my crocs. As the smell of frying eggs hit my nose. There was the sound again, a rooster crowed outside. "Oh my God, it's a rooster," I mouthed under my breath. "Yes, and look, we have fresh eggs this morning," Jay said. "Wow, those smell so good," I said. "We have plenty for breakfast and we can put some in the fridge for later," he added.

Everyone else was waking to the smell of eggs, frying and fresh coffee on the stove. I sat down on the sofa where all the dogs were laying. Tator jumped up in my lap. I snuggled him. "How are you guys holding up?" I asked, as I pet all three of the other dogs on the head. "I let them out the run and play this morning, so they should be good and tired for the trip," Jay said. "So did you all check out the house last night, nobody in there?" I asked. "Yeah, there was someone in there," he said. "You don't want to go in there," he added. "Oh," I replied.

Andie and Sean were the next to come out of the bedroom. "Did you guys sleep on the floor again?" I asked. "Why didn't you pull out the sofa bed?" "We're good," Sean said. "It's not too bad," Andie said. "We stayed up talking to Dre and Mom pretty late last night," Sean said. "How is Dre feeling, and how's your mom's leg?" I asked. "I think he will be up and around today. Mom's leg is looking really good, healing well," Sean replied. "That's good. It was scary what they both went through," I said.

After we all ate, Andie and I took a walk around the yard. Being that it was now almost September, flowers were blooming in the flower garden. "If she has a flower garden, I bet she has an actual garden. You think we can find any fresh veggies?" Andie asked. "Let us go look," I said as we walked on the other side of the farmhouse. As we turned the corner, we saw it, a small greenhouse. "Oh man," I said as we walked faster toward the greenhouse. Andie opened the door and our eyes widened. Although I didn't like most vegetables, when you're hungry you will eat what you have. There were pots with tomato plants, pepper plants, and all kinds of herbs. Most were withered because of no water, but we were able to salvage a few. She had chive plants, dill, oregano, and parsley. "Do you think if we take these back and give them some water, they will survive?" I asked Andie. "I don't know. We can try," she replied.

I grabbed the best-looking plants and sat them on a tray. Most of the tomatoes and peppers we gathered, we put in a pot. "Let us go see what is in her garden on the other side," I said as we walked outside. The garden was vast. There were rows of lettuce, carrots, okra, peas, and green beans. A little further away was a smaller garden with broccoli, cauliflower, and potatoes.

On the side of the greenhouse were some 5-gallon buckets. Andie and I went row by row and picked what looked eatable and put it in buckets. When we thought we had enough, we each carried three buckets in each hand and the tray of herbs back to the bus. "Look what we found," I said, setting the buckets down. Liz came out of the bus with a big smile on her face. "Oh, the food I can make with these," she said, picking up a head of broccoli. "See if that well pump works over there, and we will wash them," she said, pointing over to the side of the barn.

I walked over to the pump. It was just like the one my dad had put in on our Kansas farm. I lifted the handle, and nothing came out, then I heard gurgling, all of the sudden the water spit and sputtered, and ran out. "Yay!" I shouted. Liz and Andie carried the buckets over and started washing the vegetables. I was standing there and movement out of the corner of my eye caught my attention. I turned my head and saw a horse grabbing an apple from a tree. "Look," I pointed toward the orchard. "Apples!" Andie squealed. "Let us get the veggies on the bus and go get some apples," Liz said.

We carried the vegetables to the bus and set them out on paper towels on the table to dry. Then took the buckets and headed to the orchard. I knew the horse was most likely not supposed to be in the apple orchard, but I didn't want the horse to starve, so I opened the gate so the horse could get out and into the green pasture.

We picked the apples we could reach, and the ones the bugs hadn't gotten to. A couple of rows over were peach trees. "Peaches," I said, as Liz and Andie both let out a "Hurray!" "Do you think we can make some kind of pie out of these?" I asked. "We should," Liz said. "We have dry milk, and flour and sugar, and now some fresh eggs. I bet I can whip something up," she said as my mouth watered. I picked an apple off the tree and bit into it. It was so sweet and tasted so good. I had eaten the whole thing before we got back to the bus.

With all our goodies on the bus, Liz started making a stew with the canned meat we had and all the veggies we found. Once it was all in the crock pot, she started on the pie. The bus smelled so good. "Can you cook as we drive down the road?" Jay asked. "Yeah, it all works as we drive," Liz responded. "Load it up people, let's hit the road," Jay shouted to the group.

We drove out of the drive. Everything outside seemed different in the daylight. You could see farmhouses you didn't know were there at night. Cows and horses in the fields, eating the grass like nothing was going on. The countryside passed by like nothing had even happened two weeks ago.

We reached the town of Socorro, where we needed to take Interstate 25 south a little and then turn off on Highway 380. The town was like most of the towns we had driven through, cars in the street, crashes, some businesses, and homes burnt. People outside of churches and schools. Everyone watched as we drove by. Every once in a while, an older truck or car drove by. Everything was feeling normal, not the old normal, but a new type of normal. "It's that time again," Jay said, interrupting my thoughts. "We need to find some diesel," he continued. "We are almost at the edge of town. There might be a truck stop up here before we turn off," Sean said.

We drove a couple more miles and, sure enough, there was a truck stop up on the right. This kind of truck stop was one of my favorite truck stops. On long trips, I would get audio books on CD and listen to them. It made the trip seem not so long. Which gave me an idea. There was a CD player on the bus, and so far, we hadn't listened to anything. "Maybe when we stop, we can see if there were any left inside," I thought. Jay pulled the bus in and drove close to the doors. The door's glass was smashed all over the ground. My hopes were dashed as I thought people probably already got everything. "Wait here till we make sure it's clear," Jay said as he and Sean got out.

A few minutes later, they came out and waved us in. Andie, Casey and Liz and I got out. "Not much left in the way of groceries," Jay said. "I'm not looking for groceries this time," I replied as he gave me a strange look. As we went inside, I looked for the display of CD and audio books and, to my surprise, they were there. They had been knocked on the floor, but they were there. "Casey, come here," I shouted to Casey as she was looking for a candy bar. "I know it's been really tough on you, and if you are like my teenagers were, music is a big deal to you," I said. Casey's eyes got big as I handed her a music CD. "But how am I going to play it?" she asked. "Look," as I pointed to a glass case that had not been broken. Hanging there were old time portable CD players. "Stand back," I said as I took a piece of shelving and smashed the window. Liz screamed, "What are you doing?" "Getting some entertainment," I said.

I went around to the counter and grabbed some bags, and then stuffed them full of all the CDs and audio books we could find. Even though we didn't have a DVD player, we grabbed some movies also, just in case. I reached in the case and grabbed all the CD players and noticed on the bottom shelf was a portable DVD player. "I guess that makes sense," I said. Truckers probably have them in their trucks. Casey pulled out all the batteries she could find. Liz and Andie searched for anything useful as we stuffed all we could into the bags. "I think we got enough," I said. "Come on," as we all walked out the door carrying big bags full of stuff.

Jay and Sean, and with a little help from Dre, had found diesel. Filled up the bus and all the cans and put them back in storage. I helped the girls get the bags on the bus. "You won't believe what we got. Hopefully, they didn't get fried," I said. As he turned to look at all the lute, we had all over the table. Casey had a big smile on her face that we hadn't seen since we met her.

She was opening the package to the CD player and installing the batteries. She didn't know how it worked and looked at me. "Oh Lord girl, you're making me feel really old," I said, laughing as I took the player and the CD from her and popped it in and hit play. She put the headphones that came with it on, and a smile so big came across her face.

She started bobbing her head to the music. My heart was full. It wasn't much, but she seemed happy again. I showed her how to do it, remembering that all teenagers had to do now days, was turn on YouTube or some music app. She got up and went to our bedroom and crawled on the bed with the dogs, snuggling and tickling them.

We got back on the road. Andie and Dre got the DVD player working and Liz and Vickie sat at the table talking about the recipes they could make with the veggies we had gotten. I opened another CD player, put batteries in it and popped a Johnny Cash CD in it. "My Son would love this," I thought as I closed my eyes and listened to the music.

Every time we got close to a town, or what looked to be a group of vehicles, Jay or Sean would say, "look alive, be ready." But so far, so good, everything had gone uneventfully. As I listened to different CDs, I looked out the window at the landscape. Most of it in this area was brown and desert, like Arizona and Nevada. Occasionally, we would go through some trees as we topped a hill. I played the ABC game with myself as I watched billboards go by. Then I saw a billboard announcing a golf course in Ruidoso. My mom and dad went there many years ago, I thought, which brought me back to thinking about my childhood.

My parents were typical parents back in the seventies when I was in high school. I was the oldest and the only girl. I loved playing sports as well as my brothers. My parents came to all our games, even the away games. I remember my dad working up in the booth at the football games. As I cheered our team on. The high school I went to was tiny. In fact, in my graduating class, there were only thirteen of us, five girls and eight boys.

Everybody knew everything about everything in such a small community. I grew up on a so called "farm." We had horses, cows, and pigs, and to this day, the reason I hated chickens, we had a rooster that was very mean. My middle brother, Mike, used to run up and down the fence as the rooster would chase him on the other side of the fence. But, that one faithful day, the rooster got out. My brother ran as fast as his legs could carry him, screaming all the way. He climbed a tree and cried cause the rooster stayed at the bottom just waiting. I don't remember what happened to that rooster.

y childhood was great growing up. I had so many wonderful memories. My brother Mike was a hell raiser. He was 5 years younger than me. And Jace, the baby, was 7 years younger than me. We were always doing crazy things. The worst memory I have of Mike was the time I believe I was in high school. My dad worked shift work at the local refinery in town. So sometimes we had to go feed the pigs or the cows. Well, this time, we were out feeding the pigs. And anyone that has pigs knows they need a mud hole to get in to keep cool in the summer. They say pigs are one of the cleanest animals, but you couldn't tell by the way their mud hole stunk. Well, I don't remember exactly how, but I ended up falling face first in the mud. My brother Mike, stood there laughing his ass off at me, didn't offer to help me or anything. I was so mad. Covered in mud and pig feces, I dug my way out of the pen, grabbed the only thing close, which was a pitchfork. I chased that little son of a bitch all the way to the house. If I could have caught him, I would have one less brother today, I swear. But I got him back not too long after that.

My parents were good friends with a couple that had a boy a year younger than me and a boy the same age as Mike. Kyle and Paul. Mike and Paul loved to ride their bicycles in the alfalfa fields, where we had many bike trails. One night, Kyle and I strung a rope across the gate entrance to the field, knowing they would ride right through it. He lay on one side and me on the other, hiding. When the two came riding through the gate, Kyle and I pulled on the rope. Just like you see in the movies. It caught them both in the neck and knocked them completely off their bikes. Kyle and I ran as fast as we could to the house laughing all the way, as Mike and Paul lay on the ground crying.

When Mike and I would get together, we always brought up old memories and laughed about them for hours. I don't think my parents knew have the stuff we did to each other.

"Look alive," I heard Jay say, as it brought me out of my memories. I took my headphones off and grabbed the rifle. We were getting ready to pull into Roswell.

Roswell was a big town. As we drove through it, we saw more people out walking the street, more stalled cars than we had in previous towns. But people looked hollow. They looked still in a daze like state. Walking around like zombies. Once we got closer to the center of town, we noticed burned-out buildings, and most buildings and business looked like they had been looted with trash all around the fronts of the buildings and into the streets.

As we turned the corner to get on highway 285 and head out of town, we could see a few blocks down what seemed to be a mob of people blocking the street.

"Shit!" Jay said, "What the hell is this?" Jay brought the bus to an abrupt stop. "I don't know if we should continue. Will they move? What are they doing?" he said. As we all stared out the front windshield, we noticed the mob was moving towards us. We could see that a lot of them carried baseball bats, large sticks, and a few had rifles. "Oh crap, here they come," he shouted. "Step on it, just go through them. They will either move or get hit. It's them or us. I have a feeling," Sean yelled. "Hold on everyone, this might get ugly," Jay hissed.

The crowd was screaming and yelling, waving their sticks and bats as they headed toward us. Jay stepped on the gas and drove straight for them. I was petrified, sitting there watching it all unfold. There seemed to be at least thirty people. Men, Women, and even so older teens. Most of them looked disheveled and dirty, with contempt in their eyes. Jay laid on the horn as he approached them. Most immediately moved. But some with guns and bats did not. "Oh my God, we are going to hit them!" I screamed. "Well, they better move," as he slowed down just a little, enough that if he hit them, it would just be a hard bump, and hopefully they would move. A couple of men with bats started hitting the bus as we drove by. The bangs made the dogs go crazy, barking and growling.

Dre moved to the bedroom to make sure no one would attempt to come in from the back. "We need to just get out of here," I cried, "Jay, go, go, that one has a gun aimed right at us," Sean yelled as a man with long greasy hair took aim. "Everyone on the floor!" Jay screamed. As the shot rang out, Jay floored the bus, hitting several people that stood in the way. You could feel the bus jump like it had run over a speed bump. But we knew it wasn't a "speed bump." Jay watched in his side view mirrors to see exactly who he ran over, and if they were going to get up. But not letting off the gas, kept going. "Everyone okay?" Sean asked. Everyone was in shock but seemed to be fine.

"What did we hit?" I asked Jay. I could see he was visibly shaken. "I think it was a woman," he said as his voice trembled. "Look Jay, you had to do what you had to do to keep us all safe. Don't think about it. We would have surely died if we would have stopped," Sean said, trying to console Jay. "He's right, Jay, you did good," I added. Jay shook his head. But I knew this would probably haunt him for a long time.

Once Jay had gotten far enough away, he stopped the bus. "Let us check out where the bullets hit, make sure everything is alright" he said. Getting back in, Sean got in the driver's seat. As Jay sat on the couch. I grabbed him a cold bottle of water and handed it to him. "I think I need something stronger than this," he mumbled. "Do you need to smoke?" I asked. "Or do you want some gummies or chocolate to help you relax a little?" I added. "I think so," he said as he got up and went to the back bedroom. After 30 minutes he hadn't returned, so I checked on him. I opened the door and he and the four dogs were sound asleep on the bed. He was exhausted. I would let him sleep. The door to the bunkroom was open, Casey was on her bunk, with the headphones on her head. She hadn't taken them off since we got them. Dre was on his bunk, sound asleep. He still slept a lot since his head injury but was doing much better.

Vickie and Liz were both on their bunks reading prepper and survival books that Nadia had left us. "He, okay?" Vickie whispered as I walked by. "Yeah, he's just exhausted, needs to sleep," I replied. "It's getting close to dark. Are we going to stop anywhere?" Liz asked. "I sure need a shower or something," she continued. "I will go talk to Sean and see what he thinks," I replied.

I walked back to the front. Andie had moved to the Passenger seat, and I sat in the recliner behind her. "Do you think we should stop for the night?" I asked. "We've only gone a few miles. I would like to get more mileage between us and that town," Sean replied. "Yeah, you're probably right," I added. Sean swerved and slammed on the brakes several times to avoid debris in the road. Suddenly he swerved again, but the driver's side of the bus bounced up. "What the fuck was that?" I asked. "I don't know. It looked like a bicycle or motorcycle. I tried to miss it, but I must have just clipped the corner," he replied. "Crap, crap, crap," he said, "I think it punctured a tire," as he was coming to a stop.

I met Sean and Andie outside. "Yip sliced the side," Sean said as I approached the rear tire. "Damn it," he continued. "The spare is probably in that back storage area," I said as we walked to the other side of the bus. Sean opened the door and pulled out the lawn chairs and saw the spare tire laying in the back. Almost crawling in the storage area, he reached in and pulled it out. It was flat. "Damn it, what else could go wrong today?" he said.

I jumped from fright as Jay came walking around the side of the bus. "What's going on?" he asked. "I hit that freaking motorcycle laying over there. I didn't see it till I was right on top of it." He continued, "and to top that off, the fuckin' spare is flat." Jay walked around to the side to look at the deflating tire, then back up the road from where we came. "How far out of town did we get?" he asked. "Only about 10 miles," Sean responded. "I don't think we have much choice but to walk back to town and find a tire. Maybe we can find one that will fit on a truck or something along the way," Jay said. "Hopefully that mob is gone," he added. "Well, if we can get there in the dark, maybe we can sneak in," Sean said.

We all went back to the bus. Everyone else was waiting in the living room for us. "Sean and I are going to have to walk back to town, unless we can find one along the way and get a different tire," Jay said. "The tire is shredded, and the spare is flat. Will you guys be okay here by yourselves?" Jay asked. "I think we can manage it," Dre said. "Yeah, go, don't worry about us. We got guns and Diamond; we should be fine. Just hurry back." I replied.

It was getting late in the afternoon, soon it would be dark; the moon would come up in the east. We turned off all lights in the bus and sat outside in the cool evening air. We turned off the generator so not to make any sound. I put the three little ones back on the bus after Casey took them to potty. "Why don't you stay inside with them," I told Casey. Liz and Vickie sat in the living room, and each looked out a window.

Andie sat at the front of the bus, Dre sat at the back, and Diamond and I sat by the door. Each of us with a rifle in our laps. "Diamy, keep your ears and eyes open," I said, and I patted her head. She laid her head in my lap and let me caress her head. Diamy was a nickname I gave her, and Jay sometimes would call her, Dog Dog. Once I heard my youngest son Jordan call her Dodo, and I asked him why he called her that. He thought that is what Jay called her, "No silly it's Dog Dog" I said, as we laughed. But he continued to call her Dodo from that time on.

Occasionally, Liz or Vickie would bring us out a cold bottle of water and a snack. Jay and Sean had been gone for over 3 hours now. The moon was directly above us. Sitting in the quiet, all you could hear were the bugs and the noises a forest makes. Sean had gotten the bus to the side of the road on the shoulder before it came to a stop. Sitting by the door, I faced the forest. I could only see the first row of trees, and that was only when the moon shone down.

Diamond laid by my feet and every once in a while, would perk her ears up and looked towards the forest. It gave me chills not seeing or hearing what she heard that got her attention. She would then lay her head back down and shut her eyes. "I got to go pee," Casey said at the top of the steps. We didn't want to use the black tank that much, so I said, "just go over there by that tree," as I pointed. It was only about thirty feet from the bus, but it was dark, and I knew it was private.

Diamond watched as Casey walked down the embankment and out of sight in the dark. Diamond stood up, and the hair on the back of her neck stood up. She was looking in Casey's direction at the edge of the forest and growling. "What is it, girl?" I whispered. "Casey, you need to come back up here now," I yelled. No answer. "Casey, come on," I shouted again. Holding my gun ready. I stood up. Diamond wanted to take off and run into the forest, but she knew better after the last time, plus I had her tied to the steps of the bus. Her growling was getting more intense. I untied her and let her go down the embankment a little to the end of her chain. Once she couldn't go any further, she started barking aggressively. Then, I saw it too.

Jay and Sean had almost reached the edge of town when they came across an 18-wheeler with a load of sheet rock on a flatbed trailer that had overturned in the ditch. They climbed up on the trailer with the tire iron they had been carrying from the bus. Examined the tire and knew it would probably work. "Why don't we grab two of them just in case? We can roll them back to the bus," Sean said as he loosened the lug nuts. Once they got the tires off, they pushed them to the ground, then rolled them on to the highway and headed back towards the bus.

A Man walked out of the forest. I recognized him as the long greasy haired guy that shot at us in town. I took aim. "Stop right there," I yelled, as he walked towards me. He laughed. "Look little girl, there is one of you and there are four of us, plus you don't want these pretty little girls to get hurt, do ya?" the man said as he waved to one of the other guys just coming out of the dark. One of them had their hand around Casey's mouth and was holding her tight as she fought to get away.

Behind her was another man with Andie. She looked like she was out of it, and blood was coming from her mouth. "This one is a little hellcat," he said, dragging her. "What did you do to her?" I screamed at them. "She got a little fisty. I had to settle her down," he said. Andie could hardly stand on her own. "Where are your men? You know, the one that ran over my sister," he said angrily. "They should be here any minute," I yelled back. "Well, we are just going to take these two fine looking women back to our compound, an eye for an eye," he said, "and if you know what is good for you, you will not try to come after them, we will kill them."

Casey was now in fight-or-flight mode, she stared punching and kicking the man that was holding her. Diamond saw Casey struggling and took off toward the man, breaking free from her collar. Before anyone knew what was going on, Diamond had his arm in her teeth. "Get this fucking dog off of me," he screamed as Casey broke free and ran towards the bus. At that same moment, the greasy-haired man took aim and with one shot, Diamond fell to the ground. "NOOO!" I screamed and aimed and fired at the long hair man. The shot hit him in the arm. "You Bitch," as he turned around and lifted his gun towards me. I pulled the trigger again before he could get a shot off. He fell to the ground but was still moving. He had dropped his gun, and it was out of his reach. Dre took aim at the guy that Diamond had attached and shot him right between the eyes.

The man dropped to the ground. As we both aimed our rifles toward the man that had Andie. Liz came down the stairs at the same time with another rifle. Andie knew a little about what was going on, and dropped to her knees, which left the man wide open. Dre pulled the trigger. He went down with a thud, releasing Andie, who also fell over to the ground. Dre ran over to the man that was moving towards his gun, "I don't think so," and with one last shot, shot him in the head. Liz and I ran to help Andie.

While Casey, screaming the whole time, ran towards Diamond. I watched. "Go," Liz said, "I got Andie." I ran over to Diamond on the ground with blood coming from her chest. The shot killed her instantly. "Oh my God!" I dropped to my knees and held Diamond's head in my hands. "No, God No," I cried. Casey came up behind me and held me as we sobbed together. "I can't lose my dog," I cried.

I sat on the ground with Diamond's head in my lap for the longest time. Casey had gotten up and went to check on the other dogs. Liz and Dre had helped Andie onto the bus. Vickie came over to me where I was sitting on the ground holding Diamond rocking back and forth. My clothes were soaked in her blood. "Come on, D'Ann, come back to the bus. There is nothing you can do for her now," she said. "Give me a minute," I cried. "Okay, Jay and Sean should be back anytime, hopefully," Vickie added. Vickie walked back to the bus and left me with Diamond.

I caressed her head like I had done so many times before. I buried my face in her fur and sobbed. "Oh, my poor girl," I kept repeating. I don't know how long I was there, but I felt a tug and then I heard Jay's voice, "Oh D'Ann, I'm so sorry you had to deal with this, and we weren't here to protect you," Jay whispered in my ear. "Come on, let me get you to the bus and get you cleaned up and get her buried," he said. "No, I don't want to leave her here. I can't." I cried hysterically. "Isn't there some way we can take her home and bury her? Please, please," I pleaded with Jay.

Sean had been standing behind Jay and heard everything. "Jay, what if we put her in some trash bags and strap her up on the roof?" He said. "I guess we can try. As hot as it's going to be in Texas, and we still have a long way to go, she may stink," he said, looking at me. "I don't care. I want to take her home," I pleaded. "Okay, we'll do it," he said. Sean got on the bus and brought out 4-5 trash bags. Jay lifted her and put her in the bag. As I watched, I couldn't hold the tears and sobs back. "What about those men over there?" Sean asked. "Fuck em, leaving em where they lay. They killed my dog and hurt your wife," Jay hissed. The guys changed the tire, put Diamond in several bags, and strapped her to the roof of the bus. I had gone to the bedroom to lie down in the meantime. Casey and the three dogs crawled beside me. Casey put her arms around me, and again we cried together. We both fell asleep as we felt the bus moving down the highway.

Sean drove a few more hours until we finally reached the Texas state line. "Texas!" Jay said as he saw the Welcome to Texas sign.

CHAPTER SEVENTEEN
One dead, One Injured

Day 15

I could hardly open my eyes. They seemed to be matted shut by the tears from the night before. I found myself in bed, alone. No Jay, and no dogs, and the bus was not moving. I lay staring at the ceiling, going over in my head what had happened the night before. Tears again filled my eyes as I thought of Diamond. As people walked up and down the hallway, I heard talking and felt the bus move. I slowly sat up in the bed as my head hurt. I slipped on my crocks and opened the door. Vickie, Liz, and Andie were sitting at the table going over the maps. I grabbed a bottle of water from the fridge and noticed there were only a few left. The Tylenol bottle was sitting on the shelf about the sink. I shook three out of the bottle and put it back. As I put them in my mouth and took a big drink of water, I could see out the kitchen window. A huge windmill was just outside. I looked harder out the window and could tell they surrounded us. Jay, Sean, and Dre were putting the last of the diesel from the cans into the bus. Casey and the three little dogs were running and playing.

"How are you feeling this morning?" Vickie asked. "I have a horrible headache," I replied. "Did you guys find the rest of the route home?"

I asked. "Yeah, we are trying to avoid any big cities, but there is a heck of a lot of small towns we must go through," Liz answered. "We still have about 8 to10 more hours to go," Liz continued. "Looks like we need some supplies," I said. "Yes, we do, and diesel," Jay said as he walked up the stairs and onto the bus. He walked towards me and held out his arms to hug me. "We're almost home, baby," he whispered in my ear. I turned towards the door as I heard the dogs come pounding up the steps. I sat on the sofa and all three jumped up in my lap and started licking me and seemed excited to see me. I gave them all kisses and hugs and as much love as I could. Casey handed me the treats as I looked up at her, tears in her eyes. "NO, we are not doing this anymore," I said to her, "We gotta look out for these three now," as I smiled at her, and she smiled back. "Everyone ready to hit the road, we got several more hours, and we gotta find supplies," Sean said, crawling into the driver's seat. "We have about 450 miles to go," Liz said. "I think if we get one more full tank and the gas cans full, we can make it the rest of the way," Jay said.

We had been avoiding the major highways, sticking to the back roads that didn't go through any major towns. Watching out the window as we drove, we passed farmhouses that stood in silence. No one seemed to be around, seeing no movement. Wondering whether those families were gone, or they had somehow been prepared for what happened.

I would see livestock roaming around the pastures. "Why wouldn't the farmers eat the cattle instead of starving?" I thought. "And what is it going to be like when we get to the deer lease? Will there be enough food to sustain all of us, plus everyone else that showed up? Is it far enough away from the big cities that we won't have to fight for our lives every day?"

The realization was hitting me. For the last 2 weeks, all we focused on was getting to the deer lease. Now that we were almost there, I wondered what we would find when we finally got there. And what is going to happen in the weeks, months, and years to come? It was getting too overwhelming thinking about it. I closed my eyes and tried to think of happier times. Days we struggled with even a month ago, compared to now, seemed carefree. We didn't have to worry where our meals were going to come from, or if we had to find water. Life seemed so much easier just 2 weeks ago, I thought as I drifted to sleep.

Startled awake, I heard shouting but couldn't quite figure out what was going on in my sleepiness. "GET DOWN!" Jay was screaming as shots rang out, hitting the windshield. I felt a tug on my arm as Andie was trying to pull me out of the chair. I got on the floor, as the bus came to a screeching holt.

Jay and Sean both returned fire out their side windows. "Drive, Drive!" Jay yelled at Sean. But the bus didn't move. Glass and windows were breaking everywhere around us. From the floor I looked towards the front and could see Jay pulling Sean out of the driver's seat on to the floor. Blood was collecting on Sean's chest. "Oh my God!" I screamed. Jay jumped in the driver's seat, put it in drive and stepped on the gas.

More shots rang out. Hitting the side of the bus, breaking the kitchen window, and lodging in the refrigerator door. Andie crawled towards Sean, as I noticed Liz was still sitting at the kitchen table, just staring at the front. "Liz, Liz, get down!" I screamed, but she didn't seem to hear me. I crawled towards her, reached up and grabbed her arm. I pulled it towards me on the floor, as she just fell over. Then I noticed it. Blood was running down the side of her neck. Her eyes were open, but she made no movement. "Liz, Liz!" I screamed. Vickie eased under the table and crawled her way to me and Liz.

I tried shaking Liz, but there was no response. "D'Ann, stop, she's gone," Vickie said, grabbing my arm that was still shaking Liz. "No, no, that can't be," I cried. I heard several more shots ring out and hit the back of the bus and busting out the bedroom windows. Casey let out a scream, and the dogs were barking. "Casey, are you okay?" I screamed toward the bedroom. "Yes, we are on the floor. I'm okay," she yelled back. "Dre, are you okay?" I yelled. "Yeah, I'm okay. What is going on?" he asked. "I don't know," I replied. "Try to crawl up here and help us with Sean. He's been shot," I yelled.

Jay pushed the bus as hard as it would go, weaving in out of stalled cars and trucks. The gunfire had stopped, but he kept going, trying to put as much distance between whoever that was and us. Once we had gotten about five miles away, Jay pulled off on a country dirt road and drove about another mile till he came to a long drive and at the end was a farmhouse about ¼ mile away.

Sean was lying in the middle of the floor. I grabbed some towels and a pair of scissors from the drawer. Andie was too upset holding and rocking Sean's head to help. Sean was breathing and was awake, but in a lot of pain. I cut his shirt so we could see where he had been hit. Soaking up the blood as it poured out a hole in the upper part of his shoulder.

Vickie grabbed one of Nadia's medical books for survivors and searched what to do for a gunshot. "Well, I've seen them on TV. Take a bottle of whiskey or alcohol of some sort and pour it into the hole to clean it." I said. Jay got up and went to the cupboard above the stove and pulled out a bottle of Jack Daniels and handed it to me. I looked at him with a puzzled look. "Do you think it's okay?" I asked as I grabbed it. Jay just looked at me. It looked like he was going into shock, as well. "Vickie, did you find anything?" I asked. "No!" she replied. "Jay, turn on the stove and put that spoon on the flames. We have to stop the bleeding." I said. "What the hell are you going to do with that?" he asked. "We are going to cauterize the wound, to stop him from bleeding to death," I said. "Here, make him drink some of this," as I handed Andie the bottle of Jack.

Sean winced in pain as Andie helped him raise his head high enough to drink the whiskey. "Here, give him some of this also," Jay said as he handed Andie a bottle of tequila. Sean took several big drinks. "Okay, it's hot," Jay said as he handed me a potholder and the handle of the spoon. "Hold him down, this is going to hurt," I said. Jay and Andie held Sean's arms and chest down as Dre and Vickie worked their way to his legs and held them down. I looked up to heaven. "God, please let this be quick and as painless as possible and stop the bleeding," I said out loud as I pressed the red-hot spoon over the hole in Sean's shoulder. "Hold him," I screamed, as Sean screamed and tried to move. I lifted the spoon, and it looked like it did the trick.

The area looked like it had been burned, but the bleeding had stopped. Everyone released Sean as he passed out from the pain. Everyone stood up, but as I was getting ready to stand, I saw blood on the floor underneath Sean. "Hold on," I said to everyone. "Help me turn Sean over," I said. Jay and Andie gently turned him over. Another hole was on the back side of his shoulder, and blood was coming from it as well. "I think the bullet went all the way through," I said, "Which could be good cause it's not lodged inside of him. But we need to stop the bleeding on this side too," I said. I handed Jay the spoon. He put it on the flames again. When it was good and hot, he handed it back. Sean had already passed out, so Andie just held him in her arms as I pushed the spoon on the other hole. "Jay, in the top drawer in the bathroom are some bandages. Let's get him bandaged up," I said. "Look, here is the bullet," Dre commented as he pulled a bullet out of the driver's seat. We got Sean to one of the bunk beds, as Andie stayed and put a wet cloth on his forehead. Now it was time to help Liz. Liz was gone. She had gotten shot right in the neck, and it looked like she died instantly. "I think we just need to dig a grave here and bury her," Jay said. "I agree," I replied.

Jay grabbed a shovel out of the basement storage, and he and Dre found a place under a nice tree and started digging. Vickie, Casey, and I finagled Liz out of the dinette and onto the floor. We pulled her to the steps and waited for Jay and Dre to help carrier her out.

Vickie read from her bible as we all stood around Liz's grave. I found some more branches just like I had for Curt's grave and tied them together to make a cross, as Jay pounded it into the ground. The others went back to the bus to check on Sean while Jay and I checked out the bus. We found several bullet holes, and they broke most of all the windows. But the tires seemed to be okay and seemed none of the major engine parts or gas cans were hit. "What was that?" I asked Jay. "It was an ambush of some sort. People are getting desperate now. We could run into more of this before we get home," he said. "I don't know how much more of this I can handle," as I cried. He reached out and pulled me into his arms. "I know, I know," he whispered. "You've got to be strong. I need you," he continued. "Should we get back on the road, we are almost there," I said, looking up at him as he kissed me softly. "Yes, we need to go," he replied. We pulled back on the highway and drove in silence. Every time we approached a town, the nerves started in. My stomach did flip-flops until we were out of the city limits. A couple towns, we saw a few people walking around like zombies. After going through what we had just experienced, we didn't want to take any chances stopping for more supplies. We checked our supplies and if we really rationed them, we could make it to the deer lease on what we had.

"We are going to be coming up on Interstate 45 in about 30 minutes. I don't know what to expect, just hope there are no roadblocks or ambushes like we just experienced. But you need to be on the lookout," Jay yelled back at us. I sat in the passenger seat with Jay's AR, Vickie, and Dre both had rifles and, after cleaning all the glass off the sofa and dinette sat ready at the window. I had asked Casey to stay in the bedroom with the dogs, and Andie stayed with Sean in the Bunkroom. Not a word was spoken as we all sat nervously, waiting to see what was ahead.

Interstate 45 ran through Corsicana. Daylight was getting away from us as we approached the interstate. We could see military vehicles on the overpass and a roadblock right at the entrance and exit to the interstate. "Okay, here we go. Don't show your guns, let me do the talking," Jay said as a soldier motioned for him to stop. Jay slowed the bus down and came to a stop.

"Can you tell me where you folks are heading?" the soldier asked. "We are trying to get home over by Henderson," Jay replied. "Are we able to get through?" Jay asked. "Yes, you can continue on this highway, you just cannot get on the interstate," the soldier replied. "We have a tent next to the CVS on the other side of the interstate that has water, and some food, place to shower if you need to," he continued. "Would you have a doctor?" I asked, as Jay gave me "don't tell em anything," look. "Yes, you can get medical attention there as well. Why? Is someone hurt?" he asked. Jay looked at me and then back at the soldier, "We ran in to an ambush a couple hours back, and one of our guys is hurt," Jay replied. The soldier keyed up his radio and told the medical tent that a bus would come with an injured person. The soldier waved us through as another soldier waved us towards the area of the medical tent.

"Everyone stay inside. Let us go check this out first. Make sure it's safe," Jay said to the others. Jay and I walked towards some soldiers standing outside a tent. One soldier opened the door and let us in. Once inside, we saw a desk with a couple soldiers and beyond that was cots with a few people laying on them, nurses and a doctor walking around talking to them. "We have one of our guys got shot by an ambush. I think the bullet went all the way through, cause there was a hole in front and a hole in back," I said. "We can see him if you want to bring him in," the nurse said. Jay and I looked at each other and then around the room. "Okay, we will see if we can get him in here," Jay said as we turned to walk out. "What do you think?" I whispered. "From the looks of thing, I think it's okay," he replied. "Well, I think he needs to see a doctor just so the wound doesn't get infected." I said as we walked to the bus.

Sean was sitting on the sofa when we got back on the bus. "He's in a lot of pain," Andie said. "Can you walk?" Jay asked. "I'm a little lightheaded, but with some help, I think I can make it," He replied. Dre and Jay helped him down the steps and into the tent.

The doctor examined him and suggested he stay the night and let them pump some intervenes antibiotics in him to keep from getting infected. At first, Sean didn't want to stay. But after talking to him about how this might be his only opportunity to get antibiotics, he decided he would stay. "But just one night," he complained. "I'm going to stay with him," Andie said. If you guys go through that door, there are showers set up and food and water. "Oh, man, we could use a shower," I said.

We got Sean settled in his cot and went back out to the bus. Jay moved the bus over to the parking lot. "I think someone needs to stay on the bus in case anyone gets any ideas," Jay said. "You go take a shower, get some food and then come back to watch the bus and then I will go take a shower," he continued. "I'll go sit with Sean so Andie can take a shower, then I will," Vickie said to Andie.

After a short not to hot shower, but still refreshing, I grabbed a couple bottles of water, and MRE and went back to the bus with Casey and Dre. It was dark out now, and we were all exhausted. Jay stayed up and kept watch first, then Dre and I took turns keeping watch. While Vickie and Andre took turns sitting with Sean. Although we felt safe for the first time in a long time, we still were not 100% sure if anyone would try to take our stuff.

CHAPTER EIGHTEEN
Almost Home

Day 16

Morning came early as we saw lots of military personnel rushing around calling out orders and speeding off in military vehicles. "Good morning," Jay said as he was standing, looking out the window. "What's going on?" I asked. "I'm not sure. Lots of movement out there. I'm going to go out to see if I can get any information," he said. "Okay, I'm getting up and taking the dogs out," I replied. I put the leases on the three kids and, quietly trying not to wake the others, took them outside.

In Texas, there were lots of grassy areas the dogs seemed to love. They would roll around in the grass and run and play. A female solider saw me standing in the grass with the dogs while they were playing in the grass and walked towards us. "Those puppies are so cute, Shih Tzus?" she asked. "Yip, they're little monsters," I replied. "I'm Anna, where you guys from?" she asked. "We were living in Las Vegas, but we are from Texas, just trying to get back home," I replied. "We are almost there, about three more hours. I'm D'Ann, nice to meet you," I continued. "Where are you from?" I asked. "I'm from North Carolina, but I've been stationed here at Ft Hood for almost a year now." She answered.

"There was a lot of commotion and moving around this morning. What's going on?" I asked. "I can't really say it's pretty confidential, even I don't know everything that's going on." She answered. Anna was a young girl, I guessed maybe in her early twenties. She looked to be of Hispanic descent.

Tears started welling up in her eyes, "I just want to go home to my family," she cried. "I understand. It's got to be hard not knowing. I haven't heard from my kids either," I said, trying to comfort her. "You remind me of my mom," she whispered as she sniffled. I reached out and touched her hand. "It's going to be okay. You have got to stay strong so you can get home. We are all in a state of shock right now. Do you know, or have you heard what happened 2 weeks ago? We came across some air force personnel several days ago, mentioned it might have been an asteroid hitting the Hawaii area. Have you heard that?" I asked.

She looked up at me in my eyes, with tears still flowing. "It wasn't an asteroid. I know that for a fact. Please don't tell anyone I told you. I will tell you what I know. I could get into a lot of trouble," she pleaded. "No, I wouldn't say a word to anyone," I replied. "I heard some senior officers talking in a meeting. It was an attack. They set off some sort of EMP through the 5g towers that fried the electronics," she whispered. "Who are they?" I asked. "Well, that's the part that confuses me," she replied. "They were talking about another country, and then said that it could have been our own government. They weren't sure, but they kept saying we needed to be ready because something big was coming, even bigger than what had just happened," she continued. "What?" I gasped. "Our own government? Why would they do that?" I asked. "I don't know. Please say nothing," she cried. "Anna, I promise, we are leaving today as soon as they release our friend from the medical tent. I won't say a word." I said. "All I know is you need to be very careful. They talked about there could be an invasion if it was another country, and not to trust even our own government," she said.

I stood there in shock, not knowing how to respond. "I hope you get home soon," I said as we hugged. "Thank you," she replied, "You too," as she walked off towards the medical tent.

I walked the dogs back to the bus, where Jay and Dre were checking it over. "Hey, I saw you talking to that soldier for a long time. What were you talking about?" Jay asked. He could tell by the shocked look on my face, it was not good news. "I'll tell ya when we get out of here," I replied. "Have you checked on Sean? Are they going to release him soon?" I asked. "They said not till later this afternoon, they wanted him to have a good 24 hours of intervenes IV antibiotics first," Dre replied. "So, what are we going to do until then?" I looked at Jay and asked. "Just hang out, I guess. The nurse said they have somewhat of a grocery store for the locals set up in that Dollar General across the road. We could go over there to see if we can get some supplies," he said. "Okay, let me get the dogs inside and feed them, and then we can walk over there," I replied as the dogs, and I went up the bus steps.

Jay and I walked across the street. There were two soldiers standing outside the doors, and as we approached, they opened the doors for us. Jay stopped before going in and asked the soldiers how this works. "There are a few supplies you can get, water, some MRE, and some toiletries. There is no charge, but they limited you to three items per person," he replied. "Okay, thank you," Jay said as we stepped inside. We could tell the store had been gutted, probably by looters, before the military got there. There were stacks of six pack bottled waters down the middle, and 10lb bags of rice and beans on one side and packets of travel size toiletries like toothpaste, soap, shampoo, and a toothbrush on the other. "I think we mainly need water. I'll get 3 6-packs, and you grab some bags of beans and rice."

Jay and I said thank you and carried the items to the bus. We startled Vickie sitting in the recliner dozing off when we opened the door. "Oh, hey guys," she said in a sleepy voice. "Any word on Sean's release?" I asked as I sat the beans and rice on the table. "I think it will be around 5pm, is what the nurse said," she replied. I looked at the only working clock sitting on the countertop by the sink. "Well, that's in a little over 2 hours," I said. "Maybe we should catch a nap also," I suggested. Jay put the water in the refrigerator. "Sounds good to me," he said, shutting the door. We headed back to the bedroom, shooed the dogs over, and were snoring before our heads hit the pillows.

The bedroom door opened. Casey peaked her head in. "Hey guys, Sean is ready to be discharged," she said. "Okay, we're getting up," Jay replied. Jay and I slowly put our shoes on and walked out the door. All of us were at Sean's bedside when the doctor came over and said he could go as soon as the nurse brought him some pain and antibiotic pills for him to take with him. "We are going to go get the bus and move it closer, so you don't have to walk so far," Jay said as he and I turned and walked away. "We'll meet you on the bus," Jay said.

Jay pulled the bus as close as we could get to where the group came out. Dre and Andie helped Sean up the steps. "Everybody ready to go?" Jay asked as everyone settled in. "Let go home," I replied.

We still had about 2-3 hours in the dark to go, bearing no more trouble, and one big town to go through. Jacksonville. Casey went back to the bedroom to see the dogs, while Sean and Andie crawled into the bunk. Dre and Vickie took the other bunks, which left me and Jay up front. "What do you think it's going to be like when we get there?" I asked Jay. "I just don't think any of our family made it all the way from Galveston up here," I said. Jay just sat and listened, not saying a word and no expression on his face. "If they didn't make it, are we going to go get them?" I asked. Still nothing. "I'm so excited to be almost home, but I'm scared, too. Life is going to be so much different." I said.

Jay slowly turned his head and looked at me. "So, what did that soldier say to you earlier? You said you would tell us when we left," he asked.

"She told me she heard it wasn't an asteroid that it was a terrorist attack, but the military is being hush hush, whether it was a foreign country or our own government. For some unknown reason, she thinks it could have been our own government. They were able to set off an EMP through the 5g towers and all the computer chips and electronics fried. She is scared. She told me not to trust the military or any government official. I just don't understand why anyone would do this to us. Many people have died and will die. The last thing she said to me was something big is coming."

Jay sat in silence, driving. I turned away from him and looked out the windshield with all the bullet holes and cracks. The night was black. We drove in silence for about an hour. Several times we had to go slow to maneuver around vehicles blocking the road. "We are coming up into Jacksonville in a few miles. Just have your gun ready just in case," Jay said. I grabbed his AR and sat it between us, and then grabbed one rifle and held it in my lap. We knew the way through Jacksonville by memory we didn't have to look at any maps.

Jay slowed down, trying not to draw any attention to us. The houses were dark, no movement in the shadows. It was so quiet it was eerie. We turned on to the main street, which went north and south, just a few more blocks, and we would turn east again on Highway 79.

As we came to the turn, we could see straight ahead several blocks, a large group of people with torches. They seemed to be walking up the street. "Look," as I pointed towards them. "It's a good thing we are turning here," Jay said as he turned the bus on to highway 79 and hit the gas. "I don't want to wait around to see what that was about," he added. "Right!" I commented. We had been on this stretch of road many times before, and knew we were just 30 minutes from the deer lease. My heart was beating fast, my stomach was in my throat as we got closer and closer to the county road that took us to the deer lease. Once we turned off the highway, it was only one more mile to the driveway. We crossed over the last bridge; Jay slowed the bus down and made the turn on to the county road. I looked at him and he at me and we smiled at each other. "We made it," I said, smiling at him. A half mile more over the next hill. Looking out the window towards where the drive would be, something didn't seem right. We topped the hill and looked toward the drive. "OH My God!" I screamed.

DAY 17.

To be continued: 17 Days from Galveston.

www.ingramcontent.com/pod-product-compliance
Lightning Source LLC
Chambersburg PA
CBHW071856220626
47052CB00002B/151